Brunanburh

Chronicles of the English: Book 1

Dedication

For a man I never met, who inspired my love of history,
George Fullerton.

Contents

Prologue

September 925 Kingston upon Thames

The church is full, the smell of incense heavy in the air. Expectant faces look my way, some friendly and open, others more hooded although none are overtly hostile. These are my people, and I rule them as king. This ceremony will officially mark me as anointed, raised above them by Almighty God. And for the first time, I'll be crowned as king of the English, with an actual crown. No helmet will grace my head, marking me as a warrior before a king, for all that I am a warrior, and proud to be one.

No, my holy men have decreed that it's time for a change. A new coronation service has been constructed, and a new crown has been moulded and fitted to my head. It's made of the lightest gold and embellished with the finest, though understated, jewels. It is beautiful to behold, and probably the worst kept secret in my kingdom.

It will fit me perfectly, and it will mark me like no other king has yet been marked. Not my illustrious grandfather, Alfred, who bought his religious conviction to bear in crushing the Viking menace and holding Wessex complete against the attack, nor my father, Edward, who continued my grandfather's work, and added Mercia and much of the Danish lands to his kingdom.

My father. A man I respected and loved, and yet who decreed that despite my grandfather's expectations, I would not be sole king after him. No, he gave that position to my half-brother; a youth younger than I, though barely, less tested in the ways of war, but more in the skills of the diplomacy of the Wessex court. And the men of the Wessex witan voted for him.

I didn't curse my father for his choice, but it did confuse me until the men of the Mercian witan voted that I was to be their king. And yet, dividing the only recently united realm seemed wrong somehow, counter-productive. However, I didn't have long to question my holy men or decry my father's good sense, for my half-brother, as I say, a youth younger than I, shortly joined my father in his heavenly splendour, and then it was I who acceded to the kingship of Wessex as well as Mercia, almost as if my Lord God too decried the division of our mighty realm.

Not that it was as easy to achieve as I've implied. The men of Wessex were unsure of me, a youth raised at my aunt's Mercian court, following my father's second marriage. His decision to crown my step-mother as queen, a position denied my mother, long dead now, somehow making my brother more 'throne worthy' than I, a child born of the union between a young man who was not yet king, and his wife, who would never be a queen. A king born of two consecrated parents is to be preferred where there's one available.

I'm a youth tried in the battle against the Vikings and the Danish and yet somehow, not tried against the wily nature of the men of Wessex. But I shouldn't dwell on that now, not when I'm at my coronation.

And now the land is united again under one rulership, my own. And this is my moment of divine glory.

A prayer is intoned by the Archbishop of Canterbury, Æthelhelm, appealing to God to endow me with the qualities of the Old Testament kings; Abraham, Moses, Joshua, David and Soloman. As such I must be faithful, meek, full of fortitude and humility while also being wise. I hope I will live up to these expectations.

I am anointed with the holy oil and then I'm given a thick gold ring with a flashing ruby to prove that I accept my role as protector of the one true faith. A finely wrought sword is placed in my hands, with which I am to defend widows and orphans and with which I can restore things left desolated by my foes.

Further, I'm given a golden sceptre with which to protect the Holy Church and a silver rod to help me understand how to soothe the righteous and terrify the reprobate, help any who stray from the Church's teachings and welcome back any who have fallen outside the laws of the Church.

With each item added to my person, I feel the weight of kingship settle on me more fully. I may have been a king for over a year now, but this, this is the confirmation of all I have done before and all I will be in the future. It is a responsibility I am pleased to take, but a responsibility all the same. From this day forward, every decision I make, no matter how trivial will impact on someone I now rule over. It's much for a young man to think about.

The prayers continue around me, but I'm looking at those whom I now rule, my second step-mother Eadgifu, little older than me for all that she produced nine children for my father before his death, is resplendent in the front row of the Church. She's serene in her place as king-mother; for all that, she's not my mother. I have her support and the support of her sons and daughters. She will rule my household for me, and in payment, and in part to fulfil my wishes, I will stay celibate, choosing never to marry. After all, I have half-brothers a plenty who can rule when I'm dead in my grave. And if I live to old age, then their sons can rule in my stead.

I catch her eye with a solemn nod of my head, and she inclines her head in acknowledgement that the new king has marked her with special favour. She's a woman who knows the worth of her good looks and uses them to the best advantage. She dresses carefully, the colours sombre but pleasing to look upon.

She is pleased with the way events have played out. I think she misses my father, her husband, but she must have known when they married that in all likelihood he would die before her. But with our agreement, she's lost nothing. She's still the Queen of the Anglo-Saxons, as she was consecrated, at my father's command, still the mother of kings and likely to be the mother of kings for many long years yet to come.

And I? I am king of the English, as my archbishop proclaims to rousing cheers from all within the heavily decorated church, festooned with bright flowers and all the wealth this church owns, gold and silver glitters from every recess, reflecting the glow of the hundreds of candles.

I am more than my father was, Edward, and I am more than my grandfather, Alfred. I am King of the English, King of a people not a petty kingdom.

It is done. I am an anointed King, and I will protect my land, and with God's wishes, I will extend its boundaries yet further, clawing back the land from the Danes and bringing the kingdom of the Northumbrians back under my command.

As the cheers reverberate throughout the confined space of the church, I hold my joy in place. It would not be kingly to sit and grin at everyone. Instead, a regal expression touches my face, a small tug of my cheeks to show my understated joy at becoming king of this proud people.

Chapter 1 – 927 – Eamont – Constantin

It's a sobering thought to realise my advanced age compared to this young king, who styles himself of the English. He's courteous and treats me with respect, as he does all the other kings he's called before him, at this meeting place, high in the north of his lands, but too close to my own for comfort. And yet, for me, his respect just reminds me of how very old I am compared to him and the other kings. I will list them all, just to mark myself amongst them. Hywel of the ancient southern Britons, Owain from my puppet kingdom of Strathclyde and Ealdred of Bamburgh, the northern most tip of the once mighty land of the Northumbrians so called for they live to the north of the tumultuous river Humber.

So many of us all together in one place at the behest of the young Lord. It's an uncomfortable thought and a remarkable achievement for how little blood has been shed to bring it about. I wonder if our people are tired of bloodshed and distrust or whether he is emboldened by the knowledge that his God blesses his every move and brings about its success.

His respect annoys me. My advanced age should mark me as wise and wily. I've been able to hold my own against my enemies for more than twenty years, yet I can't help but think this young man thinks me too old, too weak and too easy to subdue. He, who has gained so precipitously from the deaths of his half-brother, and his brother-in-law so that he now stands as king over the old lands of Wessex, Mercia, and the kingdom of York, looks at me a little too closely. I want to assure him that I'll not be the next to give up my earthly crown for a more heavenly one, but, he might just have a valid argument, for of all of us here, I am most likely to die next.

As I said, it annoys me. As does having to be here at all. Why should I bow to this king of the English? I am King of the Scots and have been for nearly thirty years. I've governed well and kept my people safe so why should I now submit to an 'overlord'? I've never feared to fight in the past and don't now, and yet I'm here, as are the other kings. We've decreed that we'll all reach an accord with each other, but I can tell from the shifting feet and sideways looks of my fellow attendees that this might all be a ruse.

Athelstan is not untried in battle. In the past, I know he's encountered the men of the ancient British kings and those of the Dublin kings as well. Alongside his aunt, Æthelflaed of Mercia, he's done great deeds and secured more land for his kingdom. But she's been dead for many long years now, and he stands alone against us all.

I too came to terms with her once, over ten years ago. She was a wise woman, devout and assured in her powers and she trained her young nephew well. But, the accord did not last. They never did. The shifting sands of allegiance and counter-allegiance run contrary to any agreement lasting too long. Perhaps the shifting feet have the right of it after all.

I met the young king's father once, Edward, King of Wessex and Mercia. Seven years ago when bloody Ragnall and his Norsemen were causing havoc amongst our borderlands. Edward, Donald of Strathclyde and myself reached an agreement to curtail his raiding activities amongst any of our lands. If he attacked one of us, we would all respond. Or so we said.

It worked, in a fashion, for later the same year Ragnall came to an independent agreement with Edward. Again, it was short lived for Ragnall had the audacity to die the following year. Since then Sihtric has ruled the York kingdom, the land that was once the ancient kingdom of Deira. Coerced into Athelstan's Kingdom via marriage to his sister, his death was not long in coming, and his kingdom not long in joining Athelstan's lands for all that he had repudiated both his wife and his new found religious fervour for my Christian God.

And my point in recounting all this? Athelstan's aunt and his father were more my age, and their respect was genuine, one contemporary to another, not as a son to a doddering father. I have sons enough of my own to know the difference.

Still, he's a finely wrought man; long blond hair graces his head, and he's tall and well built, apparently still training each day so that he can wield his sword and spear as and when they're needed. For all that he wears fine clothing, I hear chosen and embellished by his second stepmother, the raw energy of his muscles can be seen flexing and stretching the fabric of his deeply dyed royal tunic. He almost compels me to train as often as he does, instead of passing the duty to my sons, who are more of an age with him. I wish I could feel fatherly towards him, but I don't. I can respect him, providing he respects me.

And so this treaty. Why am I here? Is it because he swept into the old Danish kingdom of York or Jorvic after his brother-in-law's death and effectively annexed the land back to his kingdom, and I fear what he will gain if he pushes further north or is it because he vows himself a Christian king, and I too am a Christian king, of the old Ionian school no less, and it would be a good and Christian thing to live in peace with my neighbours? I don't yet know, but what I do know is that few have died an untimely death to bring about this understanding, and so, in the spirit in which it's offered, and provided it does not become too onerous, I'm prepared to accept the hand of friendship extended by Athelstan. It will be easily done and can be just as easily undone. I risk nothing by being here, and I may even grow in acclaim if this union is a success.

I will wait with baited breath.

Brunanburh – Athelstan – 937

I rise from my knees before my portable altar, the noises of the busy camp flooding back into my consciousness. Grimacing, I wonder how I've managed to ignore it for so long. Men shout at each other, dog's bark and horses shuffle in their temporary paddocks. The press of men and animals can be felt even within my private tent.

My personal priest, Beornstan, watches me. He's not alone. My ealdormen and my commanders have spent much of the last week looking at me surreptitiously, thinking I'm not aware of their scrutiny. I don't believe they expect me to crumble with the stress and the knowledge of the battle that must come, but they are looking for something. I hazard it's my confidence. And so I must hold myself firm and let not one flicker of doubt of the victory to come show in my face or my actions. That is why I seek the comfort of my Lord. Only to him can I profess my anxieties. But never out loud. Only when I speak to him with my mind can I ask the question that taunts me, 'am I doing the right thing?'

Not that I can act any differently, not now. Those who should have sought my protection and my overlordship have tested my patience. They have gone against me, as I somehow knew they always would. Not all of them, but even those who were my close allies have become distant of late, avoiding my messengers and sending responses that reach me too late to be of any use.

I would blame myself, but none of this is of my making. They gave their word. They broke their pledge. They must be punished. They must know that the English are not to be ridiculed and ignored. The English are a truly dominant race and we must be respected as such. We've grown since our near annihilation at the hands of the Vikings during my grandfather's tenure of this land, and we will not retreat or run from any who attempts to encroach on our land.

I would blame the arrogant Norse king of Dublin for all my ills, but he's not so persuasive that he could have made men act against their nature. He's just the excuse they needed for their current actions.

I've not been ignorant of the man's increasing success in his native land, and I'd been warned that once he felt secure there, he would attempt to claim back the land that he believes is his birthright, the Viking kingdom of York. I can admire his misguided hopes while acting violently to repel him. There is no irony there. He'll not have back what belongs to my people, and I. York is a part of the ancient Saxon kingdom of Deira. It belonged to my ancestors, the Saxons, and we'll keep it or die trying to protect it.

My ealdormen and holy men agree with me. Most are here with me now, even the more militant of the holy men have come and will fight alongside the men of the fyrd and the men of the household troops that guard my person, or their lords, my ealdormen.

The only aspect of the entire coming battle that surprises me even a little is its position. I would have expected the battle to occur near York, close to the heartlands of the kingdom that he wishes to claim. Instead, we'll meet in the battle between the source of his power across the sea, Dublin, and the land he wants, the old kingdom of York, or as he names it, Jorvik. It's a strange place to make battle, and I smirk a little. As Edmund advised, it's proven to be to our advantage to hem them in a little and make them take a stand in an area that I can't imagine is of their choosing.

Sadly, it's close enough to the sea that Olaf might either send for reinforcements or retreat that way, but my men will be deployed in such a fashion that they might be cut off.

It's an excellent day. A good day for a battle, if such could exist. I pray the Lord is showing his support for my actions in everything from the blue sky dotted with sporadic clouds high in the air, to the gentle breeze rustling the ripening crops, to the light and welcome heat coming from the sun. We'll be cool when we attack our enemies. Sweat will not quickly bead our faces unless the fighting becomes fierce.

I'm fitted out for battle, ready and willing for it to start. My coat with its closed woven together metal rings fits me perfectly, pulled tightly together by my decorated belt, complete with pouches and hooks from which my weapons hang; a small, richly decorated bone handled knife, a sword made for my hand and height, a carefully constructed piece of workmanship made by the finest metal worker in the land. I even watched him make it, bending the molten metal and hammering it into place, allowing it to cool and then repeating the procedure, time and time again until the sword was complete. And then to top it, he added a handle made of blessed bone and wound a coil of metal tightly around it so that the blade stays true to its handle.

If I must make war, then I will do it with the best weapons possible.

On the small wooden stool sits my shield, polished, sanded and repainted, the colours are bright and gaudy, the reds and oranges and blacks of my Wyvern standard easy to differentiate. Any whom I meet will know that they fight a man of the ancient Wessex line.

My clothing reflects the colours of my shield. A little less bright, they still mark me as a man of Wessex, a man of England, and many of my warriors dress the same. My gloves, now safely stowed inside one of my waist pouches are the deepest black, better to hide the blood and gore that will cover me before the day is done.

My hair is neatly tied back, secured with bands of twisted rope, and for the occasion, I have shortened my blonde beard a little. In battle, it's important to deny the enemy even the smallest means of killing a man. Without being able to gain a fist hold on my beard, they'll not be able to grab tightly and hold on and force my head into positions of weakness.

These men who swore their oaths to me ten years ago, and who tested me three years ago, shall not defeat me here. They swore a holy oath, and they were guests at my Witan, honoured guests no less and yet they turned against my gentle Imperium and sided once more with the Dublin Norse.

But I'll not upset myself further now. We've arrived at this moment, and honeyed words or overtures of friendship will not sway me – not again and not when they dare to enter my lands in hostility.

We've been marching for the last two days, my troops and the members of the fyrd arranging themselves in a position where we can clearly watch for the enemy, as I must now call them.

We know where they are, the forward scouts have seen to that, and so with the help of my ealdormen and leader of my household troops, and my warrior half-brother, we've argued back and forth calling for a number of local guides to explain the lay of the land, and finally I've had my way.

This spot, high on a steep hill, overlooking the lush countryside is a place my aunt once exclaimed with delight at seeing, musing that it would make both a fine muster point and a wonderfully defensive position. This will be where I defeat the pretentions of the enemy; Constantin the old grizzled warrior, Olaf the upstart from Dublin and any others who feel that my sway is too great over their lands and that mine, are for the taking.

Beside me, Edmund is being fitted with his war gear, his byrnie, and his sword holster and thick gloves. He wears the same colours as I, his belt as encumbered with pouches and hooks as my own. Many may think that to fight with a sword is all that is needed, but my brother and I have small knives, a war axe, a sword, and also matching shields. He looks a little grim, but his actions are decisive. He's as committed to this battle as I am.

I watch my men with pride. There's a purposefulness in them all. They share my desires here, more so than when I attacked Constantin's lands three years ago. Many didn't appreciate my taking the ship and land army away from our lands. I can understand their reluctance. They didn't want their land undefended, not when so many enemies surround us. They also didn't want a greater area of land to defend and they didn't want people who didn't want to be ruled by me added to my domain for they could only cause trouble.

I understand. I don't agree. And I will, God willing, prove to be correct.

Chapter 2 – 927 – Eamont – Athelstan

It feels a little like my Coronation again with all eyes on me, only here, the eyes are all hostile.

Or are they? Perhaps there is the hint of approval in a few of those eyes. I hope there is. It doesn't bode well if everyone is here against their will, grudging in their acceptance of my desires, even if so little blood has been spilt to accomplish this meeting of the kings.

In the two years since my Coronation, I know I've accomplished much and that some of these men probably begrudge me that success, particularly when it's come at their expense. I believe that only by working together can we repel those who try to take our land from us. And anyway, my most recent acquisition has come at the expense of none of these men. York is now mine, the man who thought he should succeed to Sihtric's throne, Guthfrith the King of Dublin, has fled, possibly seeking sanctuary amongst some of these kings before me, but for now and in the interests of diplomacy, I'll not press the matter further. They've assured me they don't have him, and until proved as liars, I'll accept their word.

I've never been as far north as Eamont before, almost in the land of the Strathclyde king, but I know of these men and have heard much about them. Constantin is the man I know most about. He's an elegant older man, more of my father's generation than my own. I know they met in the past, just as he met with my Aunt on occasion as well. He eyes me with interest from behind his wrinkled eyes and creased face. He's the most careworn of them all and possibly the most cynical of events here today. I hope to prove him wrong, but neither am I a fool. I know these men change their views with the wind, just as our enemies power their ships by the self-same winds.

Hywel of the ancient Britons is a man very much like myself. His age falls between my own and Constantin's and he's ruled his lands almost as long as Constantin. Rumour has it that he's wise and well educated, an avid believer in the one true faith, and someone I would like to know better. He acknowledges me with a genuine smile that I return fully. Here, at least is a man who holds the same ideals as me. He wants the menace from Dublin contained as much as I do, especially as his lands have a vast coastal area, almost opposite the Dublin king's stronghold, separated only by the sea. I don't envy him and imagine his problems are similar to my own with regards to keeping the plentiful sea routes under close guard. There is only a limited supply of warriors to watch the coastal lands, and they can't be everywhere at once.

Owain from Strathclyde is someone I little know. Rumour has it that he's much under the influence of Constantin, and I wonder at the truth of that. He's here with his retinue, and he seems kingly enough, not once looking to the man who may, or may not, hold the reins on his reign, but still, it's a perplexing problem and one I hope to get to the bottom of during my time here.

Ealdred of the old royal family of Bamburgh is a man I know more of, and he knew my father as well. Now that I've taken back York on the death of Sihtric, we're neighbours. As with all these men, he's a close ally of Constantin. They've fought against Viking raiders in the past. They share common goals and needs and seeing them all arrayed before me makes me wonder who will be true to their word, and who will not, and whether, one day, I'll have to face their combined ire against my expansion plans.

By rights, we should all hold much in commonality. It should be natural for us to unite against the Viking raiders, whether they come from the lands of the Dublin kings, the Outer Isles or the homeland of the Danes and Norwegians. I doubt we'll stand and fight battles if the other's land is attacked. It is more likely we will look only at our borders and assist only when incursions threaten our existence and our property. My purpose here is to prevent that from happening, to decide on a goal we can all agree upon.

I hope we will have a unifying force at our command. I will remind these men of our love of the one true faith, and I will have them visit my Witan, and see the strength of my control over my lands, and those newly come to my kingship. For now, I will feast them and show them my wealth, and extract promises from them that we will act in concert against the Raiders. And those who please me, I will propose marriage alliances with, and those who displease me, I will take their sons or grandsons as my hostages, and raise them at my Witan, under the watchful eyes of my step-mother. They will be treated honourably as if they were my brothers, and they'll return to their lands one day, in awe of my kingship, keen to emulate me and stay friendly with the English, and while their father's resent me, they'll show nothing but love for me. I will gain their support no matter what.

The day is fair and warm, the breeze gentle on my face. My household troops are close to hand, ever vigilant and armed well. My archbishop is here too, a warrior clad in a holy man's clothing, but no less devout for that. And surrounding us, in a circle of my devising, are the men who look to these kings. They watch everything either with distrust or with ease. After all, we are merely men.

I've brought precious gifts for these men, as they have for me. They've already been exchanged in more private arrangements, and we all know where we stand with each other. Am I content with the gifts given to me? It would make me an unchristian man if I weren't, and yet, perhaps I'd hoped for some greater commitment to my cause here, some more substantial gifts from amongst these men. But for now, I will eat and smile and laugh and joke as best I can. Later, I will scrutinise the actions of my fellow king's. Later.

Brunanburh – Constantin – 937

From my vantage point, I watch the English King with interest, noting the gleam of swords and shields, battle coats and war axes. I suppress a self-satisfied smirk at his precious order and picky ways. We'll show him what a real battle is, here, today.

I'm dressed in similar equipment to the English. I notice it dispassionately. I want to stand aloft from them, completely different, but in warcraft, there is not much that separates one warrior from another. We all have swords, war axes, shields and rings of metal around our upper bodies to deflect the sharp points of swords and axes. Gloves of padded leather cover my hands, and they too will deflect initial sword strokes and knife strikes.

Not that I plan on fighting today. I am too old and too slow, and I have sons and grandsons to fight on my behalf. But I must dress the part and show that I am willing to face my enemy. My warriors expect it of me, and I would feel a fraud if I sat on the side wearing jewels.

Athelstan, when I think of him, my blood boils afresh, and I have to offer words of apology to my Lord God. He wouldn't approve of my battle-rage, but I can't stop it. Not now, when we've come to this.

Three years ago he took it upon himself to run rampant through my lands and around my land by ship. I'm still unsure what he hoped to gain by it, but if it was simply to raise my ire, then he succeeded. Completely.

He may have no lasting token or land gain from that attack, but here today, he will see the budding of the seeds of anger he sowed. Here, today, my people will reveal how deep their hatred of him lies.

His audacity in riding through my land, surrounded by his warriors, sending his ships to trail his every move, will be punished today. Never in any of the histories of my people, or the tribes who came before our unification, has a man of the southern people of this island done anything so inopportune.

The old Northumbrian kingdom attempted to win more land for itself but was stopped every time. Athelstan instead seemed to take a leisurely stroll throughout my lands, assessing as he went, seeing what riches I could lay claim to, almost as if he meant to stake his own claim to it.

My sons met him in battle, and when that failed, I was forced to come to terms with the man, journey with him back to his heartlands and bend my knee before him at his royal council.

Never again, I vowed that day. Never again would an English king inflict such dishonour on my people. With Olaf's help, I will erase the stain on our collective memory of his half-hearted attack. Today, I will draw blood and force Athelstan to his own knees.

Chapter 3 – 927 - Eamont – Hywel

The English King is smiling. Constantin is smiling. Even Owain is smiling, and so must I, Hywel, King of the Southern Britons, known by the name 'Welsh' by the English and the Scots.

It's strange, this collection of men who hold sway over so much land on this island we call our home. We are, for once, amongst equals in rank and prestige, piety and warcraft, statesmanship and power. Our lands may be vastly different, but we have the same hopes and fears. Will we keep our kingship? Will we die as embittered old men in cold and lonely beds or in a trail of glory on the battlefield? Will our neighbours remain our friends or covert our lands? Will our successors rule as well as we have done or will they, heaven forbid, outdo us?

Behind our smiles, we plot and evaluate and consider our options about how to get the best possible outcome from this gathering of great men.

Beautiful drinking horns are passed between us as we toast each other and our accord. The wine is sweet and blood red. Perhaps not the best choice in the circumstances. Athelstan's cleric will shortly present us with an elaborately written and beautifully decorated script for us to put our mark upon, and with that mark, the bargains made here will be sealed. Possibly.

I for one am keen to make this agreement. I have more spiritual cares that I plan to turn my mind towards. I have seen my lands, and some of the English King's but I wish to set forth and journey across the lands of our nearest neighbours, see their religious wonders and eventually seek the physical embodiment of our Lord on Earth, the Pope. If I can leave this place, confident that these kings will not invade my land in my absence, then I plan to leave as soon as possible. If.

The sun is warm on my exposed head. My heavy garments, suitable to show my wealth and power, a little uncomfortable in the summer heat and I would welcome something more thirst quenching to drink than the too sweet wine.

We are gathered outside to take advantage of the warm weather, and yet, we are surrounded by exceptional goods and valuable gems. We sit on fine crafted wooden chairs, before a large, well-built and functional table and above our heads, a small half tent flaps in the almost non-existent breeze. Our followers are similarly arrayed on wooden benches, in rows, as if they sit within a great church and they too share in drinking horns of the fine, sweet wine.

Athelstan sits erect, listening calmly to the words of his cleric, while his eyes dance between us, and behind us, noting those with us and calculating the strength of our fighting forces. But I do not come to fight. I support him and his plans. I might be the only one here who does.

Athelstan has with him a small collection of the relics of the saints that he collects and I would rather spend my time in discussion with him about those relics than listening to the droning of the charter that is being read to us. It uses the language of the English king. I understand everything being said, for I am fluent in more than my tongue, but the flowing words and convoluted sentences are unappealing, and for those who do not speak the language this must be a laborious process.

I wish the cleric would just get to the point. Nothing he says will be unexpected, as we've agreed to the words already. Diplomats have been busy working, rushing between the courts of all gathered here to ensure that this meeting runs as smoothly as possible. It may only have been a month since this gathering was conceived, but much has been done behind the scenes to make the actual meeting of the kings appear as flawless as possible.

Constantin sits as contentedly as I do. He's assured of his position and loved by his people, fearless in the face of his enemies. Owain is more unknown. He's regal and proud but maybe just a little too proud. And then there is the figure of the House of Bamburgh. He's younger than all of us, but his face wears a frown of thought as he squints in the bright sunlight and I'm not the only one to mark it. What must he think of his future? Constantin on one side and this young king on the other? Is it much different from when he had the Dublin King with the weight of his homeland at his back, to having this English King with the might of his united kingdom? Time will tell, I suppose. As it will for all of us.

At last, the voice of the cleric dies away, and Athelstan looks at us expectantly. With a fluid movement, he rises first, to add his mark to the charter with a flourish and no hesitation. This is the only part of the proceedings not to have been pre-ordained. Who will rise next? Who will rush to mark themselves as a little subservient to this English king? I glance at the other kings with interest, and when none makes a move, I rise myself and bend to add my cross where the cleric indicates with his long, ink-stained finger. I am a little surprised that this great man of God has clearly written this charter himself. Surely he has others who could have done it for him?

With a flourish, I add my mark in the bright green ink, careful not to stain my sleeves or my fingers. It's no lie that this ink can mark the skin as clearly as it can the scrapped parchment before me. And it burns as it does so, a sharp pain that nothing can dilute until it's done eating away at the flesh it comes into contact with.

Athelstan extends his hand of welcome to me, and we clasp as brothers should, arm-to-arm, shoulder-to-shoulder. A faint word of thanks from the English king and I realise that he was worried that none would mark the agreement. Again, I'm surprised. His supreme confidence in the face of possible rejection astounds me, and I reappraise him once more. He's a worthy grandson of King Alfred, a man I've heard so much about and whom I hope to emulate in his love of learning and law. He's a man I'm pleased to call my overlord. He's fair and honest and courageous.

Behind us, a small skirmish breaks out as the other three men now vie to have their marks on the charter next, and I smile again, as does Athelstan. There is a feeling of relief that the deed is now done, a freely taken breath of the clean air. Now, we can celebrate our unity in the face of the Viking raiders. We can drink as we please, converse about holy relics as we please, for we are now allies, witnessed by God and each other. Allies, a word to mask many.

Brunanburh – Olaf of Dublin – 937

I narrow my eyes with displeasure as I watch the English upstarts force before me, he who stole my birthright without thought.

Years it's taken me to mount my counter-attack against him. I might be ten years later than I might have hoped but this is retribution, and he mustn't think any differently. York is mine. It's been in my family for far longer than this English king might think and I will have it back.

I curse my ill luck that I was unable to pursue my claim sooner, but events in Dublin needed my urgent attention, and until Gothfrith's death three years ago, the claim was his to pursue, not mine. My father, a man who did not live up to his heritage. That he failed to do so means that it now falls to me, and Athelstan's now dead brother in law Sihtric's son from his first marriage, another Olaf, to seek victory where he found only defeat. Olaf Sihtricsson adds, even more, credence to my claim. He will be a constant reminder that upon his father's death, Athelstan stole the land from the Dublin Vikings. As before, the combined kingdom of Dublin and York can be ruled jointly, I in the more prominent role in York and the younger Olaf in Dublin, now that I've quietened the dissidents who wanted to rise against my rule and made it peaceful for him. Now that he's in my debt.

But, I can't deny that the English king is well provisioned. He has many, many men encamped upon their chosen ground. The scouts have attempted to count them all, but they shift and move so often that it's not easy for them to tell whom they've reckoned up and who they've missed. Still, I imagine in my mind that he has at his command the same amount of men that Constantin of the Scots, Owain of Strathclyde and I can rely on combined, at least five thousand men. This land of the English, now combined into a greater whole than it ever has been, is rich and well endowed with land and riches that I can only hope to have at my command.

I've been forward with my scout and looked at the English King's camp with some dismay. It is neat and tidy and massive, square tents stretching almost to the horizon, their canvases coloured with the orange, red and black of the wyvern that the ancient house of Wessex claimed as their own. As if a family could claim such a mythical beast and call it his or her own. The arrogance astonishes me.

And the number of horses and carts that carry provisions worries me as well. These men could stay here forever and never need to leave. My men are in daily need of supplies, and our ships have only enough if we need to make a hasty departure. Just enough water, mead and food to return across the sea. I take a moment to think how pleased I am that the sea is at our back. Initially, the knowledge had worried me, but now, in the face of such huge numbers, I've changed my mind. Not that I plan on leaving here without my birthright.

I'll be happy with York. For now. And the King's death, of course. That goes without saying.

Chapter 4 – 927 - Eamont – Ealdred of Bamburgh

My hand is steady as I mark the charter before me. It's a beautiful piece of statecraft, finely decorated around its edges, with emblems deemed to show the peace we've agreed upon. Even my rudimentary understanding of the written word is stirred to admiration, and I'm minded of some of the more elaborate designs I've seen within the walls of the monasteries that dot the landscape of my homeland.

My homeland.

The king needs to appreciate that while we may now be neighbours, I've no intention of gifting to him my homeland. My family and I have held it against the ravages of the Raiders, the pretensions of the Kings of Dublin, Ragnall and his men and even against the forces of Constantin's countrymen of years ago. My family. Not his, and I will guard it as well as my ancestors have done. Not for us the submission to Dublin kings and Viking raiders, not like other lands that once formed the mighty kingdom of Northumbria.

And yet, I will come to terms with him. For now. I'm not sure how long it will be to my benefit to do so, but that little concerns me today.

My mark made, I step away from the table, holding the pen out to Owain. He will sign last and is unhappy about that; I can tell by the scowl that mars his face. He's a man who truly wears his heart on his sleeve. Does signing last mark him as least of the five of us? Let him think about it, and perhaps next time, he'll be quicker to act.

Athelstan and Hywel are conversing quietly amongst themselves, so I turn to Constantin for want of anything better to do. He seems as comfortable with proceedings here as the other two kings.

"This is a grand plan," I mutter softly, watching Constantin's wise eyes wrinkle in amusement.

"Yes it is, but these kings of the Angles and Saxons, or the English as they now like to be called, do like things to be grand. His grandfather, father and aunt were the same."

"I knew his father, but I don't think his aunt, and certainly not his grandfather."

A loud chuckle of amusement,

"And I, contrary to reports, did not meet the grand old man either. But I've heard much, and we can't deny, no matter how much we'd like to, that the kingship of Wessex still stands and flourishes."

"No, we couldn't deny that," I mutter darkly as Constantin laughs again.

"I know, don't tell me again, about how long your family survived, and marooned as you were between my lands, Strathclyde's and the limits of Dublin-York."

"I wouldn't dream of it, Constantin. After all, I think you're only too aware."

"Yes, your father never tired of ensuring all and sundry were aware. And I think when you came begging to my Court for my help to reclaim those lost lands from Ragnall, that you too might have made use of that same argument."

"Ah, well, he was on occasion a little too sure of his family," I reply, ignoring the jibe about my time at his Court nearly ten years ago.

"And you will not fall into that trap again?" he queries, eyebrows raised.

"I hope not. The might of this king will not take my land. And neither will you. Nor the bloody Vikings."

"Don't want it!" Constantin re-joins smartly.

"Well tell your retainers that then will you?"

"Gladly, Ealdred. And now, let's not mar the proceedings with an unseemly argument. Remember, unity is the key to success."

As he says, Constantin and I know each other of old. We are uneasy neighbours and mostly allies, with more in common than I have with this new king, with his pomposity and sense of superiority.

Do I resent adding my mark to this accord of his? Yes and no, all at the same time. The idea is a fine one, and yet, it seems unworkable. The lands around me push and shove, hoping to claw back my domain, and they do the same with all the other land around them. There seems to be a march to be as united as possible in what I can only see as a 'land grab'. The rights to govern the lands are legitimised by reference to forebears who had no clear right to claim the lands, and so to me, at least, it all seems a little laughable, a little too much.

Not that I say this out loud. My lands are my own, and I plan to hold them well. Would I like more? That's not easy to answer. I know my lands and my people, and I trust them with my life as they trust me with theirs. Why would I look to add people hostile to my regime to my command? And yet clearly, most others do.

I'm a warrior, never doubt that, but I don't look for unnecessary trouble.

Brunanburh – Edmund of England- 937

I like this position insisted upon by Athelstan. I've argued against it, as all good men of the Royal Witan should, but I think it is the best option available to us, and I've made my opinions known.

The Norse and the Scots combined will be an excellent fighting force. We need to use every advantage we can gain from every facet of the coming fight. The land we choose to fight upon will be important, perhaps the most important aspect of the battle. My experience of the Scots is that they fight much as we do. The Dublin Norse, I've not yet met in combat, but I imagine that men fighting to the death fight much the same. It must all boil down to one man fighting for his survival against unimaginable odds, in the terrible confusion of battle where it's not always skill with a sword or an axe that determines whether a man lives or dies.

Once we'd recovered from our shock that the Norse of Dublin didn't seem to be moving any closer to York, where we'd first thought to mount our defences, we made all haste to reach this side of our land.

It seems a strange place to meet us in battle, but then, the Dublin Norse and the Scots, for all that they say otherwise, make uneasy allies. I imagine that wily old bastard Constantin does not want the Norse to close to his lands, and I believe that Olaf knows it will not be easy for him to effect an entry into York, not unless he comes as the victorious commander to claim his spoils. Athelstan has been king of the place for too long now, and the people have become used to him.

He does not change their lives or alter their livelihoods, happy to let the people alone provided they turn to his one true faith, and pay their taxes when they're due. He's not a cruel king; there's little point. He must rule alone, but with the consensus of his Witan and if his people are unhappy with the way he rules they can speak out against him. He's worked hard to stamp on all factions within the Witan, worked hard to quiet the voices of my disaffected half-brothers, but their supporters still fester. And wait for him to make a mistake. York would be a perfect mistake, and so he governs lightly.

He governs with the same gentle touch in the old Mercian kingdom for all that they love and respects him anyway, seeing in him an embodiment of his aunt, the great Lady Æthelflaed. By rights, her daughter should have taken her place, but my father thought differently and secreted her away. Few know where she is or where she went or if she lives and I know the lack of knowledge bedevils Athelstan. He was her cousin, her playmate and yet he was powerless to intervene when our father decided that she should not succeed her mother. In a similar way, he was powerless to intervene when our father chose our half-brother as king of Wessex.

I think it's a stain on my father's memory and I'm not alone to think as such. It does little good to overturn every stone looking for her. The damage has been done, and Athelstan works to right the wrong. And the people of Mercia know and respect that. He investigates every rumour and searches as far and wide as he can. Goodness knows what would happen if he found her, but I think she must be long dead. No one could keep a secret for over fifteen years. No one.

The borderlands with the ancient Britons, the Welsh, are a little more problematic for my brother. In recent years, since his attack on the lands of Constantin, there has been a cooling in his good relationships. I think they fear him and his pretensions and that's a shame. All these years of trying to show them that he simply wants to live in peace have come to this. They will not stand with him against Olaf, although neither will they stand against him.

Instead, a bitter battle will be fought on the slopes of a small rise in the sight of the sea that has brought the Dublin Norse to our lands, and near a river that they can navigate to come further inland, but have chosen to stop beside. Constantin has brought his troops here, and some of them have come via ship too, while others have come over land, collecting the Strathclyde forces along the way. They will all have an easy means of escape should any live to walk from the battlefield. I doubt they will. And we've already decided that we'll move into position to prevent them from making a retreat over to the sea if we're able to.

Years and years of training will come to fruition here. Men who first blooded their swords on the foray into the lands of Constantin will get another chance for glory and victory. And more will get their first chance. My brother will not stand in this battle alone, and I'm proud to be here to serve him. Our half brothers from our father's second marriage are dead now, my full brothers still deemed too young to fight in the shield wall and anyway, they are more loyal to their mighty older brother than perhaps even I am. They've fallen entirely under the sway of the illusion of his power, and I can't begrudge him their admiration. I only hope that one day I can follow in his footsteps with the same charisma.

With decisive moves, I check my equipment is in place, my rounded shield, painted in the colours of Wessex, my sword, gifted to me by my father, my knife and my war axe. Everything is where it should be, and, as it should be. And then one of the young servants hands me my leather gloves, and I thank him, realising that without them I would have been severely hampered when I went into battle.

I walk to where my brother is himself waiting and ready, watching the movements of the enemy in the early morning sunlight. Today great deeds will be done, and tonight, I hope that I will still live.

Chapter 5 – 927 – Eamont – Owain of Strathclyde

I know a scowl mars my face as I reach over and add my mark to this ridiculous piece of scraped parchment before me. The scowl is more than skin deep, running through my blood and permeating as far as my churning stomach. I feel sickened by the blood red wine and sickened by my presence here.

The smiles on the faces of the other kings and would be kings is doing nothing for my aggravation and annoyance. Even Constantin, the old bugger, who said he had no taste for this alliance, is smiling wildly and enjoying himself. He leapt up, keen as a young squire, to sign his name to this superfluous bit of parchment. I fear I've been played for a fool and it does not sit well with me. Not at all.

When Gothfrith came to me, after his defeat at the hands of Athelstan, begging me for help and assistance, I offered it gladly. Anything to discomfort this upstart Wessex king who styles himself 'of the English'. Not for one moment did I think Constantin would pull rank on me, and demand that I send Gothfrith on his way.

Our relationship, until that point, had been amenable, and I had almost forgotten that I owed anything to the king of the Scots. But now, he's not only reminded me, he's also brought me into this laughable alliance with other kings, constantly under risk of attack from the Dublin Vikings. Now I seem to have two overlords, whereas only a month ago, I could think I had none.

The hearty laughter of the other men resounds loudly in my head, and I'd like nothing more than to call my war band to me and demand that they kill all these men here, or at least take them as hostages. Then we could net ourselves some fine coinage and jewellery, and this journey to the far southern borders of my lands would at least have been worthwhile.

Turning to look at the gatherings of my now supposed allies, I note that Athelstan and Hywel are stood almost nose to nose perusing some ancient text that the Wessex king's holy man has in his hands. In hushed tones of awe, they confer about whatever it is. Besides them, Constantin and Ealdred stand a little more aloof from each other, but laughing and conversing all the same. I imagine their fake smiles hide the truth from the Wessex king about what they discuss. I hope it's an idea to attack Athelstan, drive him back from the lands of the York kings, and send him back to Wessex mewing like a kitten. I doubt it, but I can hope all the same.

As another holy man works to seal and store the parchment we've just signed, Constantin gestures for me to join him and Ealdred. I go, but unwillingly, and I'm right to be sluggish in my response to his command.

"Come Owain; a smile would look better on that face of yours. We do good work here today."

A tight and sardonic smile touches my constricted face in response to his words. He's baiting me, or he knows me too well. Neither thought is appealing.

"It may well be good work, but I do not look forward to the repercussions from across the sea when Gothfrith returns to his lands."

"I'm sure that you've little to worry about. Why would he want to come anywhere near your lands? You know as well as I do that the raiders enjoy a land crossing from Chester to York that's now in the hands of Athelstan. It's him who should be wary. Not you."

Is that a hint from Constantin that his intentions here are less honourable than they appear?

"Indeed Owain. It is Athelstan and myself who should be worried, not you," Ealdred offers as well.

"You don't share a coast with the marauding bastards," I grudgingly counter.

"No but I do have a coastline to protect, and it's just as open as your own. It might take a little more thought, a little more time and effort, but if they wanted to attack me, they could sail around the top or bottom of this island, and cause havoc wherever they went. And anyway, what of Hywel? He seems little concerned, and his lands are just as exposed as your own. In fact, more so."

I turn to look at Hywel then and notice that Owain is correct. He seems happy with this arrangement!

"He'll probably just be pleased to get the Wessex men off his border, and the Mercians."

"The English, Owain, you must get used to calling them the English. They're now one race under one king." Constantin offers the condescension in his voice clear to hear.

"You can call them what you want, but I see them for what they are. The men of Wessex and the men of Mercia, and now the men of York, all looking to one king but only while he's powerful and winning this war against the men of Dublin."

"Now, that might well be true Owain, but you'd do well to accept it for what it is."

"I would much rather it had stood for longer than a few months before I accepted anything." In a lower voice, out of Athelstan and Hywel's hearing, he continued, "You'd do well to do the same, Constantin and Ealdred. He'll not be happy with what he has. He wants all our lands."

"That might well be true as well, but this accord binds him as surely as it does us. He can't take our lands. There's nothing mentioned about annexing his allies lands if the agreement is broken."

"No there isn't, but look at York. His sister was only married to the old king for a span of months, and then she was cast out on the wishes of Sihtric's retainers and Lords. And now, somehow, that gives him a claim to those lands. She doesn't even share a child with him. No, his sons are older and by another woman."

"He might have used the marriage as a basis for his invasion, but he won the battle for the land. Gothfrith was wounded, and his men deserted him. That's hardly Athelstan's fault."

"But he shouldn't have been there in the first place?"

"Are you telling me you'd have let an opportunity like that pass you by?" Constantin queries, his eyebrows raised in admonishment.

"No, I wouldn't, if I'd had the men and the finances. But that doesn't make it right."

Constantin is laughing merrily now, fuelling my anger further and only a quiet hand on my arm from Ealdred prevents me from stomping away in anger.

"Why do you let the old man bait you so much?" Ealdred queries into the quiet summer's day. "You know what he's like. He enjoys seeing you outraged. Why give him the satisfaction?"

I turn to glare at Constantin's smirking face and take a moment to calm my anger. Ealdred's right. I always let Constantin upset me with his snide remarks. After all these years I really should have learnt to control my temper more. I continually play right into the older man's hands.

"Why didn't you march on York?" I counter to Constantin, only slightly less aggressively than I'm feeling.

"What, and upset my good friend Ealdred. I think not."

"What about your sons then? They could have gone in your wake."

"Yes, but they're hot headed and rash and more likely to cause more problems than solve the current ones."

"I'd have thought that would please you," I offer, raising my drinking horn to my lips as I speak.

"The only thing that pleases me is keeping my borders safe. If that means keeping my sons well and truly tethered, then so be it." Constantin's voice had lost its merriment, and I glance at him through narrowed eyes. Good, the old man was as liable to bad temper as I am.

"Then I suggest we raise a toast to the future of our alliance. Long may it stand!"

Constantin's grin was instantly back on his face, and Ealdred's eyes were dancing with amusement.

Passing the drinking horn along, he toasted the future of the alliance with the other two men, and then Athelstan and Hywel joined them, Athelstan quickly glancing from one to the other of his new allies. I suppress a smirk of amusement. It was good to see the cocky bugger looking a little unsure of himself.

Brunanburh – Athelstan, King of England– 937

It's still early in the morning, early enough to call the last council before the battle commences. Edmund is grim-faced at my side, and although I know he mirrors himself on my deportment, I childishly reach over and whack him on the back. He jumps a little at my touch, but when he sees my smile, he impulsively grins back. I love my brother Edmund. Of all my father's children, apart from my full sister, he's the one I care for most.

"Brother, this battle will go well, I assure you."

His eyebrows rise at my confidence, and he smirks.

"Surely it's better to be a little less confident, and then when we prevail you'll be surprised," his tone is as light as my own, the ramblings of men elated and scared about what is to come. And it's my turn to smirk as he flings one of my favourite comments back in my face.

"Ah, today it feels a little difference. I think overwhelming confidence is called for."

His mouth turns down a little as he considers my words, although his eyes still dance with mischief.

"Then I'm glad you feel like this. I feel a little nervous, a little apprehensive, but your confidence bolsters me. Especially when it's so rarely seen."

My brother is right. I'm not one to gloat before something is completed. This righteousness flooding through me though is too good to ignore.

"We will beat them, Edmund, never fear that. But, there will be a great slaughter here today, of that I'm sure. There are too many men here in one place, two enemies who face each other, for slaughter to be avoided. For all my confidence, I command you to keep yourself safe and well. Do not fear to attack but do not take risks that are not needed. Do you understand?"

My tone grows firmer as I speak. My belief in victory is one thing, but I can't countenance losing my brother to accomplish it.

He sobers at my words, and I curse myself for a fool, until he smiles again, real mirth transforming his face.

"And I, as the king's heir and atheling both, command the same of you."

I stare him down for a long moment, but I admire his courage. He will fight exceptionally well for me today, and he'll be doing it for me, as his king and as his brother in equal measure. At no point will he even consider that he's fighting for his inheritance. His reminding me of whom he is just his way of highlighting its irrelevance to him.

"Then I will do as my heir commands," I reply testily, my thoughts already on the clash of weapons that I imagine I hear even though we've not yet joined in battle.

Other men are starting to enter my command tent now and so Edmund, and I drop our line of conversation. They are dressed as we are, with helms under their arms and their shields hanging down their backs. These are the men I trust above all others within my kingdom.

The first inside are my ealdormen, the brothers. I always feel a little more warmly towards them than my other ealdormen, simply because like Edmund and I they are brothers. Athelstan and his brother Ælfstan, both ealdormen over difficult lands, only recently clawed from the hands of the Vikings, they are both vicious warriors and religious men as well. They wear their weapons and their armour with the same ease that they wear their miniature crosses and outward religious mementoes.

Edmund greets the brothers emphatically. They are childhood friends of his, having been raised at the royal Witan together, their father serving my own in the Western lands. My jealousy of their friendship has long since faded. It's not, after all, any of their faults that I was banished to the Mercian lands, away from my brothers, in virtual seclusion from both the Witan and the Royal Court.

The brothers look more alike than Edmund and me, but then they are full brothers. They share the same auburn hair, intelligent blue eyes and have many of the same mannerisms. I've made a small study of them. It's good to know how men think and act, whether they show all their emotions on their faces or whether they mask them and act opposite to how I might have thought.

"My Lord," Ealdorman Athelstan speaks first as he tugs on his gloves and makes ready to meet the enemy, "My men are ready and keen. I would request that you let us lead the assault."

His tone is formal, but his eyes glint with the joy of the coming battle. I smirk back at him. I'd like nothing more than to give him the command he wishes but Edmund has already demanded it.

"My thanks, Athelstan, but alas, Edmund has beaten you to the position you want. Is there another that would satisfy you?"

"No, but I'll be pleased to take the flank beside him."

He's eyeing Edmund with a challenge, and I feel my eyes roll in my head. The childhood rivalries they once shared can still reassert themselves at the most inopportune times.

"It would be my pleasure to fight with you at my side," Edmund counters a little aggressively, but luckily Ælfstan steps in before I need to.

"I think you should both step aside and let me have that position," he argues, watching my face to see how I'll react to his efforts to further muddy the waters. Instantly I feel my temper fray, but then I notice all three are smiling at me, and I know that they've decided to lighten the mood with their particular sort of humour.

I quirk a smile. It is after all expected of me as their king and commander to enjoy their attempts to distract me.

"I've a mind to let Ealdorman Osferth take that position now," I say to outraged cries of protest. Now it's my turn to cause a little mischief.

"He is, as we all know, a great warrior."

Edmund scowls at me then and so too does Ealdorman Athelstan. Our names confuse all apart from ourselves, as we're lucky enough to know who we mean when we talk about the other.

"Fine, fine," I capitulate, holding my hands in the air, "Edmund can keep his place, and Athelstan, you, may go on his flank. And Ælfstan, where do you wish to station your men."

Ælfstan stands silent for a long moment, eyeing his brother and my brother, and then he says,

"I think I'll stand behind the two bloody fools and make sure they don't let the Scots or the fierce Norse through." Now it's the turn of the other two men to look outraged, and I hide my burst of amusement in place. Ælfstan speaks his mind as no other man I know ever has, even if it is, occasionally, unwelcome.

"A fine plan," I concur. "And behind you all, I'll place Ealdorman Guthrum. He'll make sure that none of you let our enemies in."

It's the turn of the three to act outraged again at my words, but I know they'll agree with me. After all, all this was decided upon yesterday, and now we only pass the time until the other ealdormen arrive, and it's time to make final battle plans, for make no mistake, a battle is to be joined today and we all hunger for it.

Chapter 6 – 927 - Eamont – Edmund of England

My half-brother makes a resplendent figure amongst the small crowd of kings gathered just outside the tent covering, his clothing has been carefully selected, the finest of everything but as with all of his preordained actions, it is understated enough that some might not even notice. He's relaxed, but wary and I don't blame him for that. Expertly arrayed against us is a large force of men who could, at any moment, turn on him and murder him where he stands.

The sun is warm, and the day a little too bright for my liking. I'm forced to squint as I watch him from my place amongst his household men who hover protectively around the proceedings, ready to act should the worst happen.

He wanted me here, to see the successful completion of his statecraft, but he did not want me too noticeable. None of these men has met me before. They know my name and could name me as my half-brother's intended heir, should he be murdered here, but that's all. And that gives me a mask to hide behind.

Athelstan bid me watch the men to determine who would be true to their word and who not. It's an interesting exercise, but I fear I might not yet be able to read men as well as my brother. To me, they all appear uneasy, as though they've been dragged here against their will. He assures me that's not the case, but I'm not convinced by the shifting looks and nervous laughter.

In my beautiful clothes, I sweat profusely and wish the sun to diminish in heat, or my brother to hurry up and conclude the ceremony upon which he's insisted.

My mother is safely back at home, in Winchester, gleeful, if such a noble lady could be, that Athelstan has managed to extend his kingdom so effortlessly. She's also pleased to have my half-sister back with her, now that she's been 'rescued' from the clutches of Sihtric's York. She will be another pawn for her to play with in her dynastic games that extend far beyond the borders of our land. My father was a virile man taking to his bed three wives, and any number of mistresses. Sometimes I think my family could populate Winchester single-handedly.

When the scribe sent home the words extolling my brother's glory in battle, my mother was pleased and ordered a mass to be raised in his honour. When he commanded that I meet him on the borderlands, to watch him receive the submission of these kings, I was keen to follow his instructions, for all that my mother clucked at his command, thinking it a little foolish to have us both in the same place at the same time.

I believe he was correct to command me to see the Kings who've agreed to his submission. They've come with the intention of being almost equals and only a little subservient. There will be a baptism of one king's son, a sign of submission, and yet others will leave a hostage in their wake or pay a small geld. My brother will come out of this as a man rich in wealth and allies.

When we leave this place, we will travel to Hereford and there begrudgingly receive the submission from those kingdoms of the Welsh disinclined to give it. This is something that Hywel of the South Britons and my brother have agreed. I think that perhaps when I compare this meeting with that one, I'll know more about the real feelings of these men.

Essentially, they're all strong enough to mount an attack against our lands. They have resources and the wherewithal to defend their lands if they must, only they've chosen not to. The scattered old British kings, with their tiny kingdoms, have no such luxury. They must submit to the greatest king my lands have yet known. It fills me with pride to watch my brother, and hope that one day I'll be as great a warrior as him. One day. But not too soon. I wish to learn more and gain experience of managing men and land.

But then my brother is much older than me. If my father had died and made me king, I would have had need of someone older to govern in my stead, and it would not have been as smooth or as orderly as Athelstan's acceptance to the kingship has been. And in all likelihood, I would not have had a chance of gaining the throne. My other half-brother, Ælfweard, who was to have ruled Wessex had he not died so soon after my father has another brother. Without my mother's alliance with Athelstan, it would be he who was destined to rule in his stead, Edwin. A brother I little like and tolerate only because I must.

For now, Edwin ferments trouble within the Witan, and it is my mother's primary role to undermine his attempts as destabilising

Athelstan's kingship. That she works ultimately for my gain does not worry my brother, the king. He's happy with the alliance he made with her when he became king of Mercia and Wessex combined. Now that his lands are so much extended, he knows that he needs someone to work on his behalf when he's away from the Witan. He's a wise man. Some liken him to my grandfather, Alfred, who held back the tide of Viking raiders when they threatened to engulf this land in a wave of warriors.

I didn't know my grandfather. I know of him, but that's not the same. He was pious and determined and stubborn. Perhaps not the greatest attributes for a great king, but that seems to little concern those who write the history of that time. I grin a little at the thought. Of course, they thought he was great for his piety; they were all men of God after all. But my brother, he too is a religious man, collecting relics of the saints and fragments of the disciple's possessions. I wonder what the chroniclers of his reign will make of this moment.

And then I smile afresh. They're religious men. They'll comment on his piety, as they did my grandfather, but I know his devotion masks his fierce desire to win. I wonder if my grandfather was the same.

Brunanburh – Olaf of Dublin – 937

I've brought many of my subordinates with me to fight for my land. The irony is not lost on me that I ask these men to fight on my behalf and yet entice Constantin and Owain from their own allegiances. That is how war should be made. The strongest men should win, those who argue that their cause if the most righteous should win out. The weaker, well, in my opinion, they should be replaced.

In all, I have near enough fifty ships with their men under my command and petty kings and earls a plenty, more than two handfuls in fact. With each ship carrying up to fifty men each, I have over two thousand men at my command. The men on this island of Britain hold sway over far greater tracts of land than do the men on my own island and I fear as I stand and watch the enemy that they vastly outnumber my warriors.

And we fight over our land more, and demand more from our followers, and harshly punish those who go against us. We think nothing of burning monasteries and nothing of murdering our rivals and nothing of demolishing their Churches, even though we are men of God. We may have smaller numbers, but we have fewer scruples about a battle. It's bloody and dangerous and not at all the grand carnival that Athelstan has brought with him.

But for all that, I make a good ally. I'm strong and powerful and have men who will follow me to their death if need be. I can't for even one moment imagine that Athelstan can say the same about his men. Well, perhaps those in his 'England' as he calls it, but certainly not in the kingdoms of the old Britons, the Welsh as they are referred to.

And his luck's now run out. He shouldn't have attacked Constantin three years ago, even if the wily old bastard was playing him for a fool. No, he should have bound Constantin to him more intimately, and what would have been closer than a blood tie, a marriage between him and Constantin's daughter. Not that I'm complaining. I find the girl pleasant enough in my bed, and it has served me far better to be able to marry the king's youngest daughter than to marry another.

He told me that Athelstan stood as godfather to his youngest son and hoped to bind the family that way. What he should have done was to arrange a marriage. Although, perhaps Constantin would have been even more wary of him if he'd suggested that, for that, after all, is how he conquered my ancestral home of York. One marriage, that lasted barely half a year, and upon the death of Sihtric, he claimed my land. What would he have done if he'd married Constantin's daughter and the old bugger had died before now? Would he have claimed the land of the Scots too, united all the people upon his island home?

I have sons aplenty already to continue my family line, and a new young wife is a pleasant pastime now that I've finally vanquished my enemies in my native land. The Limerick King, another bloody Olaf, has been bested, taken as my prisoner and now he serves me here, on English ground. He will endeavour, along with his men, to restore me to my ancestral lands of York. Perhaps then, when his work is done, I might release him from his subservience to me, provided he continues to serve me and makes an oath that he'll never again rise against me. And provided he still lives!

"Olaf," shouts Constantin from inside the tent where we are to hold our final battle conference. His voice is hoary and rough with lack of use. Or age. Probably age.

"Constantin," I reply, no need for us to use king or My Lord when we speak to each other, for we are equals. In everything.

"Are your men aware of what we hope to achieve here?" His voice, stronger now, is taunting, and I glare at him.

A smile plays around his lips, and I curb my frustration with him. This is simply his way. A little humour, a little gentle teasing. In those who hate him, it works to enrage them enough that they fight well, even if it is for him. In those who revere him, it makes them fight excellently, so either way, he wins. Not that I know this first hand but my father, Gothfrith often spoke to me of Constantin, and I listened. Carefully.

"Yes Constantin, my allies from across the sea know what's expected of them. They'll fight well."

"They better," he answers jubilantly. He knows that he's annoyed me, and that adds to his personal enjoyment.

"And your own ally?" I query. "He too knows what's expected of him."

Now it's Constantin's turn to look annoyed, and I hold my own mirth in place. It's no secret that Owain doesn't want to be here. It's also the worst kept secret that Constantin is hoping for his death so that he can replace him with someone he finds more malleable, Owain's son, or perhaps one of his own sons.

"Yes, he knows what he's to do. He'll be in the front as discussed."

"Is that truly wise?" I counter. I feel he's putting a lot of faith in a man who is only too aware that Constantin plots his death.

"Don't talk to me about battle tactics," Constantin replies hotly, "I've been fighting battles since before you were a babe. I know what I need to do to beat the bloody English."

I bow towards Constantin now and narrow my eyes at the sons and grandsons who surround him. These will be in a position of relative safety, behind Owain, but I still imagine they'll need to raise their swords and axes and engage in warfare. They'll also have the opportunity to win through to the English ranks and slay their king. They have the best position and will get the greater glory, but I've held my tongue about my dismay with the battle formation. If Constantin, all grey hair, where he has any, and white-bearded, has decided that his age and battle experience makes him the expert, then I'm happy to let him think so.

I am a victor of sneaking raids and lightning fast advances and retreats. For years I've fought the Limerick king's, and they've fought me back. Small, deadly battles. I know the importance of hand to hand combat. I know the devious ways of getting your opponents to fall into your trap, and I know that I am far more a warrior than Constantin ever was, despite his victories and battles against Edward, Athelstan's father, and Æthelflaed, his aunt.

"As you will Constantin. But when will we let the battle commence."

Constantin looks around in some surprise then.

"When we are well and good."

"I think it should be now. We don't need to posture and make any final demands; we just need to attack."

Constantin watches me carefully again and then gestures for his youngest son to come to him.

"Inform my men and Owain that we make battle now."

"My pleasure father," he says, bowing low and scowling at me as he walks past on his way towards the rest of the camp.

Constantin walks towards me and holds his hand out towards me so that I can clasp it.

"May our battle be glorious," he says, his voice booming now, his dark blue eyes blazing with fiery determination.

"It will be," I comment, clasping his arm firmly. "See you this evening, when, with Gods speed, the English king will be dead, and we'll have his land at our fingertips."

Constantin gives me a strained look then, and momentarily I worry. Does he not wish the same as me? But then, the swirl of battle preparation distracts me, and I think I don't care what Constantin hopes to gain here. As long as I get York, what more is there to fight for?

Chapter 7 – 927 - Eamont – Athelstan, King of England

My brother catches my eye from his place amongst the household troops. I can see his thoughts, even though he thinks he masks them. He's wary but contains his unease well. I'm only aware of it because I share it.

Now that the charter is signed by my fellow kings it needs to be witnessed by the ealdormen and religious men that I've brought with me to this meeting. Edmund too will witness it, only later, perhaps when we return to Winchester, and it's no longer important to keep his identity a secret.

I didn't spend much time with Edmund when he was just a boy. I was away, with my Aunt, in the Mercian lands, as my father had arranged. In fact, I little knew any of my brothers and sisters, apart from my birth sister. She was raised with me and lived with me until her marriage to Sihtric, and I've always felt closer to her than I have to any of my brothers and sisters. It's good that she's now back at the Court. I'm not sure her experience was a good one, being repudiated by her husband can't have been a pleasant experience, but I love her all the more for she has bought me her husband's old lands, now that he lies dead and buried.

In their way, my siblings all have similarities to me. Edmund, I like perhaps the most, which is good, as his mother wishes him to succeed me upon my death. I know that in the end, I'll have as little choice of my successor as my father had over his. Time and fate and God have their cards to play, and the mere whims of men seem to have little part to play in those plans.

I digress, my sister's number almost into double figures, my brothers far less. They are all good and dutiful girls, raised by either of my stepmothers in a Christian way, and yet, they have the sharpness of my tongue, a bequest from our common father. Sometimes I pity the men who are, or who will be their husbands. They'll find themselves often at a loss as to how to reply to their whims and demands, no matter how reasonable they might sometimes be.

My brothers, like me, have been raised to be warlike and pious in equal measure. Edmund is a good strategist, or at least he will be when the time comes. For now, he's a little timid with his ideas and too ready to let others steal the words from his mouth.

I hear that my half-brother Ælfweard was an unpleasant character, who tried very little to make people like him, believing he had a right as the king's heir to be liked anyway, regardless of his character flaws. Still, it is wrong to speak ill of the dead, so I shall refuse to compare myself to him. Not that it doesn't make me a little proud to hear the men of the Witan profess their complete faith in my kingship, and add with a whisper their fears that Ælfweard wouldn't have made such a fine king as I do. I hope that means that they've forgotten their discomfort when they had to elect me as their king in Wessex, an almost unknown man who wanted to rule their lands, and just maybe, take away their hard won power bases.

My other brother, Edwin, who was Ælfweard's full brother, I find not to my taste at all. I wonder if he's more like his mother, but as I knew her so little as well, it's hard to tell. I know he resents my taking the kingship, but he'd done nothing to prepare himself for the honour. Calling on his brother's supporters upon his untimely death were the actions of a desperate man, and none will forget that. For all the little snippets of gossip that come my way, I don't seriously worry that any of his half-hearted efforts to oust me will come to anything. He's an annoyance to be tolerated. Nothing more.

Edmund has a full brother as well, Eadred, the youngest of all my half-brothers and half-sisters, he's still too young to have made much progress on the man he will be when he's older. But I hold out the hope that he will be more like Edmund than my other two half-brothers. Sisters can be born with patience and a little joy. Brothers, I need to be warier.

And my sisters. I hope they're pleased with the marriages my father or I made for them. One is married to Charles the Simple, at my father's instigation and another to Hugh, Duke of the Franks, at my own and only last year. I thought I'd accomplished much when I arranged the marriage of two of my sisters last year, one to Sihtric and one to Hugh, but even with those three married, there are still a further five sisters for me to find suitable husbands. It would seem an insurmountable task if only I didn't know that I could play each marriage to my advantage.

Eadgifu, my father's second oldest daughter after my full sister, made a prestigious marriage with Charles of the West Franks. They had a son together, Louis, who now resides at my Court with my second stepmother as his guardian because his father has been deposed and imprisoned.

My sister sent him to my father's safekeeping when he was no more than a babe, and I'm pleased to carry on his duties. The lad is a small thing, with barely six years to him, but he's engaging and I know that my step-mother looks at him as little different to her children.

I've begged my sister to return home and hope that soon she will. She's missing the youth of her only son, and I pity her for choosing her husband over her child. I cannot see how her husband will ever regain his throne. No, I think that monumental task will fall on the shoulders of young Louis and that only adds to the prestige of my Court, to have the rightful heir of the West Franks as my foster son.

I think that perhaps it is Louis' presence in my Court that attracted the attention of my next sister's husband, Hugh, Count of the Franks. He approached me only last year to ask for my sister's hand in marriage. On the receipt of excellent gifts and even finer relics, I was happy to arrange the wedding. I hope she fares better than her older sister and that her husband does not spend his time in imprisonment at the hand of over-mighty ealdormen.

I'll look further afield for the next marriage alliance. I know my stepmother has her eye on a suitable husband for Eadgyth, her oldest natural daughter. I only hope that we both agree on her choice. I would also suggest that my stepmother marries again, but that would remove her from my Court, and I'm loath to do so. I need a strong woman to manage my domestic arrangements. I could, of course, ask my full sister, Ecgwynn, a widow at such a young age, but she was only ever the wife of the king of York, never a Queen as my stepmother is. It's always about the person with the most prestige.

And of course, should I ever run out of alliances for my sisters, there's always the Church for them. It would be a fine profession, to run and manage their own nunneries and it would endear me further to my Lord God. That's always to be commended.

But I digress again, and my fellow Kings are looking at me a little expectantly. With a hasty beckoning, I instruct my ealdormen to step forward and add their cross to the Charter, a slight sheen of sweat sheeting their faces as the day grows hotter, not cooler as I'd hoped. For future reference, I need to remember that looking resplendent and noble serves as nothing when the heat of the summer is at its fiercest. Red cheeks and sweat certainly detract from the regal clothing my ealdormen have chosen to wear. It's long past time that this ceremony was concluded.

Brunanburh – Owain of Strathclyde – 937

Bloody Constantin. Bloody Olaf and bloody Athelstan. Why should I be here now, with my warriors when their arguments little concern me? I've been asking myself the question ever since Constantin appeared on my doorstep, battle ready and eyebrows raised at my unprepared state.

I'd already informed him, in no uncertain terms, that I had not one whit of interest in whatever he'd agreed with the Dublin king. Certainly not after what had happened ten years ago, when he chastised me for offering sanctuary to the fleeing Gothfrith. I vowed then that I'd not trouble myself again with the affairs of Dublin and York. But Constantin, he has a way with words, a way of persuading a man even against his express wishes.

In the middle of a sumptuous feast to celebrate the marriage of my son to a girl from the Outer Isles, I was well on my way to being more than drunk and enjoying every moment of it. That was until Constantin appeared with his battle-ready troops and his bloody demands.

Helping himself to a drinking horn and drinking deeply from it, he'd looked around my tastefully decorated hall with eyes alight with mischief. His white hair had spilt down his back, and his greying beard had been splattered with my finest wine, but for all that, his stance and his warrior's clothing had made it clear that he was the true master in my hall.

"A beautiful girl," he'd offered, pointing to the bride, all dressed up in fine cloth and with her hair intricately braided, dancing with my son and any who wished to swirl and twirl her on the dance floor.

"Pretty enough," I'd countered, not wanting to upset her father, the Jarl Sigurd at my side, the man as drunk as I was. I didn't think her too lovely, but my son seemed happy so who was I to complain.

"Aye," Sigurd had interjected, "the prettier they are, the more other men want them, and the more likely they are to stray. I'm pleased my daughters are all a little bit dull."

We'd all laughed then, drunkenly sloshing our drinks down our fronts and caring not at all that our best clothes, worn only for state engagements, were now besmirched with mead. For the briefest of moments, my dismay at seeing Constantin had lifted. Perhaps, after all, it had just been a social visit.

"If this is the send off you give your troops the day before they march to battle, then I must ensure my men don't see how well you treat them," he'd drawled when his laughter had finished, and instantly I was sober. Damn the man.

"My Lord Constantin, I have no plans to take my men into battle. Did my messenger not reach you?"

Constantin's face had turned darker in the flames from the fire as I'd spoke, and I'd known to expect trouble. We'd both known each other far too long not to know how the other would react.

"I did receive a messenger, but he was not very good at delivering the message, or at least, not the right message. I punished him on your behalf."

I'd swallowed deeply then and swept a look to the churchmen in my hall, already grimacing at the display of lewd behaviour before them. It wasn't that they were particularly unctuous in their demands for a chaste court, but what was going on amongst the young men and women was a little too brazen.

I didn't look forward to the conversation I'd need to have with them about why one of their numbers wouldn't be returning. I'd hoped that a man of the church would be forgiven his message by the religious Constantin. Clearly, I'd been wrong.

"Indeed Constantin. My apologies that the message was not to your liking, but it makes it no less true."

Jarl Sigurd had shut up by now, as instantly sober as I, he was deeply embroiled in a conversation with his wife to the side of me. I'd wished I could do the same.

"How long will you need to assemble the best warriors; a day, or maybe two?"

"My warriors are here Constantin, but we have no plans to ride to battle."

He'd eyed me coolly, his displeasure increasing every time I denied his words.

"Owain, once more I think you forget the basis of our relationship and mistake it for friendship, which it most certainly isn't. You'll do as I command, or I will replace you, and your sons will never rule in your stead." His tone had been bland, almost bored as he'd looked at the on-going celebrations.

Damn him, I'd thought to myself. It always came down to this. Normally he was a kind master, but he had no compunction about reminding me that I was his creature to do with as he commanded on the few occasions that I forgot myself.

"Two days at most, Constantin," I'd heard myself replying, cursing him all the time. I was too old for this, too comfortable in my hall, and yet I couldn't argue that for Constantin was far older than I. He's a true grizzled stag, who didn't like to be reminded of the horde of grandchildren who overran his halls even though he wore his age like a cloak of office.

"Ah, that's good. Two days I can spare. We're not due to meet with Olaf of Dublin for another six days, so two days I can give you. Especially if the mead is as good as this," he'd offered, raising his drinking horn once more to his lips.

I'd pressed my own together in annoyance and a little fear. I didn't want to go to battle. I wanted to enjoy my old age and die in my bed surrounded by beautiful women, not just functional ones.

"I take it you can still wield a sword?" Constantin had asked a little scathingly as I bit back an angry retort.

Not as well as I once did, but I wasn't going to confide that in him.

"Of course, my men and I train often."

"Good, I plan on putting you in one of the forward positions."

I'd suppressed a groan at that. Clearly, Constantin has every intention of punishing me for attempting to ignore his call to arms. I may as well inform my churchmen of my wishes for my body upon my death and which of my sons I expected to succeed me. It seemed pointless to plan on returning.

As I pondered this unlooked-for turn of events, I noticed that Constantin was watching one of my sons closely, and not the one who'd just been married. Apparently, Constantin had made his decision on my successor already. Pity I agreed with him. A great shame indeed.

Two days more at home, of drinking and satisfying my needs wherever I chose. Two days more, I'd mused, draining my drinking horn once more, and impatiently waiting for it to be refilled.

I'd thought I might as well enjoy myself as I watched the swaying of the hips on the serving girl.

And I had enjoyed myself, thankfully. For now, arrayed before our combined force is the might of England, and no matter how much Constantin, Olaf, and his subordinate kings laugh and joke at their ineptitude and strut around their tents talking of how many men they'll kill and how Constantin would be rewarded when York was recaptured, I'm far more pessimistic.

The plans for my death have been made, and I accept them. My son will inherit, and Constantin will approve his succession and dictate policy to him as he has to me. If he lived, that is. He is, after all, a bloody old bastard.

Chapter 8 – 927 - Eamont – Constantin of the Scots

I mark the looks that pass between Athelstan and his brother and heir. I'm not sure of the game that Athelstan is playing here, but I don't like it. He's asked us for transparency and an alliance without bloodshed, and yet he wishes to keep his secrets.

And it's not the best secret anyway. All those who knew his father, Edward, would be able to mark the young warrior as one of his by-blows, whether legitimate in the eyes of the Church or not.

He has the regal bearing of his father; the clear and intelligent blue eyes that Athelstan also possesses. The parentage of the king is clear to see, as is the parentage of the warrior the king has been communicating with using only his eyes and his face.

Not wishing to have my observations noted, I glance unhurriedly away and meet the eyes of Ealdred, another who knew the old king. He's not paying as close attention to proceedings as I. No; he's still a little rankled that he's even here at all to concern himself with the staging of the actual event. He wants to show his face, make his agreement with the new king of the English, and then go home and protect his lands from anything that might now come, be it my people or the warriors of the Dublin Vikings.

Owain too is paying scant attention, although I think from Hywel's surreptitious glances, that he knows what the king is planning, or is at least as aware of what's happening as I am.

I watch the king carefully. He's relaxed now, but a little wary still. He has what he wants but is that all he envisages for the future? I'd thought that I'd be able to play him, with his slightly naïve outlook on life, but conceivably I've been a fool here.

Unease dulls my enjoyment. Perhaps the joke is on me after all.

"Constantin," Hywel, says my name in conversation, and I focus once more on the convivial company of my fellow Kings. They are discussing nothing of importance. No great matters of state weigh on their minds, and I wonder for a moment if they even think of what may happen next week, let alone next year. Do these men plan for the long term, or do they think only of the here and now? Perhaps it's only my longevity as king that makes me think of a year from now, ten years from now, maybe even twenty, by which time I'll be long dead and succeeded by another. Hopefully, it'll be one of my sons, but there is no certainty in the kingship of my people. I can make my son secure concerning allies and men and supporters, but that may not be enough, and we're both pragmatic enough to realise that.

Hywel is passing me the drinking horn, and I swallow the liquid, even though it burns a little on the way down. My unease will spoil the food about to be served to us, and that makes me a little annoyed. It's been a long time since I last ate, last evening when I first arrived at the English king's camp, and I would rather savour the delicious smells of fish and pork, than worry about the effects they may have on my suddenly delicate stomach.

Swallowing again, the rich wine sits a little more easily. Perhaps I'm looking for conspiracies where none exist, but I've only lasted so long as king of my people because I can read people well, I can almost see treason being plotted, and spot those who speak only to blacken my name.

Athelstan is at my side now, and he beckons us to where the table is set for us to dine before all our supporters. They'll all receive food as well, but none will be as finely served as our own which is now being brought forth from a local house that has been commandeered for the purpose.

Again, there is an order of precedence in how we're seated at the long wooden table, with elegant carved wooden chairs for us all to ease ourselves upon. Before we signed the treaty it didn't matter where we sat for then we were all equals. Now that it's signed and we've become subordinate to Athelstan it matters greatly.

Athelstan sits proudly in the centre of the table and purposefully does not watch us as we try to sidestep each other to be seated as close to the king as we dare, or as far away from the king as we'd like. It's almost as if sitting close to the king is a sign of our subservience to him, but sitting too far away could be deemed as a physical display of our unhappiness with events here. It's a difficult decision to make on the spur of the moment. I should have considered it instead of worrying about the king's intentions.

Eventually, I find myself besides Hywel who sits beside the king. On my left sits Ealdred, and on the king's other side sits Owain. He's clearly pleased with his place so close to the king, but I'm happier with my own. My men will see this for what it is; an acceptance of the treaty we've signed here, but also a show of defiance. Both stances will keep my supporters loyal and my options wide open.

Brunanburh – 937 – Constantin of the Scots

I'm watching Olaf of the Dublin Norse with distrust. I know it, and so does he. Allies and enemies, far too easy to interchange at will.

The jumped up little upstart appears to have forgotten who I am, and to have forgotten that I have almost as many links to the petty kingdoms of his homeland as he does. After all, I was raised there following my father's untimely death, concurrent with my ill-omened birth.

Olaf's domain, Dublin, is but a tiny part of the lands of the Irish. He might have amongst his allies the King of the Islands, and the son of the King of Denmark and I might have only one ally, but at least I know him, and I know he's mostly a fool and mostly harmless. And a coward.

And really, he's not my only ally, for I have my sons and my grandsons with me as well and them I trust implicitly. They have no cause to work against me, for if I die here, there is no assurance that any of them will be king after me. The kingship of the Scots does not work in such a way as the English. Just because they are royal born does not make them throne-worthy. No, my likely successor has been nipping at my heels since my accession, my cousin, Mael Coluim. He's here with me now, as he should be, and he eyes my death with impending relish. And that is all to the good because the more he wants my throne, the more my sons and grandsons work to keep me alive.

And many of them have already fought against Athelstan or at least attempted to. When he shot through my lands, his forces more akin to the Viking menaces than the sedate English king I see before me, with his massive tents and masses of supply waggons, they raced to take their warbands against him, to tempt him into a pitched battle. Sadly, they were never all where he was. Not all together, and I count myself lucky that they all nearly survived the encounters they had.

Ildulb is the son with the greatest hatred for Athelstan, and he's the son I'm trusting with the most important role of all on the battlefield; keeping Owain of Strathclyde loyal and ensuring that he doesn't run at the first opportunity. If Owain should die, it is Ildulb who will rally the remaining warriors. Ildulb is a man who understands the way other men think. They admire him and respect him, even when they don't want to, and in the press of this battle, they will turn to him as a drowning man does to the flotsam of the sea.

And Athelstan he hates with a passion born from losing something he loves. In a pitched battle involving Athelstan's ship and land army, almost at the very tip of my land, Ildulb fought with his eldest son, a young lad keen to please and as keen to fight as his father, and in the fierce fighting, Amlaib, a boy of fewer than seventeen years lost his life. And since then, for three long years, my oldest son, the brightest of all my boys, has been withdrawn and moody, quick to anger and even quicker to raise his sword against any who go against him. If nothing more, this is his chance for revenge and I know he will take it, and I pray to God that he does.

"Father," he bows his head low as he comes towards me, the top of his head bare for now as he holds his helm under his arm. As I said, he's a good son, he treats me with honour, and of everyone here, it is only I who he listens to. He's outfitted for battle already and his seeing me is just for a final confirmation of our plans. He's tall and long in the arm and the leg, his reach surpassing that of many other men. He uses his length gracefully and chillingly. He knows how to kill.

"Am I still to have the honour of fighting at the front with Owain?" He manages not to sneer as he says Owain, but only just. His anger at his son's death has turned him against all cowards, and Owain's initial reluctance to fight with me, as our treaty dictates, still rankles.

"Yes, I do. You will take your men, and you will fight amongst Owain and his own. I don't expect treachery, but neither do I expect the man to fight to the best of his abilities. I fear he saw me eying up Dyfnwal when I went to round him up."

"Is Dyfnwal here?" Ildulb asks with some interest.

"No, he's stayed to rule in his father's stead, as your brother does for me in our lands. Dyfnwal is as much a coward as his father."

Ildulb's hooded eyes lighten a little at the taunt, and I can't deny that I'm pleased to see him show some sort of emotion other than anger and hatred.

"He'll make an excellent puppet king once Owain is gone."

"Then ensure that happens."

Ildulb nods in understanding, but never quite meets my eye and for a brief moment I wonder if I've miscalculated in taking him into my confidence.

"It'll be my pleasure," he finally mutters, openly taunting me with raised eyebrows and a mischievous grin. A scar marks the right side of his face, gained from a battle in his youth when he fought with Ragnall. When he smiles, the scar stretches tightly making it appear more a grimace than a mark of happiness.

"Good. It should be." I respond, but as he turns from me I have a moment of premonition, and before he can leave my sight, I reach out and grab him in my arms, smothering this giant of a son in my arms, unminding of his coat of battle that presses into my softening body with cold patches from the metal. My arms tangle in his shield where it's held in place down his back. I note the colours of our homeland, green and blue with a fleck of purple, and I'm grateful he thought to arm all our men in a similar way. They will be easier to differentiate in the middle of the battle. He returns the unexpected embrace fully before walking away and not looking back.

He's my first-born son. My oldest child and God help Athelstan if he claims the life of him. The man will never know peace again if he should harm another member of my family. And neither will I.

Chapter 9 – 927 - Hereford – Hywel of the South Welsh

The journey from Eamont was leisurely, but not without precautions. The English king may have chosen to hunt as he travelled, but he still surrounded himself with his household troops, especially when we passed the borders with the other kingdoms of the old British. He made a point of sending out scouting parties to ensure the boundary of the old dyke was well maintained although we travelled well within the lands that look to him. He's a careful man, a man to be watched and be wary around.

The kings from the northern lands took their leave from us at Eamont, a little look of condescension on some of their faces when they offered me their farewells. They think I'm too much a pawn in the hands of the English king, but they don't understand my motivations. Torn between hostilities from either the Dublin Vikings or the English king and his pretensions to govern all the peoples of this island of ours, I'd much rather ensure my people's freedoms by turning to the English king, without bloodshed. He has given me an assurance that he'll not mount battles against us and that is what I want, the peace for my people to flourish and my coffers to grow rich with tribute. He has the honour of his grandfather, Alfred. He'll stay true to his words.

Constantin and his newly re-baptized son were the first to leave, as they had the furthest to go to reach home. The old man was subdued in his words of farewell; for all that, they were respectful enough. He and Owain and Ealdred had all been in a conference together, that was clear for me to see as they all emerged from a tent, but of what they spoke, I could not tell. None looked as though they plotted to undermine the treaty but I don't know the men well, and it's possible that they were doing more than discussing marriage alliances and exchanging family news.

Their relationships are as complicated as those of my fellow British kings and me. Family loyalties are there to be maintained unless they go against the opportunity to gain at the expense of the others. I know the game well, and I've marked them all as complicit.

If I found it strange that Constantin left alone, without Ealdred, Athelstan did not.

When Owain left, alone as well, Athelstan watched him depart with a puzzled expression on his face. Apparently, Athelstan had been expecting more words with him. I wondered what the English king had promised and subsequently had turned down.

But when Ealdred sought the king for a quiet word, I knew of what they spoke. Ealdred's fierce determination that the English king would not invade his lands was evident to see. Athelstan was keen to give the reassurance, and his face glowed with his earnestness until he offered a marriage alliance with one of his sisters and I saw Ealdred's eyes narrow in annoyance, while he was forced to mouth the words that he would consider the king's most gracious offer. I could have laughed for joy to see Ealdred so outfoxed. It is common knowledge that his wife is barren now, having produced only one son for her husband. None would object to him taking another, more fruitful bride.

On the journey here, Athelstan and I often spoke of day-to-day matters; the weather, the hunting, what was for dinner, but a note of civility touched him, and he never let his guard down. He was a king all the time, or at least that's how it appeared to me. I'm not sure what he was like when he retired to his travelling tent, surrounded by his most trusted councillors and his brother, his mass priests and his reeve and provost. I hoped he let his guard down then, and let his stiff back become a little curved as he relaxed for the first time all day. I'm not sure he did, though.

Our arrival in Hereford was heralded by a small display of the king's power when his household troops lined the road and his ealdormen who accompanied him also arranged their household troops to swell their ranks.

The other British kings were there to meet him, and that was when the situation became more complicated for me, and the family ties that had bound, or not bound, the three northern king's, became relevant for me. One of the kings come to give his submission was my cousin, Idwal of Gwynedd. He eyed me unhappily from his place atop his horse as we rode into Hereford, but there was nothing I could do to soften the far harsher terms the English king might have chosen to exact from him. His submission had been begrudging, not, admittedly, as begrudging as the other king, Owain of Gwent, but still, and as I'd told him countless times in the last few months, he would have done far better to contact Athelstan himself. If he'd sought an accord first, Athelstan, driven by his need to be a genuinely Christian king, would have had no choice but to accept the arrangement.

When Idwal approached the king, after his takeover of the old Deiran lands, he was bloated with triumph and far less lenient.

Owain too had only approached Athelstan after he became king of the English.

They and their people will now face a far more stringent alliance with the English king, but an alliance they must have if only to counter the threat of the Irish kings and the Vikings who make Ireland their home.

Rumour has it that the Dublin lands are rife with discord, but, as the Court poets teach all my people, eventually a Norse man will either bring together the discordant factions or will simply ride roughshod over them and unite them anyway. Then they'll turn their attention back this way, toward the lands of the Northumbrians and York. It's best to be united against that threat. It's best to know that the English king has our back.

Idwal is of an age with me. He has been king for a decade, and in that time he has governed well, if without flair or ingenuity. I'd rather see him under more pleasant circumstances than this, but it's still good to see him, and as I slide from my horse, he does the same, and we meet in the middle, smiles upon our faces.

"Cousin," he greets me as we embrace.

"Cousin yourself," I reply, smiling despite all this.

"And what have you been doing consorting with this Wessex whelp?"

"Helping my people, and hopefully, perhaps a little bit, yours," is my muffled response.

Stepping back he looks at me with interest in his deep blue eyes, a little more wrinkled around the edges than in the past, but still bright and genuine. I've been told that we look much alike, the spitting image of our grandfather. Now I study him carefully, noting that he looks good. I hope that I look the same. It is acceptable to be a little vain. After all, I want women to desire me for more than just my position.

Behind us, Athelstan has dismounted onto the hard packed road that runs through Hereford, a remnant of a long ago past, maintained now by the people of this small town. I take it upon myself to introduce the king to my cousin, hopeful that even now he may be prevailed upon to make the terms of this treaty a little fairer.

Athelstan is as regal as on the journey here. He doesn't wear his crown, not here, but he does have his royal sword, and his clothing is richly decorated. When he stepped from his tent this morning, bedecked in all his finery, I understood why we had travelled so close to Hereford yesterday and yet, stopped short of it. He'd needed time to prepare himself this morning. He could not have travelled far in his stiff embroidered tunic and flowing cloak.

He greets Idwal and Idwal after a nod from me, instantly descends to his knee, while beside him Owain shows his disdain for such a show of subservience in the roll of his eyes, and his refusal to follow suit. That Athelstan is pleased by this show is clear to see, and Idwal is only on his knee for a few moments.

Owain steps forward as one amongst equals, and Athelstan's face clouds. This is not what he wants to see.

Idwal meets my eye, his face blank but his eyes dancing with amusement that his show of deference now has worked so well. I've been sending messengers to him since I met Athelstan at Eamont, trying to show him how to make the best of this situation. I don't want him to be too belittled by the English King, after all, we share blood, but neither do I want him to be acceptable just because he's my kin. He must make allowances and win the English King's trust, as I've done. I don't think it'll be an easy task, but he's started well.

Around us, the trappings of the English king are rapidly being brought to attention. The horses have been led away, and in the near distance, I can see a medium sized hall, with its door flung wide. I assume that it's to there that we'll walk and have our meeting.

The king's royal followers are busily filing inside already, while others dance attendance on my fellow kings and I. A drinking horn is passed to me, to quench the thirst of the road, and I share it willingly with Idwal.

"Thank you for your messengers," Idwal comments under his breath, as he steps close to me.

"My pleasure Cousin, but the terms are still not going to be to your liking."

"I know, but if they can be softened a little, that's all to the good. You were perhaps correct to recommend this course before."

I chuckle at his rueful tone,

"I don't think 'perhaps' is the right word, but as apologies go, I'll accept it," I comment, glancing sharply at where Owain and Athelstan are still making attempts at a stilted conversation.

"Now come, let's precede the English King inside. It'll be another way we show our subservience."

Trying, but failing not to show his amusement at such a simple matter, Idwal walks beside me into the brightly lit room.

A huge table dominates its centre, while a small fire roars away merrily, its heat not really needed for anything other than cooking. Around the table, the king's scribe is at work, and I watch him for a moment, wondering just what the king has decided to put in his treaty. Unlike at Eamont this submission has not been carefully preordained. Here, the English king is the master for Idwal and Owain have chosen to make peace rather than a war. It'll be interesting to see how far Athelstan thinks he can push them. I've heard outrageous numbers for a tithe being bandied about by men of the household troops. I only hope, for Idwal's sake, that Athelstan has shown more caution than that.

Brunanburh – Edmund of England – 937

The men of the council are severe and excited in equal measure. This battle must be a victory, for everyone in this erected tent near the boundary of the old Mercian kingdom. For all the joking of the brother ealdormen, and for all Athelstan's good cheer, I know that the weight of this battle rests heavily upon him.

Never one to doubt himself, not once in his thirteen years as king, my half-brother looks a little haunted no matter how hard he tries to mask it. I glance between the brothers, and they return my stare entirely. They know Athelstan as well as I do, for all that he likes to think he's unreadable and inscrutable.

But there is only one thing for it, to plan and prepare. There is no going back from this battle, and whether his poets from far distant lands sing our praises or lament our demise, this battlefield will be remembered for many long years and talked about for even more. Never before have so many enemies amassed in one place.

Athelstan the Ealdorman sidles over to where I stand, slightly behind and to the right of my brother. Many years ago my brother the king instructed me to stand in just such a position whenever a Witan was convened, or a more informal meeting took place. That's the only instruction he's ever given me, everything else has been a gentle guiding so that I act as he hopes. He does not like to issue me with instructions. He doesn't wish everyone at the Witan to see me as simply his image made flesh again. He wants me to be unique and my own man.

"Your brother looks keen to engage," Athelstan the ealdorman says.

"He is, yes. He has unfinished business with Constantin and even more unfinished business with Olaf of Dublin."

"So I understand. And you? What of your unfinished business?"

I feel myself tense a little at his words for all that they are kindly meant. He's my oldest friend, and he knows me as he does his siblings.

"I will see that I finish what I can, and avoid the worst of him."

"Good, and I'll have my two other brothers as your constant companions. They'll not let the old bugger Constantin anywhere near you."

I look at him in surprise. I'd not expected such care for my person. Ealdorman Athelstan doesn't meet my eye as he speaks, his tone firm, brokering no argument. Perhaps this is not a concern for my person, but a way of ensuring his future.

Angrily, I shake my head. The ealdorman Athelstan is my oldest friend, he may well have firmly saddled himself to my party at the Witan, but I know that in a case of life or death he would die for me regardless. I've simply spent too many of my years at Athelstan's sophisticated Witan where rumour and counter-rumour are always in great abundance, most of it at the hand's of half-brothers who proved impossible to tame and forced certain unfortunate events to happen that I deign not to think about now.

"My thanks, Athelstan," I hear myself say, and I mean it. Completely. Athelstan my brother and king has taken it upon himself not to discuss with me my involvement in the death of Constantin's grandson three years ago in the run up to this new engagement. I think he knows that the Scots king will be seeking my death in retaliation, and I also think that he's decided that the safest way to deal with the problem is to disregard it and never voice it. That way it can't happen. My half-brother's naivety over certain matters is laughable. Trust Athelstan, his namesake, and Ealdorman to think about the matter more. I imagine that it's plagued him ever since he received his summons from the king.

In front of us, I sense Athelstan's shoulders stiffen a little at our words, and I imagine he's heard them, and that dismay has briefly clouded his face. But he doesn't turn. I step forward and place my hand on his shoulder, and he relaxes at the touch. What a fool I am to think he doesn't think of these things. More than likely it's he who's arranged for ealdorman Athelstan's brothers to stand as my minders and more than likely he who's asked Ealdorman Athelstan to speak to me of it. He's concerned with even the smallest detail of this battle to come. He knows where everyone should be and when they should be there.

His hand reaches up and grasps mine and then it's all to business. The other ealdormen and leaders of the king's household troops are entering the tent, expressions from serious to cheerful to terrified etched onto their faces. The king has asked the ealdormen not to send their young sons and probable heirs, but when the glory of England is under attack, it would have been an impossible task for the men to keep their son's at home. I only hope that the crush and noise of the battle does not send the youths into a frenzy of terror.

Æthelwald and Eadric, the brothers of Athelstan, are watching me intently as if communicating their intent using only their eyes. I nod to acknowledge them both, and they relax their posture and look a little more pleased with the battle to come. They are similar in appearance to Athelstan, although Eadric is broader and Æthelwald narrower. I wonder if they worried that I'd reject their brother's words and demand he holds them away from me. And then I wonder why they told me at all. Perhaps it was so that my own heart would stop beating quite so fast, and I would stop thinking about my impending death, real or imagined as it might be.

Guthrum, who Athelstan spoke of earlier, is a great giant of a man, proud of his Viking ancestry, he's perhaps the most liberal and civil of the men within the small space, excluding the king of course. He's older than us all and has been one of Athelstan's ealdormen since the very beginning, an early convert to the Mercian king. For all that we joked about him earlier, I would be honoured to have the huge man fighting beside me, as would any of us. His weapon of choice is his fists, followed by his war axe. He was taught to fight by his father and grandfather, men of direct Viking descent in the Danelaw. He can do things with a shield, an axe and his fist that make men's eyes water and attempt at their peril. Even now he teaches me new techniques to employ, and I thank him every time. I think the man knows a hundred ways to kill a man.

Aelfwald and Uhtred, one an Englishman and one a Viking descendant, are the two men currently highest in the king's affections. They are as different as its possible to be. Neither man is small, but Aelfwald is English in looks, and deportment while Uhtred looks to his Viking heritage. I know that Athelstan values them so highly precisely because they are so different and so keen to speak their minds. And the words that they speak are always reasoned and concise, but still two sides of the same coin. They both come with their elite household troops and also at the head of their fyrds. They will take the difficult positions on the flank of the main attack, and neither will dare to disappoint their king.

Not all the ealdormen are here, deliberately so. Osulf and Scule have been commanded to hold the position close to the Royal Court in Winchester. Should the worse befall us here, they'll stand between any daring attacks into the deep South, either by land or by sea, and the rest of the royal family, my younger brother ready and able to be crowned king if the need should arise. Which I hope it doesn't, as does he. He took me aside and told me so, and I was honoured and relieved. I had hoped he'd grow into a man with my outlook on life, not like his half-brother, Edwin. The less said about him, the better.

Other men are here too, even some of the more militant churchmen, with their battle equipment in place and strange half enlightened expressions on their faces. I hope that God has spoken to them kindly this morning.

Bishop Theodred of London is amongst us, as is Alfred of Sherborne and Cenwold of Worcester and Odo, a man who should have been a warrior first and foremost but who instead is a warrior of God. They are militant men of God with their warriors. Whether the king approves or not it's difficult to say. I think he prefers the bishops to keep to their monasteries and churches, but their presence amongst us does add another layer of righteousness to our cause. A divine righteousness.

And then there are a few other men of note, Ælfwine and Æthelwine, grandsons of Alfred, just as I am, only a step or two further away from the ruling family, and as such, not quite throne worthy. Battle worthy for sure, they are great warriors having fought against the Scots three years ago. It's funny how they have the trust of the king whereby his half-brothers did not, but then, they don't want his crown, and never have. They'll happily fight at his side for the good of our people and their land, and they wear the colours of the royal family as well. They are men of Wessex first and then Englishmen second. Never forget they have something for which they fight.

The king calls the meeting urgently to order, but before he can utter another word, one of the outrider's races into the tent and Athelstan nods to show he should speak first.

"My lord king," the man begins, but Athelstan waves aside his flattering speech and the man, apparently accustomed to his King's ways abruptly stops and starts his message,

"The enemy is getting ready. Olaf and Constantin are donning their armour and arranging their shield wall."

Athelstan takes the words well for all that it might mean he's lost the initiative. He takes a breath and looks at the assembled crowd.

"Gentlemen, we all know where we should be and how we'll win the coming battle. This meeting was more of a chance for final words than anything else, and we don't need them. Go, ready your men, ready yourselves. And remember, we fight for what is ours, against men who do not keep their word and against men who are fickle in their allegiances. Rid our land of this menace, and do so with God's blessing." His voice doesn't rise as he speaks, but his fierce determination lends a threat to the gently uttered words that shouting them wouldn't have accomplished.

The men cheer his words and walk confidently from their aborted meeting. Athelstan the Ealdorman grins at me as he walks past but doesn't speak, and behind me, I feel his brothers take up their preferred positions. I glance at my brother the king, and he too smirks at me, and a calmness sweeps through me. My humour of earlier has been masking my fears, but now I'm ready for whatever might come today.

Armed with everything I need already, I sweep my shield onto my arm, noticing dispassionately that it's weighted perfectly, and the new layer of paint is bright and fresh. All will know that I'm a man firmly behind the king and a member of his family. My chest swells with pride as I step into the brightening day.

All around me other men act the same, stepping from their tents; fully armed, shields, swords, arrows, bows and spears either in their hand or around their battle belts. There's a glint of metal from the iron rivulets the men have woven into their battle coats.

The men are silent, or quiet as they talk to their comrades. Many know they'll not survive the day but who those will be is only God's doing.

Chapter 10 – 927 - Hereford – Athelstan

I've been to this place before, with my aunt when I was a youth, and she was busily reinforcing the boundaries against the ancient British. I think my father and I have come a long way since then, no longer on the defensive but firmly on the offensive.

The kings have appealed to me now, asking for an alliance without bloodshed. Pity, it's only after I've made my mark and taken the lands that my dead brother-in-law, Sihtric, once reigned over; after I've proved that I can best these men from Dublin, descendants of Vikings, who crawl over land that's not theirs, like ants.

I know they plague the British kings as much as they did my grandfather, father and aunt, but I'll not let them again. No chance. They can't beat me and my desires for a united land to be the envy of the people who occupy the lands across the sea where my sisters have married into the royal families.

My father, for all his apparent antipathy toward me, knew how to govern and rule well. He may not have intended to, and he certainly didn't act like my grandfather regarding his relationships with women, but he emulated him in almost every other way, regarding learning and his relentless march against those who'd taken the lands of the Mercians and the other ancient kingdoms.

I'm proud to continue his legacy, and that of my grandfather, but I will do more as well. Take back more land, either through war or peace and if, in the process, I exact some revenge for past actions, then I must.

And grandfathers and fathers have much to answer for here. Hywel and Idwal are cousins, I know this, and I also know that my grandfather Alfred was responsible for their grandfather's death. The great Rhodri whose dynasty has tried to dominate the old British lands ever since his death has left his mark on his old lands, and yet without him, they can't be held by just one man, but have fractured back into individual nations. And that is their weakness, and one I plan to exploit. That and pushing back their boundaries so that my people gain at their expense.

No longer will I allow the old dyke to serve as the visible boundary. No, from now on the River Wye will demarcate our lands. In peace, I'll gain more than the wars of my grandfather and father. Provided that is, they agree to sign the treaty.

I suppose that Idwal and Owain could change their mind, even this late in the day if my terms are too harsh. But with my household troops on display, and my ealdormen's troops as well, I hope to discourage them with my show of force.

As demanded, they do not have many men in attendance upon them, and so I would win any battle that took place here. That's good. I'd rather not fight. I'd rather have these kings as my friends, and a further force against the might of the Vikings, should they attack again. The more obstacles in the path of the Dublin Vikings when they set foot on this land, the better.

Idwal has bent his knee before me. Owain will not. Hywel did not need to because he came willingly to make his peace with me. These men rule small and disparate kingdoms. I liken it to the lands of the individual Anglo-Saxon kingdoms, which fell such easy prey to the Viking menace. I wish these men would realise that only by allying with each other do they stand a chance of beating the Vikings. And yet, I can't blame them. The king's of Northumbria, Mercia and the other kingdoms didn't realise that only through unity could they defeat the Vikings. My grandfather understood the truth of this, and I will strive to prove this correct. I'll hold my lands and keep them whole and bequeath them to my successor.

But I stray from the here and now. As I say, Idwal has bent his knee and now speaks with Hywel. They are much alike, but their terms will be different. Owain. He's another matter entirely. His very bearing makes it clear that he doesn't want to be here. I wonder why he came at all. There are other British kingdoms that have not sought peace with me. I respect them for that but know I'll have to try and undermine them in a different way. Owain. I could crush him or befriend him. Only time will tell as to which option I choose but why he's here when he doesn't want to be is a mystery to me.

Within the hall being prepared before us, I know that my scribes are completing the treaty. The long days and nights of my journey here have been spent thinking and plotting. My closest advisors, the ealdormen, the holy men and my closest friends and advisors, have all made suggestions as to how we can gain the most without losing the friendly overtures of these men. I only hope I've shown enough caution. I should have run the terms past Hywel, but I'm still a little unsure of him.

He reminds me too much of myself, and I know what that could portend.

With Hywel beside me, and his cousin next to him, and Idwal to my left, we walk into the hall. I feel a little apprehensive, more so than with the Northern Kings, even though I am in the most dominant position here.

I offer a silent prayer to God that I've acted as I should.

Brunanburh – Olaf of Dublin – 937

My allies mill around me in confusion and my frustration starts to boil. What started earlier as us having the advantage of surprise has quickly dwindled away to nothing. The English are lining up as orderly as they've made their camp, and they come almost silently as well, and their silence makes the men more belligerent to be ready. If the English would only come in a rush and howl of rage, then I know that these warriors of mine would be ready in the blink of an eye. Instead, the Englishmen's secret passage has fooled all of my warriors into thinking that this is not the beginning of a battle, that somehow it's more a display of their weapons than anything else.

My warriors argue and curse each other. None make natural allies, too used to being enemies but they assured me and promised me that they would put their differences aside for this battle. Apparently, they bloody lied.

At my side, my commanders, brothers and sons, are as silent as the English. They are ready and keen to get on with the fighting and further along our lines, Constantin and his own less than reliable ally, Owain, are also ready. I can feel their watchful eyes on me, and I'm trying my hardest not to meet the heat of their gazes. I can offer no explanation for the confusion around before me.

Ivarr, the proud son of the new king of Denmark, is busy arguing with anyone who steps too close to him. He'll be no help in the shield wall if he doesn't allow one of the other kings to fight alongside him. I don't much like him, but he brought great wealth and a full ship of warriors with him when he washed up on my shore at the beginning of the year. I was loath to turn him away although now I'm starting to wish that I had. Perhaps there was some truth to the rumours brought to me that Ivarr had been sent away by his father, the new king of Denmark, Gorm because he was causing too much trouble in their newly conquered land, his arrogance undermining his father's hard work.

Even his outfit shouts of his self-importance. His clothing is littered with precious metals, silver and gold run through his mail rings, even though they are soft metals, more likely to be pierced by swords and axes and arrows. His shield has an enormous golden boss at its centre, and from it, sprays of golden rays stretch to its edges. I hope that the gold is just a coating, but I doubt it. I can't see him surviving the day, but mayhap, his father will thank me for ridding him of the menace.

Gebeachan, the King of the Islands, is finding the entire situation far too enjoyable, and every time that Ivarr looks almost ready, with his weapons arranged as he wants them, Gebeachan steps just too close to him and knocks his arm, and the entire debacle starts all over again. I almost wish that the English would just rush across our no man's land and launch the attack. But they won't. I imagine they're too honourable to attack before everyone is ready. Bloody fools.

Finally, I can take it no more, and with quick words to my most trusted brother, he's striding towards the two men who are holding up the formation of our shield wall. No sooner has he reached Ivarr than his angry, twisted face looks my way but in no time at all, he's lined up amongst his men and next to Gebeachan. The King of the Islands is given no time to smirk at his seeming triumph for Sigfrodr speaks to him just as harshly. Suddenly he too is ready and prepared, his men in formation around him, their chosen weapons in their hands, as they hold their shield loosely or rest them against their lower legs.

I scowl at them both. If they should live through today, I'll punish them both for their behaviour. Of all the men here, the earls who serve under me, and the petty kings I oversee, it's these two who've caused the most trouble. There are many men and untried youths but none more challenging than Ivarr and Gebeachan.

Signalling to Constantin that my allies are now ready, I avoid the knowing sneer on his face as I eye the number of men he has. I'm pleasantly surprised to see so many. Not only is Owain there with the men from Strathclyde, centred on the enemy and keen to engage, but at least four of Constantin's sons are also leading their men and even some of his grandsons. He is a man rich in descendants, and yet it's Mael Coluim who will rule when he's gone. I'd like to change that, have my own son's, when they come, rule in place of their grandfather, but I know better than that.

Constantin has his standard-bearer wave in acknowledgement, and then I finally turn my attention to the amassed English.

As I said, what started with us having the initiative has dwindled to us having no initiative at all. The enemy arrayed before us are just as many in number as we are. Our lines stretch along their huge length of over five hundred men each without one or other outmatching the other.

I note where the English king stands, ready and waiting, surrounded by his most trusted warriors and I note where the object of Constantin's anger stands, off centre and to the right of Athelstan. That is where the main charge from Ildulb and Owain will be, and from squinting into the growing daylight, it appears as though the English king has taken more than sufficient precautions. Here, the numbers of men swell; for all that I do not know the names of any of them, other than the king's brother, Edmund.

On the outer reaches of their shield wall, the numbers noticeably thin and I hope that the men on the far edges have taken the time to note this. It should prove an easy place to break into their numbers.

Behind them all lies a line of raised turf and the scouts have informed us all that this is more of a hill than we would at first think from our current position. They warn that the ground can be marshy and the hill difficult to climb should the English retreat that far.

I have no intention of that happening, and nor does Constantin. We have a small force of our men held in reserve and if we need them, and the time marches on that far, then they will infiltrate the area between the men and the hill. We'll not let them climb out of our reaches.

Across the divide I see a man step forward surrounded by ten other heavily armoured warriors. My eyes roll in frustration. Does this English king have to do everything that is deemed honourable? Could he not just let the battle commence without the need to attempt a reconciliation at this late stage?

At my side, my son is as impatient as I.

"Will this thing never sodding start?" he mutters darkly, his face turned away from me, but I can imagine it scowling in contempt. Ragnavaldr has grown to be a youth with little patience, like his grandfather before him.

"All in good time," I caution, although, I like him, feel his frustration.

From behind me a small wave of chanting begins, started no doubt by my blood hungry brother, Sigfrodr. He fears death, not at all and never has. He's fought for me in the guerrilla warfare that's allowed me to quell all other pretenders to my land and throne within Dublin.

I raise my arm above my head to show that I agree with the warrior's impatience and the roar increases ten-fold. Such simple things make the men realise that I am the same as them, and my men will redouble their efforts to best the English.

In-between the two opposing forces, I see the spokesman and his entourage falter a little, and then I laugh out loud, the sound echoing around me and magnifying as other's join me. A stray arrow, loosed by one of our few archers has landed quivering in the ground just in front of the feet of the man and his warriors. For all that they wear all their armour and weapons, with helms on their heads, they hesitate at this act of war and look uncertainly back towards their king. Something passes between them, and they turn around without making contact, and more and more arrows chase them back towards the safety of their shield wall.

The noise from my men grows louder and louder, the crash of swords and hammers on shields, the undulating cry of men who hunger for blood, and suddenly we're moving forward, slowly but surely, this battle has been joined.

Chapter 11 – 927 – Hereford – Hywel of Dyfed

Even I'm surprised by the terms being laid out before Idwal and Owain. They're harsh but fair all at the same time. My admiration for Athelstan has increased once more.

He demands a tribute, a massive tribute; only it's for things that are abundant in the lands of Idwal and Owain, and myself if I must participate here as well. The gold and silver weight will be easy to accumulate, the oxen, hounds and hawks even easier. The numbers might be huge but they're manageable, and beside me, I feel Idwal relax a little that the number is only 25000 and not 50000 as it might have been. Even Owain looks a little pleased, a half-smile playing around his lips.

The only sticking point and this does concern me, is the idea that the great Wye River should now act as the border in the southern lands. Owain and I both shift uncomfortably at the thought that the English will now be so close to our heartlands. I know this is a punishment for Owain, but I'm unhappy about it too. The English king and his well-disciplined troops are all well and good, provided they're more than a day's march from my homeland.

Idwal smirks a little at his good fortune, for he still has the old Dyke as the boundary and I smile back although it grates on me. The lucky bastard. Bend his knee only now and be left almost alone! I'm outraged by his fortune. I just hope that in private, Athelstan has some reassurances for me, and they must not revolve around a marriage agreement. I've long had my sons and daughters arrayed around me. Perhaps when I journey to Athelstan's English Court, I'll take them along with me, or at least one or two of them. I need no more wives, and I'll not gift an English wife to my son's.

Once more we go through the motions of having the terms of the treaty spoken out loud before we must sign our agreement to it. Again, I plan on being the second behind Athelstan to do just that, but out of the corner of my eye I can see Idwal preparing to scamper to his feet, and my need fades away. I'll not play the game of favourites with my cousin, and he knows it. The smirk on his face makes that clear for me to see.

Instead, I sit back and work hard to relax my tense body. I want to appear as nonchalant as Athelstan about the whole thing.

The voice of the scribe drones on and on, rising and falling with the nature of the demands. Loudly he proclaims the greatness of Athelstan and quietly the terms of the treaty, almost as if he's a little embarrassed by them. I don't see why what's agreed here should affect the scribe at all. He'll be safely protected either by the king or by the community of his religious house. Why should he care one way or another about Athelstan's terms?

The king's closest advisors are still in attendance upon him as he makes this new treaty. I muse as to who is governing their lands in their absence, but I know they wouldn't be here if they feared any problems. Ordgar, Aelfwald, Osferth and Wulfgar; the king's ealdormen. I've still to determine who rules where but understand that Athelstan holds much of the old kingdom of Wessex himself, for all that he was raised in the Mercian lands of his aunt. Wessex is the heartland of his lands, and he guards it jealously.

I wonder why the King doesn't use his many brothers to govern the old kingdoms. And then I smirk at my stupidity. What could be worse than having your family rule in your stead? Just because they share a father, or a mother, or both, it doesn't mean that they're alike. Apparently, he thinks highly of his brother, Edmund, but I know little about the other brothers. I do pity him having so many close contenders for his throne.

Finally, the scribe has finished his recounting of the treaty, and with a look first left and then right down the line of king's, Athelstan rises and places his mark on the agreement. Besides me, Idwal makes to stand, but then sits again and allows me to go first, his face creased with delight at his trick. Ignoring him, and grateful he's only my cousin and not my brother, I rise and mark my name.

The treaty is a beautiful piece of penmanship, and I hesitate just for a moment before I lean forwards. I wouldn't want to drip my ink where it shouldn't be.

With a flourish, I make my mark and step towards Athelstan. He stands a few paces away watching my fellow kings with interest, a drinking horn in his hand. He passes it to me with a smile.

"Your cousin?" he queries, nodding towards Idwal.

"Yes."

"You look alike."

"As you do to your half-brother."

That upsets Athelstan a little, and I see him jump a little at my casual mention of his brother.

"I didn't think you'd noticed," he offers by way of an explanation.

"The family resemblance is too great to ignore."

Athelstan laughs then, his face relaxing for the first time since I met him at Eamont.

"We must all try and keep a few secrets."

"I would suggest you try and keep a better one next time," I laugh as I speak, swigging from the drinking horn as Idwal places his mark on the treaty.

Athelstan merely harrumphs at my words and I smile even wider. It's been a difficult few months, and now I know the work and thought I've put into everything is coming to an end. Soon I'll be able to travel to my home and bed my woman and relax.

Idwal joins us, looking from the English king to myself in interest.

Behind us, Owain stands and saunters to the treaty. He's handed a pen to add his mark, but before he does so, he hesitates and peers through the open doorway at where his small force of supporters is milling around. There is the bark of laughter and a cough of amusement, combined with the shuffling of the horses. A loud clang of metal on stone resounds within the hall, and we all jump at the loud noise and look behind us.

The cook looks our way apologetically as the cook pot tumbles onto the hearthstones, spilling the contents onto the small fire. Liquid sizzles in the heat and a delicious smell comes my way.

Owain curses loudly, and I turn back to him. Clearly, he'd marked the treaty with green ink, and the scribe shakes his head in dismay at the mess before him.

Athelstan flicks his hand, and a new cookpot is immediately in place.

"We may have to wait a little longer to celebrate our agreement," he offers by way of explanation, as a young lad winds his way through our small group, refilling the drinking horn as he goes.

"My Lord Athelstan, I apologise for my accident," Owain calls across the small space; now that he's hummed and hawed and finally added his signature.

"My scribe will do all he can to preserve the contents. Now come, we'll retire outside until our meal is ready."

Athelstan leads the way, and Owain smirks my way.

"I hope I've not obscured anything of importance," he whispers, and I suddenly realise that this little act of defiance has been choreographed. His pettiness annoys me, but it's nothing new. He can be devious when he wants to be. I look forward to the day that I can, hopefully, take the land he rules over from him, or his descendants.

It makes sense to me that like the lands of the Old Saxon kingdoms; the lands of my fellow British should be united, as my grandfather thought. Pity that Alfred killed my grandfather and his empire crumbled. But I'll bide my time and see what happens. I can act just as quickly and decisively as Athelstan if the opportunity presents itself and I hope it does and at Owain's expense, or my cousins, or one of the other king's who've not come here today. I don't mind who has to die or be deprived of their throne, provided my land expands.

For now, I wonder how he managed to convince the king's cook to drop their cook pot. And then I look again. The cook now busy at work is different to the man who was there before, and his face has flushed an angry red. Clearly, the other man was an imposter, and this is the real cook. The English king needs to be more careful here. The borderlands that divide the British and the English are a hotbed of conflicting and contradictory allegiances. Here more than anywhere else on our journey, it's important to be circumspect.

The commands coming from the king's men assure me that the risks are now being taken a little more seriously, and as we step into the dull summer's day, I watch the pretend cook being led away between two of the king's household troops.

The smug expression on Owain's face has disappeared but has worked its way over to my own. The man is a fool after all.

Brunanburh – Athelstan, King of England - 937

My heart was beating a little too fast, but now it's calm. We're ready for this. Far more prepared than the rabble who face us.

They may well have spurred the overtures of peace offered by Archbishop Odo, much to his consternation, but I expected nothing else. I warned him, but he wanted to try and being a most Christian king, I had no choice but to give him a chance.

Now he knows, as I did, that they're not interested in peace, only bloodshed and victory, for themselves. I'll not be giving it to them.

The first arrows have flown from their side, and although they've not hit any target yet, their intent is clear.

Purposefully, I've loaded the battlefield so that it appears as though there are weak spots. There aren't, but I will use guile to trick them if I must. They think me honourable, and I am, but I want to win this battle even more than they do.

In front of me, Edmund holds his own amongst a combination of my household troops and members of the Mercian fyrd. There is little difference between the skills of the warriors. The Mercians are so used to fighting against their enemies that even those who think themselves no more than farmers and would arm themselves with nothing but a hammer or a hunting bow and arrow are more skilled than men trained since birth to wield the weapons of war in the calmer southern lands.

The Mercian's are merciless and will fight to the death. As will Edmund.

From behind me, I can feel our handful of archers mount the small rise that we might use as a mustering point, or retreat to, or just drag our enemies to so that they perish in the ditch we've dug and filled with sharpened stakes of wood. For now, they will unleash a rain of arrows onto the heads of the enemy. Hopefully one or two of the enemy may flee in fear, and the opportunistic arrows may cut down one or two.

The men of the enemy are cheering derisively as their spears and arrows quiver in the bare ground before us. But their cheers quickly turn to cries of fear as the first arrows from my archers whistle amongst them. The raising of their shield wall resounds up and down their line in an echo of wood and clang of steel, and I think that now they realise we mean to beat them here today. We might be more organised than them, but that doesn't mean are less efficient, less blood hungry. Far from it. It means that we've taken the time to train for this eventuality. This is not an opportunistic attempt to land grab. Not like the Scots and the Norse.

One or two men fall untidily from the long, ragged line facing me, arrows protruding from exposed chests and backs. My well-trained men cheer now and shout insults at the enemy. And then slowly, and step by step, the advance begins. We are taking the battle to them, whether they like it or not.

Olaf and Constantin's men are a strange collection of all shapes and sizes, and colours of skin vary from the pale white of the northern lands to the darker tans of the Irish who fight for their king's. There is every shade of hair colour and every shade of shield and clothing. I wonder what they think of the uniform shields they face, or painted with the wyvern and the colours of the Wessex, and now, English kings.

I offer a final prayer to God, that my brother will fight as well as he can, and that tonight we will sit and talk about the day's dour work.

I offer a final prayer to God that all my ealdormen and military bishops will live through the battle.

And I just manage not to utter a prayer calling for Constantin's death. He is a man of God just as I am and I as much as I loath him for his false oaths, I know that he acts as he does because he believes he's doing the correct thing for his people and his God. Pity he's not as honourable as Hywel of the Welsh in his actions, but then even Hywel has been a little distant of late, unsure as to whether he should stand with the English or against us in this coming battle. He, at least, had the honour to seek me out himself and tell me of his fears and hopes, almost as if he was asking for my permission not to be here. Of course, I gave it, with a smile on my face. Luckily for him, he did not see my inner disappointment.

When we vanquish our enemies here, I will not exact further concessions from Hywel but will do all I can to woo him back to my court, if for no other reason than I miss talking to him. He is an intelligent man and has had the honour to travel further than I in his lifetime. I like to hear his tales of his trip to the land of the papacy and the communities he visited along the way. I envy him. I have my mass of relics sent from across the lands over the sea and collected within the lands of the English, but to have visited the holiest of places is something I can only dream off. I console myself with a fragment of the holy cross, a thorn from the holy crown, but in my heart, it is never enough for my religious fervour. I want to see it all.

And the other petty kings of the land of the ancient British. When I win this battle, and I will win this battle, they will be placed under far stricter surveillance. Any covert help they've given to the Dublin Norse must be stamped out. Once and for all.

Chapter 12 – 927 - Winchester – Edmund of England

My brother and I have finally returned to Winchester, to be greeted by the Queen and my remaining brothers and sister. We come in triumph, and my half-brother grins as he rides through the land. He might look more like a boy on his first horse, but no one has the heart to remind him of his position. Instead, we all share his joy, for he has accomplished much and in a short space of time.

For now, it appears our borders with the Scots king and the king of Strathclyde are secured, as is the border with Bamburgh, and the Britons. The Dublin Norse has no foothold on the island we all share, and the Northmen are quiet as if they sleep in their winter beds already. The Five Boroughs are almost reconciled with the king.

But, as with all things, peace in one place does not mean peace in another.

The Royal Court at Winchester is awash with rumours and counter rumours, and they greet us, almost like a wave of sound, when we return home.

My mother meets the King and me with a small religious ceremony in which Athelstan's favourite priest offers prayers for his safe return, unharmed and victorious. We ignore the sniggers coming from my older half-brother. He's apparently been drinking since waking and is intent on making a fool of himself.

Athelstan somehow lets the incident pass him by, but it's a bad sign of things to come. My oldest half-brother, who can be as placid as anyone, has his limits, and I fear immediately that Edwin will do his best to reach those limits. I'm not sure what he hopes to achieve. He has little support amongst the men of the Witan, and his mother is locked up tight in her nunnery and has been since my mother married the king. She has no power amongst the men of the Witan, no say at all. And he has even less since his older brother's death – the king who ruled for only sixteen days.

Athelstan does not trust him, as he does me. He'll not let him be known as his heir, nor let him lead his household troops. I pity Edwin a little. My father pampered him and his older brother. With his older brother's death, he's lost his place at Court and doesn't know how to fill the void. He's bitter and resentful, especially of Athelstan's success and military prowess.

By rights, he should retire to his estates somewhere, marry, have his children and forget that he was ever an atheling. But he won't do that. He thinks far too much of himself. Instead, he'll cause trouble and do everything in his power to unbalance the king's power.

My mother comes to me later that day, finds me in the stable ensuring my horse is being well cared for. He was a gift from my father, and one I love dearly.

"Edmund," she begins, wrinkling her nose a little at the smell, but smiling at my interest in the horse.

"Your father chose well when he gifted him to you."

"Yes, he's an exceptional animal, and an adequate reminder of the affection father had for me."

She smiled at that. She'd had much warmth for my father as well. I don't know if it was ever loving, but he pleased her, and she pleased him. I know she misses him, even though she's now freer than ever before in her life. She's made it plain that she doesn't wish to remarry and Athelstan has accepted that with no qualms. He doesn't need any more people with a tenuous hold on the throne.

"Athelstan has done amazingly well."

"Absolutely. He's resolved to uniting the Old Saxon lands."

"And he'll continue to work for that?"

"Oh yes, I think he's set his sights on the lands of the Five Boroughs now, and he's mentioned going to the south-western areas as well."

"But they look to him anyway," she queried.

"When it suits them they do. He wants to make it a more permanent arrangement."

She nodded in understanding and looked at him sideways.

"You've changed in your time away."

"I've seen at first-hand what can be accomplished with the correct ... attitude," he responded, smiling at his mother. He couldn't deny that he felt more confident than before he'd escorted his brother first north and then west and then south again. He'd seen battle, albeit a short one, and he'd met men who didn't like the English and yet who grudgingly agreed to follow them before of their military might and prowess. He felt different. He felt strong, committed and resolved.

"And what's happened here in my absence. I see Edwin is as difficult as normal."

His mother rolled her dark blue eyes at the mention of him.

"He's a fool, and he makes himself a bigger fool every day. He's lost the respect of the few who did see him as a possible heir, and that's just made him even more unbearable. I'm glad he's not my son," she said with satisfaction. "I'd be embarrassed to call him my son, and if I could, I would disavow him altogether. He's a disgrace to the royal family and your father should have dealt with him far more firmly."

"Has it been that bad?"

"Yes, and more. Every messenger here he tries to intercept, and every agent leaving, he tries to bribe to have them not deliver a message, or delay it. He works actively against the king."

"And you," Edmund said, "You've changed your mind about Athelstan too, haven't you."

A smile broke across her frustrated face at his words,

"Yes, I have, and I'm pleased to have had my opinion changed. I knew him little before your father's death, and after all, we are almost the same age. It was never going to be a natural relationship for us, but he's done excellent work. His father would be proud of him, and so am I."

"I'm glad. I didn't want to have to come home and convince you of his value as our king."

"And I'm happy that you don't have to as well. Now come. We must dine with the King and see what he has planned for the winter season if anything."

Together they walked back towards the magnificent royal hall. Along the way, Edmund stopped to clean his face and hands in a nearby barrel of water, and a young squire ran towards him holding a towel that he gratefully used to wipe the horse from him.

Again, his mother wrinkled her nose at the implied smell, and laughing, they walked out of the bright sunshine into the darkened hall, lit by sconces and with a small fire burning at its centre. Home felt good, Edmund thought with satisfaction.

Brunanburh – Edmund of England - 937

The press of bodies is just as I remember it from the brief battles in Constantin's lands, the smell, the fear, and the camaraderie. I fight with men I know, and I've trained with before. I'm not in the front line holding my shield above another's head, but I will be called upon to do so soon.

We shuffle forward, a step at a time, unable to see far in front because the man before us obscures the view, and none wish to poke their head high above another's for it makes them an easy target for the throwing spears of our enemies.

The ground is firm beneath our feet. It's been a dry summer although the land has not baked under intense heat. It's been free from torrential rains, not necessarily warm. Idly I wonder if the ground will be sodden with streams of gleaming blood later. I hope so. But I also hope it's not my own or any of these men who have chosen to stand with me.

To my right and left Athelstan's brothers flank me. They are mean, keen warriors. They missed out on the expedition to Constantin's lands three years ago, and they feel as though they have much to make up for, but they are calm in their demeanour, well trained enough to know that rage will hamper their actions.

They've been preparing for this moment all their lives, and they look the part. They are men who take their warrior skills seriously. They train every day, they run, spar, and devise their own weapons and watch the blacksmith create them. Everything they possess has been made to fit them; no other man can heft the sword of Eadric in the same way he can, for none need the heaviest part of the weapon to fall exactly in the centre of its long length. None other can grip the handle of Æthelwald's war axe, for his hands are so large that no other can force their hand to meet on the other side.

Around me, the men are far from silent. Cries of derision fly from some mouths, final words of wisdom from others, and from yet more, I hear the softly muttered prayers of those who seek God's help. I remain silent, my thoughts my own. My resolve is total. I'll not die here, I won't allow it, but I will fight until I know my own death is imminent and then I'll withdraw. My honour demands it for my king.

Our brisk walk ends abruptly, as a crashing wave of wood and metal reverberates through the air. The enemy has been met.

And now the hustle and bustle and struggle will begin in earnest.

Before me, the rows of men brace themselves and start to push. Shields protect the head of the men at the front, held there by the men behind them, and so on until my own position is reached. A little further back, there are fewer shields and more spears on display, as well as a handful of archers. These men let loose their weapons, and as a rain of thunder, I hear them thud into position amongst the enemy. Some of the missiles bang on wood, but others make a wetter sound, and I cheer them for they've found a target.

A cry from the rear of our attack and all shields are instantly raised. Arrows and spears thud down on the temporary shield roof, and my own arm quivers with the weight of one of the arrows.

A further cry and not one of the shields is moved. Another rain thrums down, and beside me, Æthelwald shakes with the blow that's struck his shield.

"Bloody hell," he shouts, shocked out of his stern demeanour, his voice loud enough for me to hear but no one else.

"Keep it up until we hear the order," I shout, knowing that he will instinctively want to lower it and remove the projectile.

Nodding vigorously he stays in position, his shield hovering both partially above his own head and partially above the man in front.

Eadric hits my arm to get my attention, and I glance his way. He's smiling, the joy of the battle upon him, as he holds his own shield in place. I can see little of his face as he's had an elaborate helm constructed that covers the top of his head and runs down his cheekbones and covers his nose. He looks like a creature from a nightmare. It's dull black; all shine rubbed from the combination of iron and leather. When he grins, as he does now, his white teeth and blood red tongue make a stark contrast, like an animal.

Still, no cry from behind us tells us that we can lower our shields. My arm more used to holding a sword than a shield starts to quiver under strain and I curse myself for not thinking to work in this position more often when I was training.

Finally, the cry resounds, and almost as one the men lower their shields, slowly and precautiously, quickly removing the arrows and spears that have become embedded within them. I pull out two arrows cleanly, but Æthelwald struggles with the spear in his own. It's deeply rooted, and after a few frantic moments, he just snaps the wood as close to the shield as possible leaving the point of the spear still embedded. He curses loudly. It will be a bugger to fight with his shield now that the weighting of his shield has been disturbed.

Before I can speak, the men in front of me surge forward two steps and I have to follow to keep our arrangement tight and secure. I spare a moment for the men who must have fallen at the front line and wonder how long the battle has lasted so far. It feels as though I've barely taken two breaths, but I know that time moves strangely within the shield wall.

Frantic activity in front of me alerts me to something happening, and I watch with a strange fascination as a man's body is manhandled back through the ranks. When he reaches me, I notice the bloody wounds on his face, and where his sword hand hangs loosely, red pulses slowly from it, although his sword is still clutched in his other arm.

His pained grey eyes flicker open to glance at me and a smile stretches across his face.

"You should have seen the other bastard, my Lord," he mutters and then his face clouds with agony, and two men run forward from our backline and pick the man up and carry him away, in the lull from the arrows and spears. I hold out the hope that the enemy has already exhausted their supply of arrows, but I doubt it. They, as we will be doing, are only trying to trick us.

I wonder if the man will live and pray quickly for him. Either way, he seems pleased with how he's fought here, and I know that other men will already be dead, face down amongst the crushing feet of both sides. We may never know their identities when they are finally pooled free from the mass of broken bones, bloody limbs and concaved faces.

A shout from behind and my shield is once more above my head and the man in front. More thudding arrows, more cries of anguish, and a rush forward two steps once more. Either we're losing men too quickly, or the other side is struggling to keep their place against us. I wonder how many more such quick steps forward will happen before it's my turn to face our enemy. To meet Constantin or his son and his grief.

I wish I knew who was winning the opening foray.

Eadric hollers beside me,

"I think we must be cutting them down like wheat with a scythe."

I admire his comparison and hope he's right.

"I think you're right," Æthelwald joins the conversation, "but they've far more arrows that I thought they'd have."

Æthelwald is correct in his assessment, and I only hope my brother has noted this development and changed his tactics accordingly.

A cry from behind, and we lower our shields. I'd not heard or felt the arrow sticking out from the top of my shield, but I'm glad all the same for the warning we've been given. Removing the arrow, I force myself not to look above the mass of bowed heads before me. My brother has assured me that if the position looks bleak for our side, as much as he doubted it, that he'd pull me out from my place amongst the men. I trust him implicitly and dismiss the thought from my head. This was always going to be a long and tiring battle. The strength of the two sides is similar, and we fight the same too. That is why we need tricks and subterfuge to win here. We could all fight the best we've ever fought, but when men with identical weapons meet in battle, with equal numbers and the same hopes, only a mistake on the part of one of the sides can lead to victory. I need to concentrate and think only of my next move, not what lies ahead. Athelstan has devised his battle tactics.

A cry from behind and I raise my shield again.

Where   are   they   getting   all   these   arrows?

Chapter 13 - 927 – St Davids – Hywel of the South Welsh

I sink gratefully into my chair before the huge blazing fire although the night has yet to start drawing in.

Home.

There were times I doubted I'd see it again. Times when I resented my being away so much that I almost decided that the sacrifices I was making for the future of my kingship and the future of my people, were just too much to take any more.

Home.

My small grandchildren rush around my feet, gleeful to have me home. My older children watch me intently. I've been away nearly the entire growing season and no doubt, they've become used to governing in my place. I'm proud of my sons and plan for them to govern when I'm dead, but still, this is my land for now, and I will have it returned to my control.

Home.

Away from Athelstan, at last, I feel that I can breathe more freely. Of all the king's who've bowed low to him, accepting his over-lordship, I'm the only one, the only one who's not let his true feelings show. Of them all, it is I who Athelstan thinks stand closest to him and his plans for the future.

That's not to say that I don't agree with him. It just means that I've decided to mask my true intentions a little more, wait to see just how this new alliance plays itself out before I fully commit.

Constantin, the wily old git, has made his reservations felt, and Owain too, as has Ealdred. And the other king's of the old Britons. They could barely be civil for long enough to sign the alliance into effect.

Athelstan, although he consulted me only a little on our journey to Hereford, did consult with me. He's not given any of the other's such an insight into his hopes and fears. And I'm pleased with how relatively easy it's been to gain his trust.

Not that the alliance doesn't assist me. I'd not have agreed to it if there hadn't been something in it for me. I need the peace as much as

Athelstan does, and I need him to ensure it remains in place while I travel.

I'll give it the winter and some of the early summer, but then I plan on travelling far afield and seeing places that other king's and indeed some men, can only dream of doing.

My oldest son Owain approaches me first, a wide grin on his face and a new bundle in his arms.

"Another son?" I ask, the corners of my mouth tugging with joy.

"No, a daughter of all things," he mutters, a little aggrieved. "What will I do with a daughter when I have only sons and only experience of boys?"

I smirk at his obvious discomfort. A girl would flummox me as well, but I'm not about to share that with him. It will be a test of his abilities, and I look forward to seeing how he manages.

"And does she have a name?"

"Of course she does, after my mother, Elen. What more could I do?"

I still a little at his words. The mother of my older sons has been dead for more than a decade, and still, I miss her and yearn for her gentle touch each day. Her loss goes almost hand in hand with my renewed interest in God and His saints. I pray for her as fervently as I can. She should not have gone so soon. There was still too much life in her while she was crippled by disease and pain.

"My thanks for thinking of her."

He looks a little less smug now.

"In all honesty, it was the child's mother who had the idea, not I. I'd not even considered the baby wouldn't be a boy."

I stand and examine the bundle in his arms. Big blue eyes stare at me and meet my gaze, and I hazard that his mother stares at me through those untried eyes.

"She's a pretty little thing. Your mother would have doted on her. She was always keen to have a girl of her own." My voice catches a little at the swirl of memories rushing through my mind, and I cough to mask my emotions. My son does not need to see how much her death still troubles me.

"And other news?" I ask loudly, hoping to drive the grief from my voice.

Owain does me the honour of ignoring my emotional stutter.

"Little and nothing. We've had no overseas visitors, and the other Britons have been quiet too. This alliance of Athelstan's is not attractive, but none had yet come before me and openly condemned it."

I absorb the information, all the time watching my other two sons as they make their way towards me. Owain has always been the most loyal of them all, but all three boys have been my most loyal supporters since they've been old enough to play a part in the royal court. They will inherit my land one day, and hopefully, if the other British kings prove as useless as I think they will, for all that Idwal is my cousin, they will inherit a greater stretch of our land, and it will be divided amongst them. Then they will have a kingdom worth fighting and defending as opposed to a small square of space that is more effort than its worth to keep.

Rhodri and Edwin greet me next. They look just like their older brother, but their temperaments couldn't be different. Rhodri is quiet and introspective; Edwin is outlandish and almost always nearly drunk. They decline to marry but have children a plenty. I make no comments on the way they live their lives. I will be long dead by the time all these children decide to vie for the thrones of their father's. That the children are all boys only adds to the problem.

"Father," Rhodri greets me warmly, a smile on his face, his words gentle and soft. It's no wonder that he can charm any woman he wants into sharing his bed.

"Son," I respond, smiling at my thoughts, and his welcome greeting.

"Father," Edwin snaps out, staggering a little, even so early in the evening. I can smell the mead on his breath but don't comment. We've had this argument too many times in the past. He is a man, and he must make his own choices and live with the consequences.

"You have been away longer than we thought," Rhodri mutters, drawing a stool so that he can sit before me and we can converse in the relative quiet around my own kingly chair.

"Athelstan was keen to take the submission of all and sundry who would come before him."

"So we've heard," Edwin growls low in his throat.

"But did you get what you wanted from him?" Owain asks. He does not share my deep religious beliefs but he would like to travel through the lands I hope to visit nonetheless.

"Yes, we've reached an accord, and I hope that this time next year, I will have visited the Pope and will be travelling home for a winter with you all."

The boys all nod as they absorb my words. It is as we discussed before I left.

"And I take it I can trust you all to govern in my name when I'm gone, but give me back my crown when I return, as I do now." There is a threat in my words, but it's not needed. Owain and Hywel both vigorously gift me back my kingdom and Edwin swoops his arm around the hall,

"It'll give me more time to drink and enjoy the women," he offers, a manic grin on his face. "This governing plays havoc with a man's sex life."

I laugh along with my boys, aware that he doesn't mean it, but also grateful that he can be so generous in returning control of the kingdom to me.

It's good to be home, but soon, very soon, I know I will feel the need to travel from my homeland and now I know I can do it without fear of any problems in my absence. That, if nothing else, was worth bending my knee to an upstart king who thinks he could lay claim to land that has never been within the gifting of the Saxon kings.

Brunanburh - Owain of Strathclyde – 937

I'm in the thick of it. My men surround me, but we are fighting for our lives, not for our kingdom. In fact, our country will be safe and secure no matter what happens here. And anyway, they'll probably be going home. Unlike me.

My arms ache with the weight of my shield, and my sword and I'm more than aware of the scrutiny that Constantin's son has me under, but I try to push it aside. I'm not yet ready to die.

Beneath my feet, the ground is slick with the blood of my fallen and injured warriors.

I came here with near enough five hundred men, and already some of them lie dead or dying. These English are confident and clever warriors. The rumours about them were true.

We've lost about ten or fifteen steps since we first joined the battle, by my reckoning, but I imagine we've lost more men than that. We need some reinforcements, but I'm not convinced that Constantin will send any. He hungers for my death, and this will be the perfect opportunity to gain it, and if it means that he has to run from here as a loser, not the victor, I imagine he might well find that concession worth his while.

A cry from in front of me, and the man who so recently stood there, a man I've known for over fifteen long years, lies bloody and dead at my feet. His face garishly split into two, one side hanging loosely from the thick neck he had, the other pulsing blood all over my booted feet. Grief clouds my vision for only a moment as I offer hasty words of goodbye to him.

And then I take his place, dismissing the final image of him from my thoughts.

The crash of sword on wood reverberates up my arm; the whoosh of spears and arrows above my head would be terrifying if I could spare a moment to consider it. I feel the dull thud of a sword on my shield and reach behind me to replace my sword and to remove my war axe from its place on my back. I've never liked the sword. No, an axe is my preferred weapon despite its shorter reach.

I lower my shield, slightly curious to know who will be the object of my death. Dazzling blue eyes face me. The helm covers the hair, the forehead and the nose of my enemy but his eyes pierce me. There's no malice there just calculation, pure and simple and I take my time to consider my next move and the one after that.

Quickly, I raise my shield again. The eyes I saw were not those of a killer and yet apparently, the blood splatters covering the man's face show me that he has killed, and will kill again. But not me. I will not die at the hands of the English rabble. I refuse.

Another thud on my shield and I lower it and take a swipe at the man before me with my axe. He quickly ducks as he tries to remove his weapon from its temporary lodgment on my shield. He ducks away from my wild swing, but I wasn't as committed to the move as he thought, and I expertly twirl the axe back and impact his head with the stump of my weapon.

His blue eyes blank, and I keep a smile from my face. The enemy never expects me to use the handle of the axe and with force behind it, I can quickly stun the best of men.

He falls beneath my feet, his shield discarded, knocked out by my blow, not killed by it. Immediately another man takes his place, and I spare not one thought for the man who still lives but who will probably suffocate amongst the press of feet and other bodies. It won't be a pleasant death if he wakes before he suffocates.

Hidden behind my shield again, I allow the thrill of the battle to take hold of me. I'll show bloody Constantin how well I fight.

A crack thrums up my arm, but I've not yet recovered my breath enough to make another move. I'll shelter here for just thirty breaths, mindful that I can't stop for long but knowing that I need to.

Either side of me the warriors who face our enemy are those of my men. I recognise my brother in law, Donald, and my son by marriage, Rhodri, and I grin at how well they both fight. Their hair and faces are streaked with blood and other men's spit. Rhodri has a slash down the right side of his face that leaks down his cheek and onto his clothing. He's tried to wipe it away but has only managed to spread the blood further. Like me, they didn't want this engagement, but they have every intention of walking away with their lives intact.

They slash with their weapons of choice, lowering their shields to pierce the skin of the enemy, to decapitate or strike a limb from their opponent's body. They don't care what they hit as long as they hit something and the enemy falls at their feet.

And then I feel the surge of the enemy as a fierce wind and must brace myself firmly on the ground beneath me, my shield securely held in place. Only it's impossible. The ground is wet with blood and piss, the grasses already flattened by the passage of the feet of the warriors around me.

Still, I place my shoulder against my shield, next to the man beside me on both my left and my right, and with the press of the man behind me, as we apply as much force as we can. Our feet momentarily hold firm on the ground, and I think that perhaps we will resist the threat from the enemy. Only then the man to my left slips and his foot shoots out behind his body. As he slides and works to regain his balance, the enemy pushes against the momentary weakness, and I exert myself further, knowing that the men behind me do the same.

We push, and we shove, and the man regains his footing and is quickly back in place, his face covered in sweat his hands shaking at his near miss.

The enemy press us for all that men up, and down our line groan with the effort, they are making, and a voice from behind us, Constantin I think, or perhaps his son, exhorts us to greater effort. I heave and strain along with the men.

Not much longer, I think, the enemy will not force this failing tactic for too much longer.

Only then axes snake their way around our shields. Above them and below, they slither, trying to pull the shields free as they simultaneously attempt to force us to take treacherous backwards steps over the bodies of our fallen comrades, their weapons in precarious positions, more likely to cut our own lower legs and feet than the enemies.

I turn in shock, not having seen this turn of events before, and I note where the axe on my shield is trying to force it upwards and then expose me to the blades of the warrior before me. Momentarily I wonder how they are even achieving this? Does one man stand straight while another wavers beneath his feet? I am confused and admiring in equal measure.

I watch the axe with mild interest, trying not to let its snaking closeness distract me from what my role here is. I must stand firm, not let the enemy pass me.

Men scream and cry in rage and frustration, and I wonder why by the Holy Saints Constantin has not reinforced the line. There are surely enough men for another hundred to be arranged behind us, ready to add their strength to our defence.

The axe on the shield of the man to my left works its way dangerously close to his shoulder, and exposed face and I know that if I were that man, I would be considering ducking away, removing my weight from the shield wall so that I could save my face and shoulder. That he doesn't do so, yet, is more to do with his impeccable training than his desire.

His face is drained of colour, fear evident in his stance, and still, he holds his ground.

One fingers length, and then another, the axe comes ever closer, rising and falling and crashing against the wood of the shield as it does so. I fear now, for if he lets go of his shield, there will be an opening through which the enemy will be able to pour.

I shout, as loud as I can and for as long as I can. Ildulb's name repeats itself over and over from my mouth. It is he who commands the Scots warriors in our advance, and it is he who will reinforce us.

I lose track of how much time passes, so focused on the axe around my neighbour's shield that I fail to note where the axe is on my shield.

Pain floods my lower leg as I feel the bite of the metal into my shins. I cry out loud, angry and annoyed in equal measure. Why didn't I pay more attention?

I stumble, my blood now pooling down my legs and adding to the sticky mass of blood and lifeless flesh beneath my feet. I can't feel any pain yet, only the warmth of my blood.

Only then I feel it. Without even looking I know that more men have come to reinforce this stretch of the shield wall. Thank the Saints that Ildulb heard my cry.

I turn to shout my thanks and at that moment a great heave of effort comes from the enemy, and I'm forced backwards. Holding my shield aloft and in place, I step back, once, twice, somehow missing the body of a fallen man, and then with the help of the reinforcements our line stabilises and the press from the English falls away.

They may have gained two steps, but we hold our line firm now.

But the tension does not let up, and down my left shin, I can feel my blood draining from my body. It needs to stop, but unless someone relieves me, I can't leave my place or duck to tie the wound up.

Behind me I hear men talking and shouting, offering words of encouragement and congratulations for not allowing the enemy to decimate our shield. But to my left and right my men are no longer there. Straining further I turn to where Donald was fighting before the English tried to force the battle to a quick conclusion, but he's no longer visible. Have all my men fallen in the brief skirmish and I failed to notice? Have they fallen victim to the sneaking tactics of the English? Did the axes and snaking knives of the enemy find purchase in their soft flesh?

Frantically, I glance as far as I can see, merely a few men to either side and not one face do I recognise. Not one at all. Well, apart from Ildulb, his dark eyes gleaming maliciously, and blood marring his once handsome face.

Perhaps I should have fallen victim to the Englishman's axe? Perhaps.

Chapter 14 - 928 – His Royal Court – Constantin of the Scots

The wind was fierce so early in the morning, screaming around the outside of his royal residence. It made it all seem possible that his God's Devil could be the vengeful spirit Constantin always imagined him to be. The screeching had woken him from his fitful sleep, and now he lay wide awake.

Settling back snugly into his warm bed, he caressed the warm body at his side and considered the future and the past. They should have been easy to differentiate but instead the past flowed into the future with no seeming end and likewise, the future flowed back towards his past. Once a decision was made, its impact seemed to reverberate throughout his past, present and future. It rankled a little that he could never cut the ties between youthful indiscretions and wiser decisions only possible with age.

At this moment, he recalled his summer meeting with the English king, and he growled a little. Although the warm body beside him promised oblivion for some time, the chance to feel truly alive during the deepest storms of winter, he could only think back to the warm summer's day of his submission.

He'd been doing the same ever since he returned home; his youngest son newly baptised and with the English king as his foster father. Never before had a decision caused him so much internal grief.

The men of his royal council were pragmatic in their approach to the English and always had been. This third alliance with them they knew was just a power play on the part of the English, and one that their king had been right to accept. If it saved lives, then it was all to the good! But for the first time, Constantin found himself regretting his decision and his part in the submission of his countrymen.

Not that the effect had been far ranging yet. In fact, most of his people would know no different. They tithed to their king, as they should. What he did with the funds once he had them was his prerogative. But the anguish burnt deep within him, and he knew he'd not be able to contain it for long.

A year or two his councillors had advised, as had Owain of Strathclyde. 'Just give them a year or two, and they'll forget all about us. They always do. The Dublin Norse will come and fight for Northumbria, and we'll be forgotten about.' Constantin wanted to believe that; after all, that's what had happened to his alliance with Edward, the English king's father, and with Æthelflaed of Mercia, his aunt.

Only the news from across the sea was not the best. The Dublin Norse was engaged in battles with everyone and Constantin could see no way that they'd be able to leave their lands to disturb the English. Not anytime soon. Not and return to them complete. If they lost all their lands, then they could come across the water, but their homelands were as unique to them as his were to him. They'd not leave them without a good fight – rather die than lose what they'd held for over a century.

That was what kept him awake at night and made him wakeful when he should still be sleeping. That and his age. He blamed his age for many of his ailments. He felt like a young man when he slept, but when he woke, his muscles ached and his back twanged. Everyone pretended not to notice, but he knew they did, and that annoyed him as well. What point was the wisdom gained with age if his body was too crippled and weak to make use of it?

Sighing loudly, he rolled on his side, ignoring the shot of pain that streaked down his back like a red-hot brand. Reaching out, he fondled his sleeping partner's breast, hoping to wake her, and for a while forget his worries, but deep snores greeted his attempts at arousal and frustrated once more, he rolled back over. He knew better than to push his luck with her.

The shadows from the fire played across the roof of his bedroom, and in the images, he saw portents and futures denied him. He knew that the Norse successor to York, Gothfrith, had finally returned home but his failure to secure York had under-minded his power base, and Constantin could predict that the coming year would be a painful one for Gothfrith and the Irish clan chiefs. He saw no possibility of them attempting to attack Northumbria when they'd be so busy fighting each other.

And that left him with the dazzling possibility that he should be the man to claim it and to threaten Athelstan. In the flickering shadows, he saw riches, and wealth, a kingdom bigger than any before held by his ancestors and that thought stirred him try and grab it, reach it and make it real.

If only he'd not allied he'd have felt no compunction about attacking. If only Ealdred wasn't quite so firmly in the way, and quite so firmly an ally.

Beside him, a small sign escaped the lovely woman in his bed, and his excitement mounted. A sleepy, warm body slid alongside his own, and he brushed the hair back from the face to look at the woman who'd been his bed partner for many long years now. She was a beauty, with no wrinkles yet around her eyes. He could have had any woman in his Court, but he fancied himself a little in love with her and so kept her close. Never his consort, for that would have brought more trouble than it was worth, but as his lover, she was an excellent choice, soft and warm and pliant, and barren, for in all their years together she'd never produced a child for him. Thankfully. He had sons and daughters enough, and now grandchildren had started to appear, a further reminder of his age.

He sighed again, and a lazy blue eye locked on his face.

"What troubles you, Constantin?"

"The usual," he replied despondently, knowing that her pity for him would drive her to greater heights to pleasure him.

"Then I must distract you, for a time at least."

Her hands slid across his flat chest, and provocatively lower and he gasped in pleasure. But this was only the beginning. He'd need to wait far longer to reach the height of his pleasure. A half-bite on his lip, and a soft throaty chuckle, and he submitted to her soothing touch. No time to think of the English king now, or Northumbria or Ealdred. Or his bloody age.

Brunanburh – Constantin of the Scots – 937

I'm watching from a vantage point to see how this first engagement with the enemy resolves itself, and I'm not pleased. It's been moments, and already I fear for our success.

My allies seem slow to react to anything that Athelstan and his men attempt, and that means that for every three steps they take, my men are taking three steps back.

I watch the advance with disdain on my face. Why I ever thought that Owain could be trusted to lead the first attack, I don't know. My dissatisfaction with him has blinded me to his faults. Yes, I wish him dead but not at the expense of my victory here. Perhaps I should have given different commands to Ildulb and been more reassuring to Owain. But he displeased me, and he needed to know. Feasibly though, I should have waited until after the battle.

These English have some strange tactics. I thought it would all be shov and shield and sword but they have more in their arsenal than that. They have spears and bows and arrows and more, they have devised a way to ensure that my men are always wondering what they will try next.

Not that I don't have my own bows and arrows. I do, I have many. My people are excellent hunters; our lands are filled with thick woods and roaming deer, and yet I imagine that for every arrow we've sent flying over their heads and amongst their shield wall, they've sent double the number back. I'd hoped this would be a quick battle, but apparently, Athelstan has prepared his men for a long struggle.

The men with the arrows are far back from the fighting, close to me so that I can command them from my place atop my horse, but they shift uncomfortably, and I know they're unhappy to be even this close.

Every so often a stray arrow or spear from the enemy passes far too close to where we are stationed for anyone's comfort.

Realizing that I need my men and their arrows far more than I need an immediate victory, I signal them to move back. I will rest them for some time, allow the men to do their work down at the front of the shield wall. Ildulb is there; he will force the men to greater and greater efforts.

I watch as dispassionately as I can, my eyes narrowed against the sun's rays. The English are doing their best to gain valuable footsteps forward. The men who fight in my name are shouting and offering each other encouragement, but it's clear that they need something more. I look for Ildulb and find him and his men standing to the rear of the attacking shield wall. He is barely even watching the larger arena, his eyes narrowed, and as I follow his line of sight, I realise that he's watching Owain and nothing more.

I curse myself once more for making bad decisions and turn to one of my other son's. He's younger but wiser than Ildulb, not carrying the anger of his bereavement about him like a standard coloured in reds bloodiest hues.

"Inform Ildulb that the shield wall needs reinforcing," I bark, my temper fraying with annoyance.

A huff of barely contained ire from my other son, and he's marching to where Ildulb stands motionless, his hand hovering over his dagger and war axe as though indecisive about which weapon to use.

As soon as Aed reached his side, Ildulb jumps a little in shock and looks back to me, an apology written all over his face. I beckon him on with my hand, hoping it conveys that I'm not angry with him. I wouldn't want him to go into battle thinking that his father cursed him. Fatherhood is a double barbed sword, so many mistakes can be made. Not having had my own father to hate or emulate, as seems to be the case with all other men, I often wonder if I'm a father as I should be, or whether I'm unsuccessful in fathering my children in any sense more than I helped make them.

Shaking the thought aside, I watch Aed return to my side, his bright eyes blazing with battle readiness. He is keen to engage with the enemy and would much rather have Ildulb's role than his own.

"He will do so," he mutters as he takes up his position next to me on the small command post I've chosen.

"Can I not go as well?" he almost whines, and I feel my tight face crack with a smile at the childish whining. Battle brings out the strangest behaviours in all of us.

"I need you here with me. Later you can face the enemy."

He growls in frustration, and I lean toward him and fix his angry eyes with my own.

"Your brother is ready?" I ask intently; I need to know that Ildulb can be trusted with his tasks, whether I now approve of them or not.

"He's fine. He apologised and said he was distracted for a moment. The thought of retribution is too much on his mind. You should have let me go." The whine has been replaced with conviction.

"That's as it may be but it's too late to make any changes now."

Sighing in frustration, Aed turns back to view the scene before him.

"Olaf seems over keen today."

And he's correct for instead of staying back from the main fray, Olaf is right in the heart of it, only further along the shield wall. I wonder how he expects to extradite himself if the English and their sudden surges against the shield wall catch him out.

"Yes, he fights with all the skill of his countrymen. He's not used to battle on such a scale. I hope he'll not injure himself or die here."

Aed smirks at my words, for all that I meant them, they sounded insincere even to my ears.

An enormous thundering crack of sound reaches my ears, and I turn back to where my son now stands against the advancing shield wall. Damn the bloody English. They've gained important strides from us. Damn them all.

Aed's eyes are blazing white hot, and I let him have his head. He has his troop of warriors, vicious and violent. They'll worm their way amongst my men and Owain's, and hopefully, they'll beat the bloody English back a few steps.

Chapter 15 – 928 – Bamburgh – Ealdred of Bamburgh

I pace backwards and forwards in my great hall, the messenger from bloody Athelstan dismissed from my presence and pleased to be gone.

The gall of the man. I will not be summoned like some hound to his master. I'm a king in my own right.

The messenger arrived with the burgeoning summer weather, almost as if he somehow knew to wait those few extra weeks so that my own land would have caught up with the warmer southern lands. All winter I've brooded on my submission to Athelstan. Far more than when I accorded his father the same honour, but there's something about him that worries me far more than his father ever did. More than likely it's the intent behind his words. When he speaks, he means it. With Edward, I was not always sure, but then Edward was older by the time I knew him, more secure in his kingship and acutely aware of its limitations, and he never, not once, summoned me to his Witan.

The messenger, a smartly dressed man on a horse more likely to be my own than reserved for a mere messenger, spoke the words from King Athelstan carefully to ensure that I understood them all as if somehow our shared language was my second language. His eyes showed no emotion, and his respect for me was impeccable. It was the content of the message that was less than acceptable for a king.

My rage already fired, he then continued with his list of demands from the English king. I've heard the reports of the huge tithe that he's forcing the old British kingdoms to pay to him, well all apart from Hywel, but I didn't realise that he would also be making exactions upon my people and my own wealth.

And not just any old thing does he ask from me, but for relics that aren't even in my power to gift. To acquire what he wants, or rather demands, I'll have to barter with the men of the religious communities within my land, and they and I, are not on the friendliest of terms.

As I pace, I wonder. Has he sent the same message to Constantin? Is Constantin as angry as I?

Rumours have also reached me of events happening in York, newly under Athelstan's command. It seems to me as though he treats those under his control with far more respect than I. Surely it should be the other way round. Surely he should want to entice me with gifts and pledges of his goodwill? Instead, I hear that he taxes them as little as possible, not wishing to add to their burdens as they attempt to readjust to life under their English master. Of course, he has asked for some changes to take place. The coins must now be of his own devising, difficult in a place where the coins of the Dublin kings have long held sway, and to melt the coins down and replace them with his own, his moneyers exact a cost. Still, and to my annoyance, few had spoken against their new king. I had hoped for an uprising, a battle, anything to make Athelstan less confident; to make him dance around me as opposed to stomp his way into my hall.

The messenger didn't even do me the courtesy of remotely looking dismayed by the message he carried.

Damn the bloody English king.

The winter had been long, cold and hard and I was looking forward to the warmer summer months, the chance to relax in the knowledge that Athelstan would be busy enforcing the peace between the Scots, his own land and myself. Now I'm not so sure. Perhaps a late snowstorm would allow me to ignore this command completely, coached as an invitation.

A chuckle emanates from behind me, and I turn to glare at my wife. She is a strange creature, alluring and repugnant in equal measure. Even now she sits wrapped in furs and adorned with jewels but she has refused to bathe for much of the long winter, and while she looks appetising enough, the smell of her has driven me firmly from her bed. I believe she's done it on purpose and not because, as she tells me, she believes that her belly will quicken if she carries out this penance. I have but one son from this union, a lad now, almost a man, and I doubt I'll ever get anymore. There's no hope I'll share my bed with her until she bathes, and she will not bathe until I share my bed with her. A tense situation and one I have no intention of capitulating on.

"I see this Athelstan must be a mighty king to command you as he does."

My blood boils in my ears. She has voiced the words that I know everyone else within my hall was thinking when the messenger opened his mouth moments ago. I'll not appear as a weak king. I'll not be seen as place-filler until Athelstan grabs our land.

"Athelstan forgets that I am a king in my own right, owing little to him."

She laughs at my words, a desultory sound that angers me.

"Athelstan seems to forget nothing. He remembers that you met him and agreed to his terms and that you've had a winter of peace and harmony."

I temper my angry response knowing that she's trying to make me speak without thinking. She'd probably like nothing better than to see me impaled on another man's spear and this peace is making it increasingly unlikely.

"My dear," I begin and instantly her face clouds, she knows that I'm not going to let her win this argument. "Athelstan has done nothing but shake some hands and obtain some signatures. The peaceful winter has had far more to do with the terrible weather and blistering storms that have kept everyone by their fires."

Disappointed, she turns her face away from me but not before I see the contempt in her eyes. Why the woman hates me, I'll never know. She hasn't always, and I wonder if it is her own bitterness that she's turned around on me. I'm not to blame for her barrenness, or at least I wouldn't be if we'd had any form of close relations during the winter. The birth of our one son was difficult on her. She almost died, but she does not see the joy in her survival, only the bitterness of her failure since.

My initial anger diminished, I return to my original seat, at the head of the hall where my men and my warriors will converge if needed. There are few within it today. Most are seeing to their crafts, their farms or their wives. It is a warm day after such bitter cold, and there is a spring in everyone's steps. I'll not let this messenger hamper my good cheer. I'll think of a way to put Athelstan off. I have no intention of running to do his bidding as soon as he asks.

Moodily I stare into the fire wondering what excuse will be most to the truth and most likely to be accepted. After all, I can't refuse point blank, that goes against our agreement at Eamont, and neither can I do as I'm 'requested', for that goes against my own intentions when I signed the agreement. There must be something for me to gain here. I just need to decipher what it is and then calculate how I'll achieve it.

Brunanburh – Olaf of Dublin – 937

I know that blood streaks my face and that my eyes glisten with the strange combination of joy and rage.

I love to battle, the feel of the weapons beneath my hands. The presence of the power of the other men I have guarding my front and my rear. If I could cry with joy, I would.

I have forced my way to the front of the shield wall. Sod Constantin and his tactics and devious ways. A battle should be fought fair and quickly. I want this thing done. I wish to ride into York tomorrow, or the day after that at the latest. It's been ten long years, and I will wait no longer.

I've already lost track of the number of men who've met my blade. At least five, perhaps six. They're dead now, or nearly so. Five or six less English to fight me for my York should they ever recover from the defeat I intend them to suffer at my hands. My gloved hands are sticky with blood, and I don't have time to clean my sword or my axe. The enemy is relentless in their intensity, although easy to kill.

My men are as keen as I am for this battle. We've had much practical experience of how to fight and win against my fellow countrymen. I can't imagine that these English fight any differently. They have the shields, the axes, the swords and the spears, and some arrows. I'm not sure I approve of the arrows. It seems a coward's way to kill a man without looking into his eyes and having him realise that he's lost his life at your hands.

An axe hooks itself against my shield, and I reach over the top of it to slash wildly at the hand of the man who dares such injury against me. But I flail and find nothing but air. Confused, I reach a little further and finally encounter a hand. Only this hand does something I'd not expected, it tugs on my hand and pulls my arm further and further forward, in the process forcing my shield lower as my arm is extended almost up to its armpit by whoever holds my hand.

Angrily, I try to kick my enemy beneath my shield, but he laughs openly in my face, spitting at me so that I can't see him.

A moment of panic envelops me. How can I prevent this from meaning my death?

Along the line a group of men are all trying the same tactic and the shield wall dances precariously close to the feet of my people, quickly allowing the man behind the man who holds my arm to reach forward with axe or sword and slash wildly at the man guarding my own back.

Irritated I cry out, hoping that my men will hear my commands against the backdrop of battle.

I twist my arm, prepared to break it if need be if only to free it. At the same time, I kick and try to knock against the forehead or nose of the man before me, anything so long as he's distracted for long enough for me to pull my arm back and regain the momentum.

The man laughs at me; his beard flecked with blood and his teeth smeared with the same substance. I wonder if he's bitten the enemy or if the blood had only stained him when he grimaced in delight at killing another.

From behind me, I can feel a flurry of activity, and then, amazingly, my men are on the same side of the shield wall as the enemy, winding their way through the ten or twelve men who've employed the same tactic. They slash wildly at the enemy, and because the strikes come from behind them and not before them, not one man notices before he's slashed down his back or his face.

People die with shocked expressions on their faces; unsure whether the enemy or their side killed them.

Snatching my hand back, I smirk in the face of the man who even now is dying at my feet. I force my shield back and kick him firmly in the face. Devoid of all life, his nose collapses at my attack, and he falls back on his bent knees, his body twisted awkwardly, blood pooling down his nose, covering his chin and dripping onto his chest.

I note with pleasure that my men have managed to reform the shield wall and now fight with renewed vigour. These English men have tricks a plenty to play on us, and we must be prepared.

My two warriors, Aodh and Dara, slip back into line behind me, and I shout my thanks to them. They simply brush the compliments aside, but I know I owe them my life and will ensure that they are rewarded for their efforts.

Not to be beaten, the English are steadily pressing against us once more, and I start to think that here, at the front of the attack, is not the best position for me. I need a little distance; I need to see how we fare and if I need to send in reinforcements yet or not. Signaling to Aodh that he should take my place, I make my way back through the advancing men as they move aside to let me pass.

As I do so, I count the men and see how many thick they still stand. The number staggers me. How can it be so low already?

Moving more quickly now, I almost run to the back of the line of advancing men, concern making me incautious over the uneven surface. I need to see. I need to know.

Spying Constantin, I note that he shows some apprehension on his face, and turning abruptly I look at the view before me.

A heaving mass of men and shields glint dully in the summer's day. The English have advanced many, many steps forward, their lines stringing out behind them with huge gaps where they once stood, now merely exposed soil or grasses.

Surely they can't have nearly won already. It's impossible.

I count my men one more time and note that of the over a thousand who first stood there, a full quarter must already be wounded or dead. The number of losses sobers me even more.

A messenger reaches me from Constantin, his son, the more intelligent one, with his flashing eyes and knowing looks, informs me that Constantin thinks now would be a good time for the other petty kings from my land to deploy their men.

I nod my head in agreement. If they don't come soon, I fear they'll be no one left standing. And then I wonder if Ivarr still lives. Him I'll not miss and hope he's dead. I've other allies who are more reliable than him. I'll have his wealth, but not him.

"Yes, go, give the order at once," I shout, fear making me forget my decorum.

"My Lord Olaf, as you reminded us only moments before the battle was joined, you must give the order."

Nodding at the words that drip with condescension from a man who apparently hates me, I turn to one of my own trusted commanders.

"Go, tell the other kings to come at once. Tell them to deploy as we said."

With a swish of air, both men are gone, and I am left reeling with shock and a little fear. The English are far, far stronger than I envisioned. For a moment my eyes alight on my ships, strung out along the river behind me, sunlight illuminating the dark blue of the water, ready to take the body of my army should we need to retreat, something I barely considered as an alternative to my gaining glory on the battlefield. Now I'm reassured to see them ready, with enough men on board to launch each ship and allow the wind to carry it home.

Not yet I tell myself. I will not run from this field of death just yet. There's still time for this defeat to become a victory.

Chapter 16 – Easter 928 – The Witan – Athelstan

Easter is a grand religious feast, one I'm always happy to both celebrate and commiserate in equal measure. I like to visit with all my relics, spend my time praying with the artefacts from the holiest of men and places but this year I feel aggrieved and struggle to find the peace that I seek.

Three of my kings from last year have responded to my eloquent messages, sent by my messengers, to attend upon me. And all three of them are from the old British kingdoms. Constantin, Ealdred of Bamburgh and Owain of Strathclyde have not responded. I suspect that there is treachery afoot. And I am bitterly disappointed. Of all the men I treated with last year, at Eamont and Hereford, my higher hopes were that it would be my allies from Hereford who played me false and that is why my demands on them were so great. I was wrong to think so; a fool to believe the peace would be upheld by everyone.

Hywel of Dyfed, Idwal and Owain from the old British kingdoms have come, the last two against my greatest expectations, keen I think to meet with the other kings. That they're not here shows me, as weak and I must do something to demonstrate that I'm not weak.

I had planned to show them the splendour of my Witan, to gift them with relics in honour of the season and I've arranged for great feasts in their honour. Now I will need to hold these feasts in honour of others, my brother Edmund perhaps, and mayhap also my stepmother, anything to save face.

The three kings did not arrive all together. First came Hywel with his larger than expected retinue. He apologised and explained that from this meeting he would be taking his leave, with my blessing, to travel overseas. I was genuinely pleased for him and a little in awe. The things we spoke of last year and which I thought were mere heated words on a hot day meant more to him than that. His conviction and his deep faith is a wonder to behold.

Next came Idwal. He apparently came hoping to be amazed by the splendour of my palace at Exeter. My stepmother has worked for many weeks to make sure the palace is correctly decorated, and the finest furnishings were available for our intended guests. I can only hope that her work has paid off. I feel as though even I inhabit a palace more magnificent than I deserve.

New tapestries have been completed to adorn the walls, and every scrap of dust has been vigorously expunged from the tiniest corners. The servants worked so hard, and so often I was on occasion concerned that I would be treated to the same punishment if I stood still for too long.

Idwal and Hywel are similar but different in important ways. They care deeply for each other, as cousins should, but I don't think that familial relationship would stop either of them from harming the other if it would benefit them. I will watch with interest to see if Idwal respects Hywel's borders when he's gone. Hywel has assured me that his three sons will govern for him but even so, Idwal may try to gain the upper hand.

And finally, and almost when the festival was being celebrated, Owain made his appearance. He apologised profusely for his delay, his eyes taking in all he could see and turning to me with an amused twinkle in his eye when he asked where Constantin, Owain of Strathclyde and Ealdred were. I couldn't help but think that he had intelligence that they'd not be attending even before I knew. And that was the exact opposite of what I'd hoped to achieve with my treaties last year. I wanted to be the one who knew everything, the one who held as much power as possible. Not the one that all the others were plotting to overthrow or harm. For the briefest of moments, a cold dread seized my insides. Had I, unwittingly and without intent, managed to unite the whole of the people within our lands against myself? Would they turn my intentions inside out and work to undermine all that I had accomplished.

Only with my relics have I found the courage to pray to my God that I've not harmed with my actions. Only to him can I admit that I have even the smallest amount of fear.

We will all feast together tonight, Hywel, Idwal and Owain, Edmund and my stepmother and my sister. The great men of my land are also in attendance, the ealdormen and their son's and wives. And before them all, I must sit and enjoy myself, even though my hopes are more than dashed.

The feast will be fine; the food will be excellent. Hywel has with him a poet who will perform tales of long ago. I have arranged for music and singing, and Idwal informs me that one of his men has the blood of the Vikings in his veins and will share stories of great adventures down mighty rivers and of trading with men very different to us. I look forward to the chance to learn something new. Tomorrow, my poet will perform the great legends of our homelands, and if I press him enough, he will speak aloud the great poem, Beowulf. It had been intended as both a warning and a compliment for the other king's, but it should serve as well for the three who have come.

Perhaps I will ask my poets to construct a new poem, one that tells of my deeds, or perhaps my father's, or my grandfather's? Maybe all three. It is time I made it clear that I am the King of the English, that my father was the king of the Anglo-Saxons, and that my grandfather was the king of a united Mercia and Wessex. All three of us, men of great talent and religious conviction, great in our desire to unite this land. These kings of Bamburgh, the Scots and Strathclyde had best be warned. I'll not be made a fool of by them.

Brunanburh – Edmund of England - 937

There's been a distinct slack in arrows overhead. It's allowed me and my men to regroup a little, take a bit of time to consider the best way of forcing our enemy backwards.

Ideally, we want them to step back, over their dead, and lose their footing in the mire of blood, guts and piss that will litter the battlefield, not to mention the broken bodies. Not only will it be unpleasant but coming face to face with someone who only this morning was alive and well, will strike fear into their hearts and have them reconsidering their place here. Will they want to die like the person at their feet did? Will they want to die and know that so little respect will be accorded to them that they will be trodden on, their faces made impossible to recognise, their loved ones never receiving a body to honour and bury.

If that doesn't work then ideally, we want them to take so many steps backwards that they encounter the slight decline on their side of the battlefield. It was I who first noticed it, and lucky that I did for it could do our side untold damage if we weren't aware of it. Any slight depression in the ground, or elevation, gives the opposition an advantage, no matter how small, that they can make use of to win the battle. If we can force them so far back that the depression, caused perhaps by an old building, long since gone to ruin, or a long ago stream that has since dried up, then the sudden bunching of their men will cause them to panic.

I also believe that this slight lull in arrows and spears heralds reinforcements being called onto the field. The reinforcements might attempt to rush the front of the shield wall and drive us backwards. If they do, we need to stand firm, hold our ground. For now, it feels as though we're waiting for something to happen.

I look behind me for the first time since the battle began, hoping to catch my brother's eye or any of the other commanders who watch our every move, but everyone is looking in a different direction or striving to see what the enemy has planned next.

At my side, Eadric is muttering under his breath as he effortlessly holds his shield in place.

"We should attack now," he opinions, and I agree with him. At my other side Æthelwald announces that he agrees, and all along the line, other men join the cry to move forward. We can all feel that at this moment, the enemies shield wall is weak. Whether it's a bluff or not we should still try to use this to our advantage.

Still, the men are well enough trained not to advance without warning. I risk a look behind me again but can still see no one who is giving any orders.

"I think we should go for it," I say to Eadric and he laughs at my cock sure attitude.

"You'll get no disagreement from me."

"Or me," his brother pipes in and suddenly I realise that I'm the man at the front line. For all the experience of the men who command our side and for all that Athelstan has proven himself an able battle commander, I am the one at the front. I'm the one who's tasted this fight and learned what its ebb and flow mean.

Decisively I turn to Eadric, as I hold myself firm and place as much tension as I can into the hold of my shield, and the grip on my sword.

"Shout to attack, now."

And the loudest roar I've ever heard from a man rumbles from deep within his chest, and I feel the line tighten and begin to worm its way forward.

Our actions have taken the enemy by surprise; I can tell because the hold on their shields is slack and in the first breath we've taken at least three steps forward. I'm focused exclusively on what I plan to do here, and I hope that my brother, the king, and his commanders have seen what we're doing and are providing the support that we need.

A line of five hundred strong men against another line of five hundred strong men.

Midway through the fourth step, our momentum is arrested, and there is a thud of wood on wood as the enemy recovers itself. Now they will try and force us backwards. Finding my resolve, I breathe evenly through the pain coursing up my arms as my shield is pressed against by the enemy. I look neither left nor right. I can only focus on my actions and hope that the men who support me are acting similarly. After all, this is why we've trained.

Beneath my feet, the grasses have been trampled, and the ground has grown sodden. I wonder how close we are to the depression in the ground I want to reach.

A sudden impact jars my arms further, and I feel that the enemy's line has been reinforced. The weight of however many new men in their line is felt as the press of men becomes that little bit tighter, the air in my lungs, a little more befouled by other men who try to snatch the same breath.

And then I hear the cry from behind us and know that the enemy arrows are about to fall again.

The man behind me shields my head, his breath hot in my air, almost the caress of a lover although in the bloodiest and most public of places.

My feet dig into the earth, and I feel strength flood through my shaking body. The shield wall is the hardest place to fight in any battle. As a child, I thought that the shield wall would be the place that heroes were made and I was right and wrong all at the same time. The shield wall forces men to become heroes. The intense fighting might take place there, but it's the perseverance of spirit and soul that is more demanding. To stand knowing that you are but two pieces of wood away from certain death makes men strong and weak and they'll never know what they will be until faced with the reality of the situation. No amount of training or even experience can tell a man how he will fare.

The greatest warrior may suddenly piss himself with fear, while the most insignificant member of the fyrd can suddenly stand tall and take their place beside those mighty warriors of fifty years ago who fought the Viking raiders in my grandfather's lifetime.

Today the strength of the shield wall floods my body with warmth and renewed vigour. I will kill many men today, and with that thought, the fourth step against the now reinforced enemy is taken, and I feel the rest of the shield wall do the same thing. Our shield wall is the stronger today, reinforcements or not. But, it will be a battle of will. We must will them to their death, to their retreat, to the depression in the ground, one small step at a time.

Chapter 17 – 928 - His Royal Court - Constantin of the Scots

A smirk crosses my face as I watch Ealdred strut in front of me. His ire is a welcome sight, and I can't deny that it pleases me. The more Athelstan pushes, the easier it will be for this farce of an alliance to crumble around him.

Back home, safe and sound within our fortresses and protected by our armies, none of us should fear him. After all, what can he do? March into the land of the Scots and confront me? My religious men and keepers of the historical records assure me that the English, or the Mercians or the Northumbrians, or even the ancient British have not dared to enter our lands within our lifetimes, and even before then, all they met was their death and defeat. My people are wondrously strong and arrogant warriors. We'd not let anyone take us unawares.

The Vikings. Now they're another matter entirely. They sneak and slide their way into my lands, but their violence is often repelled unless they reach an accord with us. And even then, my people are likely to wait until they sleep, or are too drunk to care, before they slit their throats, steal their treasure and forget the whole incident ever happened.

Ealdred continues to vent his anger and frustration, and I'm amazed, as I always am, that one man can be capable of talking non-stop for so long. I thought only the holy men could wax lyrical for so long, and only then because they were repeating a passage from a religious text that they'd memorised.

He swept into my hall with the evening wind and since then, no matter the food and refreshments offered to him, he's not paused, not once. All I need do is nod my head every so often, and he seems content. He does not expect me to counter anything he says. He wants my agreement, my acceptance that Athelstan is unreasonable, and without saying a single thing, I'm giving that impression.

At my right hand, my eldest son is watching Ealdred with amusement on his face. He too can't believe that the man can speak for so long, and yet, he's intrigued as well, listening to every word that drips from his downturned face. Every few words, he spits with his vehemence, and I only wish that Athelstan could see what trouble he's caused.

I too have received a summons to the English king's Witan, but I've dismissed it as of little import, not even deigning to send a reply saying I won't be attending. My lands need my full attention after the upheavals of the last few years. If Athelstan weren't such a cocky young upstart who knew how to run his kingdom, he'd know that it was unacceptable for me to be away from my lands this year. I have too many sons and too many men who think they should sit on the throne of an old man. I must stay here and show them all that my age is a blessing, not a curse. I've served my people well, and I'm not finished yet.

And still Ealdred shouts and stomps and moans and whines, more like a child than a grown man with his kingdom to manage. His rush to ask me my opinion about Athelstan amuses me, and excites me in equal measure, almost as if he thinks me his overlord, not Athelstan. I can use that to my advantage.

A sudden silence has fallen, and belatedly I realise that Ealdred has finally finished his diatribe and is sitting, and eating and drinking, without so much as waiting for an answer or my agreement that Athelstan is unreasonable.

At my side, Ildulb leans towards me, his smile still on his face.

"I thought you said the message from the English King was merely a request to attend his Witan," he queries, clearing puzzled by Ealdred's heated response.

"It was, and his words were simpering and respectful of my position."

"So why is Ealdred so incensed?" he presses.

"God above only knows," I muse. The same thought has crossed my mind.

"It little matters what the message said; the result is exceptional. Athelstan is on the cusp of losing an ally he's only just gained."

Ildulb fixes me with a serious stare,

"Are you telling me that you classify yourself as Athelstan's ally?" he's shocked by my choice of words.

"Better to be an ally than a subordinate," I mutter darkly, and the grin is back on his face. He's the kind of person who finds fun in everything and takes little of life seriously, apart from his children. Those he watches more protectively than a mother wolf, almost keen for people to threaten his three children so that he can step in and flay the perpetrator. I was never as protective of my children, and I'm glad I wasn't. I fear it will bring him heartache in years to come.

"That's true," he offers consideringly. "Are you going to take any action now that Ealdred is so upset?"

"No, nothing. I will make the appropriate noises and maybe add some more oil to the flames, but other than that I intend to sit tight here. I'll not be crossing the border anytime soon."

"I could go on your behalf?" my son offers slowly, and I look at him with my own piercing eyes. Why would he want to do that? Why would he want to visit the English king's Witan? Does he fancy himself my successor? I'd thought more of him.

He sees my fears flash across my face.

"Only out of curiosity," he hastily amends. "I'd like to see what royal splendour surrounds this supposed King of the English. Such an elegant title makes me think he lives in a castle of gold and silver and eats from plates encrusted with jewels and drinks from a drinking horn made from the horn of a mythical unicorn." The smile is back on his face as he continues to let his mind wander as to the spectacular palace the English king may live within.

I smirk now too, seeing the dour looking king, with his bright hair and bright clothes surrounded by so much flashing gold and silver.

"Aye, but they'd be no women," I offer as the only slight reservation.

"No women," Ildulb ponders, "a strange way to live one's life."

His tone is wistful, his eyes watching the graceful curves of a young woman as she sashays across the hall before us. My son, like his father, enjoys a good woman.

"But it does do away with pesky off-spring," I offer seriously, although my face is curved in a smile.

"A man should have children to care for him in his old age," Ildulb offers as if to counter that argument there and then.

"If he's lucky enough that his sons don't see their advancement in the early death of their father."

"Perhaps amongst the English and the Norse," Ildulb counters. This is an old argument that we have at least once a week, and our responses are always the same. "We Scots are a little more civilised." The thought of the civility of my successor in waiting makes my eyes narrow as I pick him out amongst the men sheltering within my hall. He's been waiting far too many years to become the successor, or at least that's what he tells anyone who'll listen. I need to keep him close to me and yet let him learn how to govern, all at the same time. It's a treacherous line I walk, and yet, the comfort of knowing that my sons don't pray for my death is a soothing balm to my soul.

Ildulb is always keen to highlight the differences between our race and the others on our island. The old British kingdoms fascinate him. Strathclyde, more my kingdom now than Owain's is the one he knows best and often visits, on my behalf, but the king we met at Eamont has aroused his curiosity, and he's had my scribes and holy men finding out all they can about him.

He is the grandson of a great king, the cousin of another king, and brother to the other kings in the disparate lands wedged between the sea, the mountains and the encroachments of the English. And yet for all his grandfather's accomplishments, his father appears to have been murdered at the behest of the Anglo-Saxon king, Alfred and Rhodri Mawr's kingdom disintegrated at his death, the rules of their land making it impossible for one man to inherit the hard won land complete. It seems a little strange to me. Why work all your life to unite people and land if it's all to be lost at your death? I suppose it takes all sorts of men to populate our island. I try to understand those who are very different to me, but it's not always easy.

And Ildulb is convinced that Hywel intends to claim back as much land as he can. He presents himself as a holy man, a man who acts with God's blessing, and Ildulb says that coincides with his desire to take the land from his cousins and his brothers. I think Ildulb is correct in his assessment, but I've not told him so. I want him to pay attention, watch those around him for I hope that one-day when my successor is dead that Ildulb will govern in my stead. He needs to know the motivations of the men who also govern the people of our island. He needs to know what they're going to do before they even do it.

As I did. I knew that Athelstan would not be able to let the opportunity to show off his new allies pass by him. I knew he'd summon us to attend upon him. What he didn't know, but I did, was that I'd not be attending, and nor would Owain, at my request, and nor would Ealdred. He vowed many, many years ago that he'd never step foot in the lands of the Anglo-Saxons. They may well have a shared ancestry, but the men of the far northern lands have always been a little bit different to the softer men of the South. After all, they must face us Scots on their borders all the time. We're not a group of men or women to be forgotten about or ignored.

Ealdred, full of food and mead and devoid of his rancour, comes to my side, his face softer now, his anger spent for the time being.

"We're not bloody going, are we?" he asks, more a statement than a question.

"No, we're not going."

"Good," he mutters, before turning his attention back to the fire and the mead, "I didn't want to give the jumped up little upstart the satisfaction of having even one king turn up to bow before him."

"And we won't," I offer softly, thinking about my next words, "ever."

Brunanburh – Owain of Strathclyde – 937

Any moment now I know that the English will break the shield wall. The reinforcements have come and accomplished little. They can't get to the front line because men more tired than them must hold their shields in place, and we are all too determined not to give up our places to easily hand our shields over to men who may not do the job as well as we are.

I did hear the resumption of arrows being fired, and I know that many spears have streaked through the air, but it's not been enough. Not for this part of the defence.

Behind me I feel that Ildulb draws ever nearer, I can almost feel his breath down my neck, and I'm determined that he'll have no part to play in whatever fate I must encounter today. If he gets too close, I will drop my shield and let the Englishman take me. Anything to disturb Constantin's plans. As much as I don't want to die at the hands of the English, I would rather die at their hands than at the hands of my supposed allies.

Even above the noise of the battle, I'm fairly confident that I know who is holding their shield against my own. Athelstan's brother, the one I met at Eamont, the one who obscured his true place from me.

I've followed his career with interest, wondering if he would rise against his brother and attempt to topple him from his kingship, or whether, as I decided on that long ago day, he was an honourable man. Time has proved me right. It was the other brother, Edwin, who tried to attack Athelstan and it was Edwin who paid the ultimate price, his death at his king's hands, as some say, while others say he simply met an unfortunate accident and the king had nothing to do with it. Personally, I would think more of Athelstan if he had taken out the upstart. I wished I'd had that sort of courage to act when Constantin first approached me and offered me the throne of Strathclyde if I submitted to him.

If it is Edmund on the other side of my shield, I know he'll take great pleasure in killing me. He'll think it a great service for his king, and I'll consider it a great service only to not die at the hands of Ildulb.

I strain to hear the conversation taking place amongst my enemy, to ensure that I've guessed correctly in my hope that it is Edmund. After all, the English men all sound the same, it could perhaps be anyone. But I think not. He sounds like his brother, regal and well spoken, every word weighed and tested before it's used.

"Owain, you fight like a young boy," is whispered in my ear, and with a start I turn and face Ildulb, his angry face barely a breath from my own. I can feel the steam from his anger in my ear, his foul breath almost enough to make me wretch.

"Thank you for the compliment," I retort, angry that my plans for a better death have allowed him to get so close to me without me even noticing.

"It was no compliment," he growls, and around me, the few men who were helping me reinforce the shield wall have melted away. I realise now that they were grandsons of Constantin, no doubt called into watch me as I laboured. They all shared his broad forehead and large nose. Pity I didn't notice sooner. Ildulb has been given the honour of forcing my death.

"Then it's as well that I took it as one," I reply once more, trying not to let any fear show in my voice. All my weight goes into preventing the English from advancing any further, and in some vain effort to show Ildulb that what he says about me is all lies.

"You will die here," he continues, and now I turn to glare angrily at him.

"And you will see to that, will you?"

He sneers in my face, and I note his blackened teeth and foul smell. He doesn't look after himself anymore, too consumed with grief and revenge. His clothes are days, if not weeks old, and the smell of rotting flesh hangs about him even though he's yet to slay any of the enemies.

"I will, and it will be my pleasure to send you to Hell," he offers.

"Then I'm sorry to deprive you of that," I respond, my voice harsh and filled with derision.

Now his crazed eyes look a little unsure, and I imagine he watches without understanding as I lift my shield clear and step against the shield of my enemy. The man on the other side of the shield stumbles a little as the force that was keeping him standing is suddenly taken away, but quickly he regains his position and lowers his shield to see what is happening.

Recognition flashes across his face, as it does Ildulb's too and suddenly I am facing my death. The warrior, Edmund I hope, takes only a moment to act, his sword slicing my face and then, when I put up no defence, across my body and against which I make no effort to stop the cuts. I'd rather die at the hands of an honourable man than a snake.

Pain suddenly engulfs me as I drop my shield and sword at the same time, and smile into the face of my death. Behind me I hear Ildulb's cry of "No," but it's already too late, Edmund has raised his sword again, and this will be the killing blow, the one that severs my head from my neck, the one that sends me to my God. I can't feel the blood that pours from my many cuts, but I can feel my strength waning as the sudden blood loss occurs. I feel no remorse, only joy to have scuppered the plans of Constantin once more. That I'll merely be the first part of this engagement bothers me not at all.

A flash of shining metal emblazoned by the bright summer sun skims across my eye line, and an unimaginable pain engulfs me. Heaven. All I can think of is my heaven.

Chapter 18 – 929 – The Witan - Athelstan

Once more my palace is refreshed and emblazoned with as many allusions to my great wealth and prosperity as my step-mother could fit into one wooden building, for all that it stretches to two levels. Not one speck of dust is out of place, and again, I am in her debt. She manages a home, a royal residence, spectacularly. I'm pleased she did not remarry and take her skills away, forcing me to marry or rely on my ideas of how a king should live. I will have to find a suitable gift for her to express my thanks.

While I've been making overtures of friendship to the kings of Brycheiniog and Glywysing on the advice of Hywel of Dyfed, my virtue and esteem have been travelling far and wide. With the changing season, I've been asked to accept an embassy of men and women from the newly created Kingdom of Germany. I am honoured and humbled in equal measure, while equally, I think that the king of Germany should be just as honoured that I'm prepared to barter with him for my half-sister's hand in marriage. We will both gain from any union that results.

And that is why my stepmother has spent so much of her time in recent weeks ensuring the palace is decorated, as it should be. For my part, I've arranged for my relics and my riches to be put on show. My priests have vowed to bring me the best of my collection, and place it in my great hall, and my provosts have arranged for previous gifts to be put on display. I have many from the marriages my other half-sisters made, but I also possess precious items that were bequeathed to me when I became king. I could name many such articles but for now, I am expectant about my new visitors.

I wonder if they will speak my language themselves or rely on interpreters. Will they have specific instructions from their king? Which of my half-sisters will they chose? As of yet, there are still five who remain unmarried. I wonder if they have a preference? I wonder if my stepmother has a preference.

Three years ago, when Hugh sent an embassy to ask for the hand of another half-sister, he ensured that within the entourage was a member of my own extended family, an aunt I'd not seen since I was a small boy, Aelfthryth, wife of Count Baldwin of Flanders. She eased any difficulties, and it was with joy that my half-sister, Eadhild, left the comforts of my court to start a new life with the Duke of the Franks. Hopefully, I'll hear word of how she fares when this new embassy comes, for they will have taken hospitality from the other kings and Dukes they encounter along the way. Their journey will not have been a quick one. I received news last year, and I imagine they've been travelling ever since.

I think my stepmother will push for one of her predecessors' daughters to go, and I'll not prevent her if she makes the request. It would be a long way for one of her children to go with no hope of ever seeing her again. I'll not force that on her.

Pity that no one hopes to win the hand of my half-brother, Edwin. Ever since Ælfweard's death, my co-King for 16 days, he's done nothing but ferment discord. I keep him close because I can't trust him when he's away from my sight. Younger than me by five years, he resents everything about me; my birth right, my kingship, my faith, my religion, and more than anything, my success.

He would have made a weak king, a feeble king, too self-centered, too keen to cause trouble, but he sees none of that. I've attempted to keep him in my counsels, offer him what small roles of power I can, but he refuses to cooperate. He thinks he should be king, and that drives him every moment that he's awake. It is better when he's drunk, although it is even better when he's sleeping. Then the whole court can breathe a sigh of relief and get on with their day-to-day chores.

I've had many conversations with Edmund and his mother about what the future holds for Edwin. If he would only enter a monastery, or marry, or join the household troops, but he will do no such thing. He wants to drink all day and have any woman who comes within three steps of him. He'll be kept as far away from the marriage delegation as possible for all that it will be one of his full sisters who marry the German prince.

"My king," a voice breaks into my reverie, and I turn to the source of the noise. It's Edmund.

"Edmund, you're well?"

"Of course brother, always. The weather is turning warm and the nights long. I think it's my favourite time of the year."

I share his joy of the coming summer. The winter has been long and cold, although I think that every year. I hope that this year the summer is long and slow and the harvest excellent.

"A messenger has reached us. The delegation is less than a day's journey from here."

"Have you informed the Queen Mother?" I ask, and Edmund does me the courtesy of not meeting my eyes when he tells me his outright lie.

"Not yet my Lord, but I will now."

"She'll have much to prepare," I press and Edmund shrugs his shoulders.

"I'll tell her when I'm finished speaking with you."

"And what do you wish to speak to me about?"

"Edwin."

I stay my eyes and my frustration.

"What has he done now?"

"I hear rumours from my friends," his voice is a little haunted as he speaks, and I take a moment to pity him for having to come running to me with half whispered fears.

"I know that, and you and your friends have nothing to fear from me." I regret seeing the relief that flashes across Edmund's face at my words. I'd have hoped by now that he knew he could come to me with anything that concerned him, but clearly, that's not the case.

"He intends to sabotage the embassy. He hopes to waylay them on the final journey here and make a case for organising the marriage himself. He plans on saying that as the bride will be his sister, he should be the one to speak for her."

I suppress my annoyance at his absurd ideas. Does the fool not understand that it's my standing as her brother that makes the match appealing to the delegation? Does he not understand that they'll not even know his name?

"My thanks Edmund for informing me. Could you and my household troops ride out and meet them before he can."

"Of course brother," he bows low, perhaps not realising that he's alluded to our blood relationship. I'm pleased he has, for in this there is a matter of family honour at stake. As he turns to walk away from me, he pauses, one foot in the air and I know he's considering his words.

"Thank you, brother," I say softly, and without further thought, he's striding his way from my presence. Our family relationship works both ways, and I know that it inspires him to be a better man.

I call my stepmother to me and inform her of what is happening. Her lips sourly purse as she absorbs the news, but as I know she will, she recovers well, probably already informed of the latest developments by Edmund. He is a loyal son.

"I will arrange for a welcoming feast. I assume you'll deal with Edwin?" She asks the question, but she is stating a fact. Edwin is my problem. She's tried her hardest to contain him, but he resents her as much as he does me.

"Yes, Edmund and his men will call him in."

Her eyes flash dangerously then, and I realise I may have erred.

"I don't think Edmund should be overly involved. Edwin can far more easily turn his discontent on Edmund than on you. You should have considered that."

Immediately I realise that she's correct, and before she'd left my presence I've called Guthrum to me, an ealdorman I trust.

"Guthrum, my brother Edmund has gone to retrieve my other brother Edwin before he makes a fool of himself before the delegation. Can you race after them and if possible, pull Edmund back, and make yourself responsible for Edwin."

Guthrum, not needing to be told any further, nods his acceptance, and quickly leaves my palace. He is a solid member of my royal court, keen to prove himself, even in matters of my own family. His massive size is why I've chosen him for this errand. Edwin is a dirty little fighter, keen to use his fists when he can, and Guthrum has the power to pick him up and crush him in his arms. Edwin, because he doesn't wish to be a part of my household troops, and because it is better if he isn't taught to fight properly with sword and axe, has embraced more physical forms of contact.

I could pace a little now, show my irritation but instead, I do as I should, retire to my room and prepare myself for the people who will be expecting to see the great English king, Athelstan. I will hide my unhappiness at Edwin's behaviour behind my mask of kingship.

I've had my crown removed from its safe box for this meeting, and I ask my priests to set it on my head. I'm pleased it still fits as well as it did at my coronation. I've not worn it since the Christmas feast, and I always worry, just a little, that my head will have grown or shrunk. My priest always berates me for my concerns, assuring me that once a man is full grown his head is unlikely to do either of those things. Now as he rests my crown on my nest of blond hair, he smirks a little, and I know he's thinking about my usual question. In amusement, I refrain from asking.

By the time there is a disturbance at the door to my palace, I'm attired, as I should be, in beautiful clothes crisscrossed with embroidery, with my crown upon my head and a cloak of fine purple silk across my shoulders. I feel regal until I step into my hall and spy the twisted face of both of my half-brothers.

Then I curse my father for his precocious ability to produce children. It would be so much simpler if I were an only child!

Edmund, although holding his annoyance in place, is less than pleased that I had him recalled to me, and Edwin. Well, Edwin is spitting and angry, his face showing where Guthrum forcefully enforced my will. I wince a little at his eye. It will blacken and bruise and puff, and while his eye remains like that he will continually cast dark looks my way, and blame me for every ill that befalls him, and to every man and woman who will listen to his bitching. Pity he has become an object of scorn and pity to most. They will nod and make a grunt of noise, but not one person within my Palace will agree with Edwin when he tries to blacken my name. Sadly, that won't stop him from trying.

Guthrum, as placid as ever, bows before me, and I beckon him forwards to report. He is a little dishevelled, his clothing rumpled and a streak of mud smears his lower chin. No doubt this is the work of Edwin.

"Edmund was happy to be called away," he says, and I ignore his glossing over of what must have been an awkward interview. "Edwin was less happy, and I'm afraid, we got embroiled in a little fight." Once more he downplays what must have happened.

"My thanks Guthrum for accomplishing a less than pleasant task and promptly as well."

He bows again but does not speak further.

"Did you catch sight of the embassy?"

"I didn't know my Lord, but one of the outriders did. I would say they'd be here for mid-afternoon."

And so spoken, he leaves my sight, to cleanse my brother's blood from his fists and to make himself respectable for the men and women from Germany.

Edmund does not come any closer to me, but with a slant of his head indicates that he too will withdraw and with my permission granted, he slides out of the door leaving me alone with a foul tempered Edwin, his hooded eyes glaring at me angrily, his mouth twisted into a grimace of disgust.

"She's my bloody sister," he spits, swigging from a drinking cup given to him by one of my most trusted servants who begged me for the honour of keeping an eye on Edwin claiming that she could exert her power over him and make him see reason, on occasion. Willingly

I agreed to her request, and in all honesty, she has served me well. Edwin grudgingly accepts her near constant presence, and I wonder just what exactly this power is. Not that I ask. Some bounties are best left unknown.

"No, she's the king's sister, and I am the king. I will treat on her behalf."

"It's not your responsibility," he counters angrily, and I breathe deeply through my nose to calm myself.

"It is my responsibility. She knows it, and so do all your other sisters, and my other sisters and brothers. You have no part to play in these negotiations. You didn't when Eadgifu and Eadhild were married and you will not now."

He looks at me sullenly.

"My father organised Eadgifu's marriage."

"Our father arranged Eadgifu's marriage," I say, stressing the 'our'. He'd do anything not to share a father with me, anything.

"Yes he did, and without you even being at Court," he counters, trying to raise my ire by reminding me that my childhood was spent away from my father. We've had this argument before, and I grow tired of it.

"How I was raised is no concern of yours. I'm your older brother and your king to boot. You will listen and honour me, as you should. I am the head of your family."

He spits out his mead derisively at my words, and I feel my temper start to fray. Now is not the time to deal with his feelings of inadequacies.

"If you wish to serve your king that can be arranged. If you want to serve your family, that can be arranged too."

"I wish to do neither," he chuckles maliciously. "I'm happy with my life as it is."

"And that is why you drink all day long, and whore all night long."

A slow smile spreads across his face at my words.

"Just because you do neither does not make my own life choice wrong, dear brother."

"No it doesn't, but it's not acceptable at my Court. If you wish to stay here, you will change your ways."

Abruptly sitting on one of the benches around the tables already laid for the coming feast, upsetting the early summer flower decorations placed there by my step-mother, Edwin sloshes mead all down his front and across the table. Walking towards him, I notice how his entire body shakes.

"Brother," I begin, hoping that an appeal to him on such a basic level will work, but not surprised when it doesn't.

"You're no brother of mine," he slurs, raising his hand to rest his shaking head on it. His eyes are glazed and wavering as he tries not to meet my eyes.

"As you will brother. I banish you from my Court. You will go to your land, and I will have some of my men stay with you and ensure you plan no rebellion."

His eyes flutter as I speak and before I know it, a snore emanates from his mouth. How he manages to drink himself into such a stupor day after day is a mystery to me.

Three of my servants quickly surround his lifeless body and lift him between them. I'd like to say they'd not done this before but I'd be wrong. They carry him away, and I wish I didn't sigh with relief as he goes. At least I'll be able to meet my guests without having to worry about Edwin interfering.

Rubbing my hand across my face, I plaster a smile upon it and turn to greet my real guests. Thank goodness they've arrived after Edwin has passed out. My stepmother, a hostess to the end, beckons the group of twenty into my hall and I'm all smiles and excitement. I'll think about my brother later. Much later.

Brunanburh – Athelstan - 937

I can see that our forces are advancing well, and I can see the furtive moves by Constantin and Olaf to stem the attack. I know they've many men held in reserve, as I do, but I'm not sure of exact numbers, and that makes me nervous. I want nothing more than to see these men running for their lives, and being cut down by the swords of my people as they prevent them reaching their ships.

Edmund is fighting well, as are the brother ealdormen, Athelstan and Ælfstan, ensuring that the respective ends of the shield wall hold themselves together and don't let any of the enemy past. Behind Edmund, Guthrum is ready to reinforce the line should he need to. For the time being, his men pull as many casualties clear from the fight as they can. It's to be hoped that some of the men may recover from their wounds. There are men and women with knowledge of healing, and they always amaze me with the power of their skills and their exhortations to God.

But I don't watch alone. Up and down our line I have skilled and well-trained men watching the ebb and flow of the battle. They act as my eyes and ears and to ensure that I don't miss any early indication that the fight may be turning against us. Periodically I receive hastily given reports from their messengers. After all, it's too much information for one man to manage single-handedly, just as running my kingdom is only possible with the help of my ealdormen and my bishops and archbishops, abbots and members of my Witan who serve me in any number of different ways.

I've had my men of letters painstakingly read the Anglo-Saxon Chronicle, and the works of Bede and the most learned Alcuin, who served my grandfather, for details of other battles as monumental as this one. They searched and scoured the records, but none seemed as impressive as this one, here today.

The Battle of Maserfelth, in the shadowy past where myth and fact mix so confusingly, fought between the Northumbrian king and the native Britons and the Mercians, was far reaching but it did not include every tribe on our island. The Battle of Nechtansmere, another battle in the no-mans land of possible history, was perhaps of greater import than Maserfelth.Still, it didn't result in the entire island taking to arms, and of course, it lead to the death of the then Northumbrian king, and I have no intention of dying here. The Northumbrian kingdom, or so my scribes tell me, never recovered from that defeat. I don't intend for the same outcome to befall my newly united lands.

The closest they could find was the battles between the Viking raiders and my grandfather, for then he united all he could to prevent the threat from the Vikings becoming overwhelming. I can't help but think that if the people of our land had united then, as I've tried to join them now, then the Vikings would have found no tenuous foot hold on our island and our history would be completely different. No Norse kingdom of York, no broken kingdom of Bamburgh, wrenched away from the lands of the Anglo-Saxons and no divided Danelaw, reaching across the eastern side of the once far mightier Mercia and the ancient kingdom of East Anglia.

No, my scholars have assured me, and shown me the proof. This battle will be the greatest ever fought on my land, between more people than ever before and for that reason, I will win it, and then my Court poets will commemorate this great deed, and our island will once more be united.

A cry to the left and I narrow my eyes looking for the source of the sound. Near the shield wall, I can see where one of my most skilled warriors has Olaf of Dublin at his mercy. I admire his tactic and hope that he will kill him immediately. Without Olaf, I think this whole thing will fall apart far more quickly than otherwise.

A cry to the right and I focus on another area of intense fighting. The men all look the same, and I call my squire to me. He has keener sight.

"Who fights there?" I ask him, and the lad, Alfred, named after my grandfather, keenly looks where I point.

"Owain of Strathclyde," he answers quickly. He has an excellent memory for faces and names. That is why I keep him so close to me. He is invaluable when a crowd of people surrounds me.

"Who fights him?"

There was a moment of silence then while the boy looked and considered.

"I believe that it's one of the ealdormen's brothers, but I'm unsure which one." He sounds annoyed with himself, and I offer a noncommittal grunt to acknowledge him. I know he'll stay there now until he deciphers whom it is.

"My Lord," he says, his voice showing his excitement. "I think Owain may have perished."

I turn to quickly look at where I asked him to focus his gaze, and there is a flurry of activity going on. I wish I'd not looked away though because I can't now find my area of focus. Damn. I'd hoped it would be over much sooner than this.

A messenger from the left arrives, a little out of breath, but courteous and concise in his reporting.

"My Lord King," he says, and I wave his use of my title aside. I just want to hear what he has to say.

"Olaf of Dublin has withdrawn. Reinforcements being called in. Constantin is allowing both of his sons, Aed and Ildulb, to take to the field."

"And what does Aelfheah advise?"

A cheeky smile lights up the messenger's face now,

"Nothing my Lord, he just wanted you to know that our side is so strong the enemy has to send everyone against us. He doesn't think it's anything to worry about."

I smirk at the arrogance in his voice; the youth made bold by his master's confidence.

"Tell Aelfheah I'm delighted with our success but caution him. I want to know if at any point it looks as though we might be in danger. Remind him that we have reserves too."

He bobs his head, and dashes back the way he's just come. He wants to be a warrior along with his father Aelfheah, but he lacks his father's greater skill and Ælfheah, as parents like to do, denies him the opportunity to fight knowing that it will result in his death. When this battle is done, I must make it a priority to find the boy a more fitting role within the Witan. I think he has the hands of a scribe, not a warrior.

"Athelstan," my squire speaks into the lull in the conversation, "It was Owain, I'm sure of it, but now I can't see him. He's dead, and at the hands of Edmund, I think."

The news snaps me from my wanderings, and I too turn my attention to peer into the mass of men and weapons clambering for attention almost directly in front of me. The neat and tidy rows of people waiting to have their turn at the shield wall have collapsed amongst the enemy. Instead the men mill around, some apparently desperate to have their turn at slaying my people and some doing all they can to stand to the rear, as far from the fighting as possible. I imagine these will be the men who will lead any retreat if the call for such ever comes.

"Are you sure? Does Edmund live?" I ask, a solid lump of fear almost choking me.

"I think so my Lord, but I'll keep looking to double check." My fear dissipates instantly at those words. I only hope that they're correct.

"Good. Let me know if you see him. As soon as you see him."

He doesn't reply. He's too intently focused on the dance before him, the slash and crash of swords and axes, shields and spears. Right before his eyes is a horror that any lad of a certain age would give almost anything to witness. I fight the bile in my throat. If only I were young enough not to understand the real costs of this battle, the fatherless children and widowed wives, the life-long injuries, and the inability to fend for themselves.

Chapter 19 – 929 – The Witan - Edmund of the English

I seek my mother as soon as I return from not collecting Edwin. My initial anger has dissipated but still, I need to vent, and she's the best person for that. That she shares my feelings of anger towards him helps a great deal.

I find her dressing within her room, surrounded by her servants and issuing instructions to members of the household. When she sees my face, she quickly dismisses everyone, even my sisters, although she does so with a gentler smile. Even I can say that my sisters are dazzlingly beautiful today, dressed as my mother dictates.

"It was I who asked for you to be recalled," she volunteers once there's no one else in the room. "Athelstan needs to realise that he can't include you in the feud. Edwin will find it much easier to undermine you than Athelstan."

Now I understand why Guthrum was so insistent when he caught me with my band of men on the road from Winchester. He is both a keen supporter of the king and the king's Mother.

"You have my thanks, I suppose," I mutter a little grudgingly, "still, I would have handled him as well as Guthrum."

"I'm not saying you wouldn't. But you shouldn't. There's a distinction."

Her voice is calm, and reasoning and I understand why she informed Athelstan of her unhappiness. Still, it galls to know that my brother would have allowed me that moment of freedom whereas my mother would not. Ever since the meeting at Eamont I've grown in both confidence and standing within the royal court. I'd rather my mother hadn't interfered.

"Come son, the embassy will be here soon, and I'm keen to meet these men and women from across the sea. Dismiss Edwin from your mind. Athelstan will ensure he's not at the feast tonight, and maybe not here for the foreseeable future. You need to change," she almost squawks taking in my mud-splattered clothing, and I feel myself relax at such a mundane thought. I bat away her hands as they try to pry my clothing from my body.

"I'm going; I'm going," I counter, trying to escape her clutches. All the way around the small walkway that flanks the individual rooms of the royal family, I can hear her chastising me. One day she might think me an adult. One day.

Suitably attired and smirking over my mother's outrage of my earlier appearance, I present myself to Athelstan. He eyes my clothing with approval, and I wonder if I'd feel comfortable in clothing quite as rich as his. I think not. The embroidery is stunning; the work of my mother and her women, but it is too tight for my liking and far too restrictive. I'd feel unable to breathe or sneeze or move or even eat.

"My apologies for earlier," he utters, but I wave his words aside. He was right to send me, and my mother was right to demand my return. It little matters now. Edwin shouldn't mar this happy event when he's not even in attendance.

Guthrum, his work on collecting Edwin done, has ridden back to meet the embassy and I hear his authoritative voice coming from outside the building and announcing his return. I wonder what the Germans think of him.

A massive fire burns in the centre of the room, and to either side of it, the men and women of the royal witan are expectantly waiting. Not as many as might attend the Witan itself, but enough to do honour to the king's name. My sister and half-sisters are amongst them, although my mother stands close to the king, and I stand beside her. The hall is resplendent in finery and early summer flowers; the smell from the coming feast is heavenly to my empty stomach. Somewhere amongst Edwin's exploits, and my mother's dismay, I've eaten nothing all day.

No fanfare greets the arrival of the delegates but Guthrum escorts them inside with much ceremony and then, all eyes on them, they're before the king. I watch them all with curiosity. Their travelling clothes are the same as our own, but underneath cloaks and hoods, I can glimpse brightly coloured fabrics, and I imagine they're all as well attired as Athelstan.

There are at least twenty within the group, mostly men, but some women as well. They all look a little cold and fraught by their journey and exclaim with delight on seeing the fire.

Athelstan greets them respectfully, but quickly, a young priest acting as their interpreter. He introduces himself as Brother Bruno, and Athelstan introduces himself, his stepmother and myself.

Brother Bruno then announces those who he's accompanied on the journey.

"I am honoured to introduce to you representatives of the great king, Henry of Germany." The party is mainly made up of men who look no different to every other man in the room. Amongst them all, a young woman steps forward, introduced as Gerbega, a relative of the King although I can't quite work out how too captivated by her beauty to truly listen to the words of the priest closely.

She curtsies prettily before the king, and I can feel my mother's eyes watching me, daring me to put a foot wrong in the presence of such a beauty. I flounder my way forward, never taking my eyes from her captivating eyes, aware that everyone in the great hall is watching the girl and only the girl.

Her hand is light on my own as I offer her an arm-clasp of friendship and then she's gone in a swirl of dresses and delicious smells. Even Athelstan seems a little captivated by her beauty, and I wonder if this choice has been made on purpose. Perhaps Otto of Germany hopes to further the ties of friendship between us all by offering this girl as a possible bride for Athelstan.

My heart sinks at the thought, both for my future and my own rapidly beating heart. I want to marry her; I want to know her, love her, and hold her tight in my arms. Not my brother, a man as cold and calculating as a sword in his every movement.

I manage to tear my eyes away from her and notice here are another three women within the group but none as beautiful as Gerbega, and two of them older than my mother. The other woman is more a girl, perhaps not yet even ten years of age. I wonder who she's and what possible part she can have to play in who the king of Germany's son should marry.

Beside me my mother mutters under her breath, dragging me back to the here and now and away from my sudden fantasy of Gerbega and I clasped together, discovering each other's bodies with fervour and desire. A little heated around the face, I plaster a smile on my gleaming face and turn to do my duties for my brother. I must sit beside one of the embassy and make what conversation I can to these strangers who seem to have an angel within their midst.

Embarrassed I sit beside one of the men, realising I do not even know his name. Thankfully he notices my embarrassment.

"My name is Eberhard, and I am one of the king's chieftains, or as you say, Ealdormen."

"You speak English well," I offer to mask my discomfort.

"Of course, I've been learning on the journey here. I see you are much taken with Gerbega."

"She is," I stumble slightly trying to find the correct word.

"Beautiful, yes?" he offers into the void, and I vigorously nod so that I don't have to squeak my words any further.

"Yes, very beautiful," I offer, trying to focus on the conversation and not where Gerbega sits with my sisters.

"She is the daughter of one of the king's greatest ealdormen, as you say, and she's here at the king's bequest as a surety for her father's good behaviour. It is no mark of respect for her to be here. She's an outcast," Eberhard mutters softly, and I wonder if he's cautioning me with his words. Resolved I focus entirely on him, noticing his beautiful beard and even more elaborate jewellery that flashes at his throat and the cuffs of his sleeves.

"The king thinks highly of you?" I ask, and he smiles a little.

"He tolerates me, and often sends me on these short journeys for him. He knows that I enjoy travel, and he enjoys not having to worry about any trouble I might cause."

And then it all makes sense; Gerbega must be his daughter, and perhaps the younger girl as well. I admire this German king for sending his disgraced ealdorman into exile while at the same time gifting him with the opportunity to appease him should the negotiations for a marriage be successful.

A slight guffaw of laughter from Eberhard and I know that he knows that I've correctly calculated who he is. This should make for some interesting negotiations. Eberhard will want to please his king, more than anything, and it's to be hoped that in his efforts to do so Athelstan manages to extract all he wants from this alliance.

And through it all there's Gerbega. She'll distract all but the chastest of us all. I feel my eyes stray towards where she sits, hemmed in by my sisters and a smile of pleasure touches my face. The worries of my half-brother Edwin forgotten about, I chat happily with the girl's father careless of his knowing looks when he catches me openly staring at his daughter. What's the harm in looking, I think to myself? It's not as if I'm looking for a wife, not yet, so I can enjoy what's freely offered with no fear of reprisals.

I wonder what would be happening during the feast if Athelstan were not so adverse to the effects of a beautiful woman. Hell, I wonder what would happen if Edwin were in the room. There's much to be played for here.

Brunanburh – Constantin of the Scots – 937

Fear has constricted my chest and made breathing uncomfortable. Or at least I hope that's why I feel so unwell all of a sudden.

I was watching Ildulb directly when Owain lowered his shield and allowed himself to become fodder for the English side. I watched with disbelief as he stepped into the killing blow of the enemy.

And now I've lost sight of Ildulb, but I know that my men are about to suffer a terrible fate at the hands of the English because just that one shield down has allowed the English to pour through into the ranks of my men. Because the English are now amongst them, they don't realise that they might be fighting with an enemy at their backs.

I scream for my men to notice, to disseminate the information one to another but they are too caught up in the immediate fight before them. And Ildulb, I don't know how he fares. I fear for him. He was there, the next man in line to Owain. I wish I could rush into the melee, but I know I can't. My age is too great, my sword arm too weak. I have become a figurehead, no more. I couldn't slay a baby goat if it wandered into my drawn sword.

Aed too. I can't find him, or my grandsons who wished to fight alongside their father's.

It's impossible to tell enemy from an ally, man from a boy and for the first time in many, many years I know what it is to fear and to feel impotent to act.

Olaf has seen what is happening and his allies are pouring into the growing void adding to the confusion as I frantically search for my family. I should be more distant, but I am old, I did not want this conflict. Not if it cost me, my children and my grandchildren. All I wanted was a little retribution for Athelstan's attack three years ago, a little bit of peace before my death. Not this. Never this. I should have held true to my reservations instead of blundering into this at the behest of my advisors and the upstart who would have my thrown. I didn't want to appear weak before them all. My pride has brought me to this disaster.

Cries of anguish and agony reach my ears, the crash of battle, the wet thud of falling bodies. It fills my senses and unnerves me. I try to think clearly, to think around this unlooked for development. But there is nothing but panic.

And then somehow Ildulb is at my side a crazed smile on his lips, blood smearing his face and great slashes of the fluid marring his clothing.

"He's dead," he announces as if it's the most mundane thing he's ever said.

A lopsided smile crosses my face at the news, but before me, the swirling of fighting is still difficult to differentiate.

"You killed him?" I ask, but he's shaking his head.

"No, bloody Edmund did, and I tried to take him too, but he retreated behind the shield wall, as did all the English men. The influx of Olaf's allies swung the fight back in our favour, for now."

I watch the scene with narrowing eyes trying to make sense of what I see, hoping to see that Ildulb speaks the truth.

I follow the line of the shield wall where it's stayed firm and true throughout the altercation, and as I do so I see that Ildulb is correct. The shield wall is solid once more, on both sides.

"And Aed?" I query, while Ildulb catches his breath at my side.

"I didn't see him. Why, is he down there?"

"Yes," is all I say, searching now for my other son, but before I can see him, Olaf is beside me. He is covered with the filth of battle. His beard is blood soaked, his eyes a little crazed and mud and a dark fluid, that I assume is mud, is slowly rising up his booted feet. He breathes quickly too, trying to speak and catch his breath at the same time.

"Constantin we must rethink our strategy. The English are too strong. Only the appearance of the reserves forced them back behind their line this time."

His voice is ominous and black with meaning, and I know he's trying to affix the blame on my shoulders. But I'll not have it. He should have sent more of his forces in from the very beginning, instead of just the useless bickering ones.

"There's a depression, a gulley in the ground below us. Look, it's barely discernible to our eyes from here, but you can see it if you look for it."

I watch where Olaf is pointing, trying not to focus too closely on Olaf's blood stained clothing, and sword that bears the flesh of his last kill.

"I see it, but how can we use it?"

"Let the enemy come racing towards us as we fake a retreat. They won't have seen it, and then when they stumble, even just a little, our warriors will knock them down where they stand."

I consider the idea. Olaf is talking about giving away a vast swathe of land and hoping that the small gulley will be enough to knock the English from their killing streak. I would far rather that we could force them backwards, towards the line of the hill that I can see. If the English were retreating up that hill, it would be easy to slice their ankles, or severe their feet, but clearly, that's not likely to happen anytime soon.

I look frantically around, looking for any other option, but other than a full retreat I can see nothing that would give a greater advantage over the enemy.

"It's a good idea. Arrange it with your men and Ildulb will inform the commanders here."

"Excellent," Olaf barks, already stepping away, calling his men to him as he does so. Only then he stops.

"Is Owain dead?" he inquires, his eyes on Ildulb and not looking at me at all.

"Yes," Ildulb replies, no hint of apology in his voice. "At the hands of the English."

Olaf flicks his eyes to mine then, his disbelief evident to see.

"As you say," he bows his way out of my line of sight, and I watch him leave with some dismay. I'd not realised my intentions were so well known.

"Ildulb let everyone know. We'll pull back. Make sure the men are aware of our intentions."

Wiping a bloody hand across his face he walks away without another word. He doesn't like the idea but is prepared to give it a try.

The fighting hasn't lessened with the reestablishment of the shield wall. If anything it's become more ferocious, both sides, for a moment each, tasting the triumph of victory if they could only hold onto their lead.

The day has reached its zenith; the high sun overhead and I wonder if this has been the quickest morning to ever pass during my entire life. And yet at the same time, it seems to have taken days or weeks to reach this moment. So much has happened in such a small space of time, and also so little.

A ripple of movement down the shield wall on our side, and I realise that the men are starting to pull back in as tidy a line as it's possible to do. I'm surprised that the ruse looks so orderly. Initially, I smirk with amusement as the English hammer home their victory, taking the advancement as their due, only then, four or five steps in I notice that their advance has slowed a little.

The men at the front of the shield wall still move shield to shield with my forces or those of Olaf's, but the rest of the force moves in a more desultory fashion. They take their time, measuring their pace and I wonder if Olaf has underestimated the knowledge that the English have of this land. Do they know of the gulley? Have we just given away the position we've fought all morning to keep and for no reason at all?

A cold dread fills my stomach as I survey the battlefield. There are many dead, many wounded on our side, and the English shield wall tramples over them with barely a thought. The men watch their backs, checking each body to ensure no life could breathe afresh in the supposed dead, and attack them from the rear. They shout to eat other as they work and a man at the back of the force seems to be jotting down details on a scrap of hide as they do so. Does he attempt to count the dead? Does he try to name the dead?

The shield wall advances ever backwards, a silver chain of interconnecting rings, the men exchanging sword thrusts and axe strikes and overhead, not a single arrow flies from the bows of the archers and hunters. It would be too dangerous to let them fire now. They would just as likely take down one of our men as one of the enemies. Athelstan has commanded the same thing on his side.

The men are within stopping distance of the depression in the ground and Olaf has arranged for his reserves to lay in wait there. They stand tall and proud, not yet having taken part in this battle. They must expect to take the place of the current men at the front of the shield wall, and knock the English back with their greater strength and untested abilities. I think the idea a good one. The English will not be expecting this, no matter if they know about the natural feature they will not be expecting to be greeted with a new force of fresh warriors. For the first time since the retreat started, I feel a little glimmer of hope.

We can win this.

Only then, with a handful of steps left, the English abruptly rush forward, all of them, as if someone has counted to three and said go. And not just the men at the front of the shield wall. No, all those other men who'd fallen by the wayside as they'd advanced so quickly, I see now they were only taking a moment to ready themselves for this final push, for that is what they have planned now. One last push.

The sound of them running hits me as thunder during a rainstorm, booming, deafening, blinding the senses.

They run as one, they add their weight to those before them, and they have only one thing on their mind.

Force all mine and Olaf's men to the floor when forced backwards at an unprecedented pace, they crash into Olaf's fresh warriors, and themselves slide down the gulley that they were meant merely to step over.

I cry a warning but none hears me but those within earshot. A reverberation of metal on wood, a wave of sound as hundreds fall in fear and shock and I watch, as impassively as I can, although I'd much rather be looking anywhere other than at the terrible destruction being played out before me.

Chapter 20 - 929 – St Andrews – Constantin of the Scots

The Church is silent; all have fled from the extended service I asked my priests to perform in this holiest of places.

In this location, I feel my earthly cares slip away from me, and I feel free and young again. Not an easy thing for an old man to accomplish when his knees ache, and his back thrums with every movement he makes. I would curse my old age but I can't. I'm grateful for it. To see my sons grown to men, my grandchildren scampering around the royal palace. It does an old man's soul good to see that his endeavours on this earth have not been for nothing.

My country is strong, my people united, everywhere. Athelstan of the English is an annoyance, like a summer fly when the cattle are brought in for slaughter, desperately trying to attach themselves to the shit and happy to feed when they can. A smirk crosses my face. Oh to think of the jumped up English king being compared to a fly on shit.

I shake the thought aside. I came here for peace of mind, not to dwell on the affairs of state that prey upon my mind.

Athelstan has risen far higher in the estimation of everyone, both within our island and on the lands of the Franks and Germans, the homelands of the Vikings, and the island of the petty kings of Ireland. I worry I may have underestimated him. He is more than a wasp sting; more than an irritating fly come to feed on shit. He is, although I loathe to admit it, a man grown in reputation.

I have a man close to the English king who keeps me informed of all that happens in his kingdom. I know of his negotiations with all the tiny nations of the ancient British; I know of his marriage alliances with the new country of the Germans, and I know that poets and scholars and religious men vie for his special attention. He loves learning, seeks relics wherever he can and above it all; he remains a man of his word. Celibate, and devoid of heirs of his own body. He is an enigma.

But he's loved by all, and I mean all.

He is to be feared and little trusted, and that is why I came here today. My thoughts mull over his intentions, his wants, his needs and I think myself a fool for incurring his wrath by not attending upon him as a friend when he offered it to me.

Owain of Strathclyde thinks me a fool too, not that I tell him his words are true. Never. In public I hold firm to my refusals to bow my knee further, laughing off the growing menace as something that I am too old to worry about. After all, my knees bend unwillingly at the best of times, why would I want to force them to my will?

Not that he's even threatened my land, or me directly, or my people indirectly, and yet, I have a feeling in my gut. He is a great king, and such kings must always seek ways to make themselves even greater. He's bested his father in his military prowess because of his love of diplomacy. Now he must aim to beat his grandfather, and no matter where I look, I see no enemies as great as the Viking raiders were for him to face in battle. No, I fear, or rather I know, that he will look to the North. He will want my lands, and I'm a fool for not bowing my knee to him.

And yet for all my self-recriminations, I know that my people stand by me, agree with me, and salute me for my firm resolve. They see the men of the English, the Saxons as they insist on calling them, as weak minded men, surviving in our island only by chance and the persistence of a few. They respect them not at all.

Ealdred of Bamburgh sends me messengers on an almost daily basis, informing me also of the English king's movements and also of his fears. He jumps at every rumour and scuttles to me when the fear and worry becomes too great. I wish he wouldn't. It sends the wrong signals to his people when he so callously abandons them to their fate, running to the apparent safety of my kingdom.

I fear that one day he'll simply bring all his people and his great hall with him and beg for some little plot to call his own. But I'll have no other kingdoms within my own. My people are only recently united, and still, I cast my eye covetously on the lands of the Strathclyde king, a king in name only. Soon, soon, I will make my move and add his land to my own, forever, but not at the moment. Not when the English king is so close, I feel his breath down my aching back.

The only consolation in all of this is that my contact at the English Witan tells me all that is discussed, all that happens. The king has many great ealdormen and these he trusts implicitly, and to them, he gives the governance of the ancient petty kingdoms of the Saxons. One of them, I hope, will prove false to him and come to my side, but who? Who should I attempt to steal away from their fervent allegiance to their king? My contact tells me that all love the king, all apart from his half-brother, Edwin, and he's a drunken sop and no use to me at all. He'll blab if I approach him, his mouth running away from him whenever he's had too much to drink, and I understand that is a daily occurrence.

Athelstan's patience with his brother grows ever thinner, and I think that something will happen to Edwin. I think the king will snap, tire of his constant attempt to incite rebellion when none wish to rebel. I do not see a very rosy future for Edwin. Still, he distracts the king enough that Athelstan makes no moves towards me. He sends me friendly messengers, asks for his tithe and little more. I know I disappointed him when I didn't rush to his generous invitation at the Witan last year, and for now, I hope it will only remain a disappointment.

Perhaps, after all, I should send a representative of my kingdom to meet with the English king. Offer apologies. It could be one of my sons, or even better, my successor in waiting. I wouldn't mind if the English king sought his revenge on Mael Coluim. Although, it might upset those men and women who've been vying for his patronage throughout their lives, longing for my death. That makes me smile again. Staying alive is another way to thwart Mael Coluim and one I quite enjoy. It makes up for the aches and pains, stiff limbs and loss of desire for women, to see his twisted face every time I preside over my royal court.

Or perhaps it should be Owain of Strathclyde. It's about time he did something to earn his position.

Rising stiffly from my stool, my arse numb and my hands a little frozen in the chill of the church, I walk forward to lay my hands on the altar under which I know the holy relics of the church's name saint rest. I know little about him other than that he was brought here by a man who fled here, from lands much more temperate than my own. I think him a fool for leaving the warmth of the southern territories, but then, if it was death or a bit of discomfort, then I think he probably made the correct decision. And I am pleased he brought the relics.

And in that respect, Athelstan is no fool. He understands the power of the holiest men's bones. They legitimise his kingship, his pledge to rule the English, and everyone flocks to him. Even the kings of the ancient Britons. Defiant for hundreds and hundreds of years, ever since the words of that great man, Gildas, an ancient monk with a grudge against his people and the incoming Saxon raiders, found their way into their people's thoughts, have started falling at Athelstan's knees as though all is forgiven. The Kings are practical men; their people not quite so much, and there once more is a weakness to exploit. The ancient Britons like a good fight and they fight dirty, using the natural environment to give them an advantage over any who trespass there. So the Vikings have learnt to their detriment, and so too could the English, if I just use the right words, the correct incentive.

Perhaps a sermon, as Gildas once wrote, maybe a poem. Something to worm its way into the psyche of the Britons.

Calmer than I've felt for the last six months, I turn away from my saint's relics, leaning on my elder son for support in those first awkward moments of taking steps, I take a moment only to compose myself. And then I'm all king again, mighty, powerful, old and wise. I've a little job for a poet I know and trust. He'll be bought with trinkets of gold and flashing red rubies, and then, he'll infiltrate the kingdoms of the Britons and Athelstan will be a little less sure footed. Somewhat less magnificent and munificent.

It feels good to be alive.

Brunanburh – Edmund of the English - 937

My mind still reels with incomprehension as to the enemy warrior's actions when he lowered his shield and allowed me to kill him, for he put up no defence, his eyes showing acceptance of what was to come. I killed him, as I should, but now I wonder if I should have been so hasty. Something was going on between the man and another warrior that I've not yet worked out. Why did he want to die?

Now that the moment has passed, I know whom I struck down, and I know whom I almost struck down. Owain of Strathclyde allowed me to kill him. Was there truth in the rumours that he and Constantin were no longer in agreement about everything? If there was then why did he come here? None of it makes sense, and yet I can't stop thinking about it.

Eadric and Æthelwald have taken advantage of the free passage amongst the enemy, as have a swell of men behind them. Racing through the hole in the shield wall that Owain opened, I impassively watch as they attack anyone within reach. The enemy to either side does not know of Owain's death. They do not know that as they work to defend their line, the enemy walks among them, killing indiscriminately, slashing down exposed backs, hacking at necks, slicing the backs of men's legs. The tang of blood fills the air, the iron of death and the salt of sweat. Fear and piss flood the ground before me.

I stand almost motionless, confused and stunned by what has happened. It seems improbable that I've slain another king and yet the truth is at my feet, and the look on Ildulb's face, for I have met Constantin's son before, only reinforces my knowledge. But the look on his face when Owain met his death mystifies me. Why would he have looked pleased with the death of one of his own?

A rush of men surrounds me, and I realise that into the void caused by Eadric and Æthelwald's absence, the king has sent men to protect me. There's no need for I feel as though I could happily slay the hundred men who face me through the hole in the shield wall but I'm grateful all the same and lower my sword arm as it trembles with the strain.

At my back Guthrum appears, his expression strained.

"My Lord, where are your men?"

I point to where I can see their backs fighting the enemy, too exhausted for the moment to speak. Guthrum looks at me in surprise that quickly turns to fear as our men within are jostled. I'm unsure why but at that moment our men begin to rush back through the shield wall and it all starts to make sense.

Reinforcements.

Guthrum is observing every man, ensuring that none of those coming back through the closing gap is our enemy. I'm grateful he's there, watching for the knowing tell of our coloured shields.

"You should retire my Lord," he mutters through the side of his mouth, not wanting to tell me what to do but seeing my exhaustion for what it was.

"None of the other men are allowed to," I breathe out and he turns his attention briefly to glare at me.

"None of the others are the heir to the throne and brother to the king. Go back now, eat, rest, report to the king, and then come back later."

The man speaks sense, and grudgingly I turn my back on the shield wall, my arms heavy and muscles leaden with fatigue.

The swirl of activity continues around me, but I'm paying little attention. Surveying the ground as I move towards the rear of the fighting, I keep my eyes on where I'm going, not on those who lie mangled and broken at my feet.

As I reach the rear of the fighting, the king's young squire races to join me, a cup of mead in one hand, and the other held out to take my sword, or my shield, whatever is suddenly too heavy to carry myself. I thank the boy, and he shrugs his shoulders. These are his duties after all.

"The king would like to speak with you," his high voice informs me, and I nod to show I understand.

"I'll come as soon as I'm able."

I think it'll take me just a moment to recover my strength and walk to the spot my brother has chosen as his command post, but long, long moments pass, as the battle resumes around me.

Only when Eadric rushes to my side do I find the energy to power my limbs forward.

"My apologies for leaving you," he grunts, apparently unhappy that he let the glory of the battle take him away from my side.

"It's no problem. Athelstan and Guthrum provided additional warriors."

"Even so," Eadric says, "it was wrong of us and against your brother's wishes. I will apologise to him as well."

He falls into step beside me.

"Did you slay many of them?" I ask, my curiosity greater than any rancour I might feel for finding myself suddenly alone on the battlefield. Well as alone as a man can ever be who can command all the men surrounding him if need be.

"At least five," he grins, pleased with himself. "They were not expecting to have to defend their backs as well as their fronts."

"And Æthelwald is well?" I ask, looking for his brother but not seeing him.

Eadric pauses a beat in his step and then shakes his head angrily.

"He is injured down the left side of his legs, but only a little. He would be with us, but he can't keep up."

Stopping abruptly, I turn back to face the path I've just walked down. My eyesight flickers over the death and destruction I see, seeking only one face amongst the many. I see Æthelwald almost immediately, his face sheeted with other men's blood and starkly white against the spray of bright red. He's limping heavily, but his eyes are fixed on mine, and I raise my hand in greeting. He returns the greeting, and I turn away, satisfied that Eadric is telling me the truth.

Athelstan is stationed half a field away from the front of the shield wall. Able to see what is happening, but with enough space for him to retreat abruptly if necessary. In my exhausted state, the walk to him feels onerous. I'd like nothing better than to slump to my seat here and now, and sleep the rest of the day away.

Battle is wearisome.

Chapter 21 – 931 – King's Worthy – Athelstan

The messenger looks nervous, and I wonder what news he carries that would make him cower quite so much before me. I am a Christian king, never known for having reacted angrily to any news brought before me. After all, it's not the fault of the messenger if the news they carry is unwelcome or unwanted.

The man has come from the lands of the new German king, the man who only two years ago I sent not one, but two of my sisters, in the hope that one of them would prove acceptable to his son as a future bride. I had hoped to hear last year that one of the girls was happily married and that the other was on her way home but no news came, and I only hoped that meant that nothing untoward had happened. I'd like to hear tales of this new kingdom, being formed at the same time as my own, moulded out of disparate petty chieftains and made whole.

His evident unhappiness makes me worry, and beside me, my stepmother shuffles unhappily, for all that the girls were not her flesh and blood. We've discussed the matter at length, both assuring the other that all would be well even though we weren't convinced.

Finally, having drunk his fill and eaten a hasty mouthful of bread the man steps hesitantly forward and begins to speak.

"My Lord King Athelstan, of the English and overlord of the Island of Britain, I bring word from Henry, king of the Germans. He is pleased to inform you that Otto, his son and heir has married one of your sisters, in a grand ceremony."

"That is excellent news," I speak into the sudden silence, for all within the hall are listening to words of the messenger. "And which of my sister's is destined to be a Queen?" I query, watching the messenger's face with interest.

"Eadgyth, my Lord," he stutters, and beside me, Eadgifu stands less tense, pleased that one of the girls was accorded the opportunity of marriage. It would have been a great dishonour if Otto had rejected both of the girls.

"And what of my other sister, Aelfgifu? Is she travelling home now?"

And this is where the messenger will not meet my eye, and I glance at my stepmother warily, praying that she's not perished on this journey. I might have too many sisters, but I wouldn't wish any of them dead.

"It was Eadgifu's wish, and Otto's that she remain with them, a source of comfort and a friendly face from home," the man finally spits out, and I relax my tense posture. This was not an unexpected development and provided the German king looks after my sister, as I would have done within my own Witan, I'm happy that she's found a new home.

"And is she happy to remain? I wouldn't like to think that she's being held against her wishes."

The messenger's face has cleared at my calm acceptance of his words, and I wonder what terrible rumours are circulating about me throughout the lands over the sea. I have no temper. Perhaps my sisters have filled the poor man's head full of false tales. I would chastise them if they were here. The messenger has carried his task with more trepidation than excitement.

"Oh yes my Lord," he exhales, "most pleased."

"Then that's also excellent news. Now, if you wouldn't mind, could you please talk in more privacy to my stepmother about how my sister's fare. She's keen to know everything about them."

Almost falling over himself with relief the messenger looks to my stepmother who nods her thanks, and then regally walks towards him. They'll find a more intimate setting to discuss the things she needs to know.

I settle back in my chair to think about the implications of this not unexpected development. I now have one less sister to worry about, provided she either marries into a noble German family or remains as a companion for Eadgifu. I'm pleased for her and pleased for myself. This family of mine is huge, with tendrils reaching across the lands across the sea. My nephews will be kings, and my nieces will marry well. My grandfather would be pleased with our wide range, and so am I.

Only then Edwin enters the hall and my mood sours immediately. He's still a constant thorn in my side, and one I'd much rather not have to contend with. I've not seen him for some months but it is the Witan, and he'll come, as he always does, to glare at all those who refuse to rise against me at his whim.

He's an unwelcome guest, but I have other guests who are also coming, and they're far more welcome. For the last two years, I've worked hard to cultivate the kings of the smaller kingdoms of the Ancient Britons. Not an easy thing to do when I was forced to exact such a high price on the heads of Idwal and Owain after they initially refused to accept me as their overlord four years ago. But I've done it, and at my Witan, they will come, as Hywel, Idwal and Owain did two years ago, and present themselves before me, and all the men and women of my kingdom will see that I am king of more than just the English.

Along with Hywel, Idwal and Owain, I am also expecting to see Morgan, king of Gwent, and it is to be hoped that Owain of Strathclyde will also attend. I've expended some time and effort on enticing him to my cause. It will amuse me if I can undermine Constantin on the borders of his land. His arrogance still chaffs. Not one word of apology did I receive from him when I invited him to my Witan in 928, and barely a word since. He sends his tithes and ignores everything else I do. Hopefully, and if Owain of Strathclyde comes, Constantin will see that my alliance is not optional.

I would also like to see Ealdred of Bamburgh, but rumours have reached me that he's ill, sick, and worn-out with the worry and stress of governing his kingdom. I don't know if the rumours are correct or not, but certainly, little of import has reached me from his country for some time. It is to be hoped that if he should ail and die, his successor will be more open to my plans for the future, and less under the thumb of Constantin of the Scots.

I should very much like to isolate Constantin. He's an ancient man, as old as my father would have been had he still lived, and not worn himself out with too many women and too many battles and his scheming ways.

Edwin stumbles into my musings, and I glare at him, but he raises only an insolent eyebrow and belches his feisty breath into my face.

"Brother," he exhales, and I curb my irritation. He uses our familial connection when he most wishes to annoy me, and ignores it when he thinks he should be king in my place.

"I hear our sister is happily wed, and the other is staying behind as some ealdorman's whore."

His tone is accusatory and insulting all at the same time. When the embassy came, he begged me to let him leave with his sisters, begged me to let him marry the beautiful girl amongst the entourage. I refused on both counts, point blank. I'd not relent to Edmund's wishes, and he at least deserved a pretty wife, there was no chance that I was going to allow Edwin to be rewarded for his treasonous activities against my reign. Even now, a month does not go by that I do not hear rumours that he plans to set sail for lands across the narrow sea. I only wish he would go now, perish, perhaps in a shipping accident; drown his worthless body in the salty tang of the sea. It would be little different to the way he lives now anyway, drowning in mead and the best, and often the worst, of the wines.

"Don't speak of your sisters in such a way," I admonish quietly, noticing with relief that no ire can be detected in my voice, no matter his accusatory nature.

"You approve of your unmarried sister living amongst those barbarians?" he tries again.

"They are our ancestors, as you well know, no more barbarians than I. I would have said you and I, but I don't know what you are," I say a little provocatively, only for the first time in years Edwin laughs at my attempts at rancour.

"Well, well, big brother, I see that you're not all quite as sweet as you portray yourself. I'm impressed to hear some barb to your voice."

"Edwin, it is, as ever, my only intention to amuse you."

Now he laughs out loud, and I watch him with narrowed eyes. What is this? What new trick has he devised in his drunken stupor?

"Brother, I'm bored and wretched. I've decided to outlaw all drink from my house, and live a faithful and chaste life. If I succeed," and here he pauses and takes a deep breath, as though he's trying to believe in his words as he says them, "will you allow me back into the family."

I'm amazed at his words. I'd no inkling whatsoever that he'd even considered changing in such a profound way. Not that I think he's capable of giving up his debauchery and drinking, but I cannot, in Christian conscience, detract from his plan. With only a moment of pause, I nod slowly.

"If you can stay sober for more than six months, with no hint of a rebellion or a woman in your life then yes, I will consider allowing you back into my more intimate circle of family and friends."

His hooded eyes light a little at the answer I give, and he reaches his arm out to clasp my own, a way of sealing the bond.

"Then Athelstan, my brother and my king, I will see you in six months, when I am free from my vices."

Without another word, he stumbles from my presence, and I watch him go with narrowed eyes. I'm uneasy; I see treachery everywhere for an excellent reason. I'll need to ensure that my servants in his household are even more vigilant than normal. It's clear to me that Edwin is busy plotting something, and this time he's put far more thought into it than ever before.

With a snap of my fingers, Edmund is at my side, his eyes watching the swaying back of Edwin as he ambles from my hall.

"He's planning something."

"When isn't he?" Edmund asks sourly. Our half-brother causes rancour amongst all his surviving half-brothers and sisters.

"Can you arrange for someone you trust to attach themselves to his household and report back to you?"

"Of course. Why what's he said this time?"

"He'll sober up, and he wants to become part of the family again?"

Edmund's eyebrows rise in surprise at the words.

"That's a new one," he exclaims softly, and I share his shock and disbelief.

"Yes, it is. This time he has something more monumental than normal planned."

"I hear he's been entertaining men from the north," Edmund offers, "Ælfstan has just reported it to me," he clarifies, almost apologising that I'd not yet been informed of the news, even though Ælfstan has only just arrived at the Witan.

"From the north of the English or do you mean men from Constantin's lands."

"Both," he answers ominously, and I look at him pensively. This is an unwelcome development.

"Perhaps send two men, or maybe a woman," I reconsider, and Edmund is nodding in agreement as he absorbs those words.

"A woman, yes, but also two men. A woman he will be instantly suspicious off, but if she's married and with one of the men he'll see it as a challenge before he considers anything else."

With that he strides from my presence, intent on his errand. I watch him with interest as he leaves. He's a good-looking young man, all the women say so, and my stepmother has often had to caution him from enjoying himself too much with the young ladies of the Witan.

Still, since his upset when he was unable to do more than look and fawn over the lovely Gerbega from the German embassy, he has little looked at any of the women with great interest. He thought his infatuation love, and the girl's father did all he could to make it seem so. In the end, I dispatched my two sisters with the embassy only because I couldn't afford for my acknowledged heir to marry unwisely. It was better to have the delegation gone than deal with their quibbling about the beauty, intelligence and birthing stock of the two, almost identical sisters.

It took some time for his infatuation to die down and for him to look at me with anything but petulant eyes, but I could no sooner marry him to the family of a disgraced ealdorman of another king than allow Edwin to marry. It would have thwarted the plans for a union between the royal families.

I must ask my stepmother for her ideas of a suitable bride for her son. After all, he'll need to marry and ensure the continuation of our father's line. I wish him luck. Women as sisters and mothers are more than enough for me.

Edwin's departure will cause me no discomfort now that I know he'll be watched for any sign of treachery. All I can hope is that he leaves quickly, today if possible. My allies are on their way, and I want to make a good impression on all of them.

Brunanburh – Athelstan – 937

I can easily see where Edmund is slowly making his way towards me, clearly exhausted and weary but very much alive. I'm relieved and pleased in equal measure.

And behind him, everything seems to be falling into place.

Messengers have come from both the ealdormen at the flank and Guthrum in the middle. The enemy is making an orderly retreat, we can all see it, and they hope to trick us into making a hasty dash forward and have us flounder in the small dip in the ground that's been pointed out to me by the local guides. They are oblivious to the fact that we know about this gulley and can just as easily use it to our advantage.

I make as quick a decision as I can, my eyes attempting to peer into the future so that I can take the full benefits of this hoped for change of tactic.

Even as I watch Edmund stagger towards me, I'm sending messengers back to my ealdormen to tell them how we'll now proceed. It's nothing new, we'd discussed this possibility, and I'm ecstatic that we get to try the bold approach.

My eyes slightly narrow as I watch the messengers reach the ealdormen, and then they circulate the information to their chosen seconds and commanders of the other men of the fyrd. Even as the enemy takes the first few steps back, I see my men slow their movements so that while they still benefit from the enemies staggering backwards steps, they do it slowly, routinely. Those at the front of the shield wall still stand, shield to shield against the enemy, but those further back take a moment, a swig of water, or just an elongated look at where they stand in relation to where they started, to look for fallen friends.

They know that the next action they take may well end this battle. Many of the men are weary, it's been a long, slow slog to reach this moment, and I'd feared that the two sides would reach an impasse. After all, two groups of men, both as well armed as the other and with the same weapons, will always find it hard to win against their foe. One side needs an advantage, something small or large, such as the death of their leader or their injury, to force the side to crumble under the onslaught of the opposition. It's my hope that this small, two-foot wide ditch will be the undoing of my enemy.

Edmund has reached my side now and has taken food and mead from my young servant. He's exhausted, but his keen eyes are picking out what's happening on the battlefield.

"Are they falling back?" he queries with interest, his exhaustion clear to hear.

"Yes, and intentionally so," I reply distractedly.

"Are they going for the ditch?" he asks, the exhaustion that had marked his earlier words, completely gone.

"It appears so," I say, trying to keep the excitement from my voice but utterly failing.

"Then I must return to the front line," he says aggressively, reaching for his shield and sword only just discarded on the ground before me. I'm not going to deny him his opportunity to kill another of our supposed allies, and so I don't add my thoughts about his exhaustion.

"Take care," I call after him, but he's gone, with his warriors at his side, Eadric striding along with him, collecting Æthelwald as they go. As Edmund walks, he's pulling on his gloves, checking his weapons are within reach, and pulling his helmet firmly over his head and face. I hope he reaches the front line of the battle before it reaches the ditch. When we discussed this possibility in our counsels before the attack, he was keen to force the men to their knees at the ditch. He thought it gave us the quickest way to defeat the enemy.

I too am getting myself ready for battle. All morning long I've sat and watched, biding my time, waiting for the most opportune moment to enter the heat and blood of combat, and I think this will be it.

At my side, I have a small force of my warriors and bodyguards. Some are men I've fought with since my youth, and others are newer and younger, just as able to fight as the older men, but a little more lively on their feet.

They've been stood all morning, battle ready and keen to go at a moment's notice.

But still I hesitate a little longer; I want to know for sure that this is the part of the battle that will be decisive.

The men held back away from the shield wall are barely moving now, but the enemy has nearly reached the ditch. My men need to go soon, or they won't gain enough momentum to take full advantage of the enemy's orderly retreat.

I wait, nervous that we'll miss our moment, but know it's not yet come.

A few more steps are needed, I count slowly to five, and then my banner man signals the ealdormen and commanders, who've been waiting impatiently for my order, and suddenly over two thousand men are racing behind the snaking shield wall as it retreats.

The combined weight of my fyrd crashes into the shield wall, driving it closer and faster towards the slowing enemy, more intent on where they step than what comes towards them. They don't want to falter in the self-same ditch that they hope will rescue them, and which I hope will cause their death.

A slow smile steals across my face as vast swathes of the enemy fall under the onslaught of pure momentum, the sound reaching my straining ears as little more than a whisper, a complete contrast to the carnage being played out before my joyful eyes.

The enemy trip and fall, rushed off their feet by the suddenly violent attack, entire contingents of men tumbling as though the wind has taken them, one after another, like leaves in the early winter, being shorn from their summer home along the tree's branches. Those who fall grab for help from those who stand next to them and force them down as well, like a row of long and deadly icicles falling from an outside roof when the weather turns, one part shearing off and then the rest following suit, unable to hold on without its neighbour for support.

The ditch has done much of the work for us, pulled the warriors down and into a crush that'll cause the death of those at its bottom, and will injure those fighting to escape from its grip. It might only be two feet wide, but I think it at least four feet deep, enough to lose a sheep or a child on a summer day. Or to kill a man weighed down with his weapons when other men fall on top of him.

And now it's time for me to be involved. Shouting for my warriors to join me, I begin to step across the mass of broken and bloodied grasses, neatly avoiding the healers who work their way through the injured or dead. My eyes barely notice the fallen, so focused am I on the part I'll play in the battle.

Edmund has already rejoined the battle in front of me. I can see where a small line of our men has parted to allow him to reach the shield wall. And I know where the enemy line is faltering, fading away, unable to stand tall against such an unexpected attack.

Now that I'm almost level with the fighting, I can't see the total effect of our battle strategies, but I know they're working. I can feel it in the sighs of the men we face and the battle hungry grins on the faces of my warriors and fyrd men.

Guthrum greets me in the centre of the battlefield, a ghoulish grin on his white face, streaked with dark blood. He holds his sword in his hand, but it's his right hand, glistening with his blood that shows the fighting he's already taken part in. His knuckles are bruised and bloodied, and his nose shows the slightest hint of blood at its tip.

"They fell for it, my Lord," he crows with delight, and I nod as regally as my excitement allows me.

"Now let's win this thing," I growl, and then I'm rushing forward, keen to be at the front of the hand to hand fighting now that it's finally underway. I've not got my shield in my hand. It would make my progress slower as I'd need to dodge around the men who fight in small, tight groups in front of me. My sword is in my right hand, and in my left, I hold a smaller version of a war axe. I can fight with both weapons simultaneously, even though their weight is very different. My left hand is the weaker, and yet, it can throw out wild strikes that can split a man's nose and cause his forehead to crumble. My right hand, I can use to sever the head from a man. It's not a pretty job to accomplish, but I can do it. Even those blessed with the neck of a bull.

My men cheer me as I race through them, a huge roar of noise that brings a grim smile to my face. My appearance on the battlefront will give them a renewed purpose, and God willing, this battle will be over soon now that the stalemate of the shield wall has been broken.

Quickly I take stock of the situation at the front of the fight. The shield wall has disintegrated, it's warrior against warrior. And the number of enemy fighters is rapidly diminishing.

With a howl of joy, I spy a warrior who must be a king or an Earl of somewhere. He's clad from head to foot in ringed mail, his shield newly painted and bright, and a helmet covers his head, but not his eyes, or his nose. His weapon looks fresh from the forge, and I know that he'll be a man who's never fought for his life before. A bully no doubt, a man who holds his position by commanding others to do his dirty work for him. I look forward to killing him.

A clear path to him suddenly opens up before me, and I step into the breach, my warriors choosing their targets and ensuring they are close to me, should I need their help. They know I won't, but a king must do all he can to protect himself from the unexpected, especially in bloody battle.

I raise my war axe and step forward at the same time. The enemy warrior fails to notice me; his attention focused on something happening behind me. I step over the dead man on the floor, and I'm before him, my axe echoing on his loosely hanging shield as it pierces the fresh wood with a wet smell. Not the strongest of shields.

He howls with rage at being attacked, looking blankly around for those who should have been guarding him, but all his men are engaged with my own, and he stands alone and unprotected. Not the greatest warrior in the battle but an easy kill is still a kill when the man is your enemy working to undermine your life's work.

He raises his weapon and pauses for a beat, deciding how best to attack me. Into that gap, I step ever closer, making his sword almost useless in his hand. It can't reach me with its deadly force, as I stand almost within the embrace of the man, making it more likely that the sword will hit him before it hits me, as he swings it to attack me.

I yank my war axe free from the shield, and I drive it forward again, trying to force the new made shield down. I can tell now that it's newly made and weak for all that. Shields, like swords, gain from a long life before battle. The extra use, the extra tarnish that must be applied after every practice session, every battle serves to make them stronger, less likely to bend or snap. The wood hardening with the years of use it gets, not weakening, but settling into its shape, and learning to grab hold of the iron boss that crowns it and holds its tendrils of wood into place.

The man strains before me, the veins on his neck standing out starkly under his long blond hair and close fitting helmet. He's holding the wrong weapons, and I'll not give him a moment to change them.

As I force my weight onto the shield, I quickly swap my sword for the smaller dagger on my belt, and once more, I raise my axe and then crash it down onto the shield. Splinters of wood fly into the air and meet my spit as they do so. The man's eyes are bulging at the strength in my left arm, and while he tries to hold his own, I take advantage of his distraction and slide my dagger across his throat. Blood immediately sprays forth, covering my face with a warm wave as I glare into my enemy's eyes, feeling his muscle sever under my hand. I want him to know that he died at the hands of the English king.

He slumps to the disturbed ground, a look of disbelief on his face, as I kick him to ensure he's fully down. I step over him and move onto the next warrior, forgetting all about him. I might find out later who he was, but then again, I might never find the body again. There are bodies everywhere, piling one on top of the other, some in the ditch and others just before and behind it. Perhaps, when it's time to bury the fallen here, it will be best to simply widen the trench and throw the rest of the bodies in.

Another man steps into my line of sight, a grimace on his hairy face as he tightens his grip on his war axe and battered shield, the paint streaked with death. He's a huge giant of a man, and I wonder what his weakness will be.

He attacks first, raising his left hand with his war axe to hammer against my chest, as my shield is still on my back. Without fear, I grab my sword again using its longer reach to slash with my right hand at the barely exposed left side of his body. Not a natural stroke, but one I've practised with before. Before his axe has swung half way back into his massive stroke, my sword has impacted and sliced open a wound on the exposed side of his body that shows red and bloody on the bright summers day. His rings of mail have worked to arrest some of the strokes, but my sword hit hard enough that I feel the weapon's silky smooth cut through his skin.

His face shows his pain, his eyes bulging although he remains silent. And now his axe has reached its full swing, and he grins at me a little, delighted in what he thinks is about to happen. Only it doesn't.

I raise my axe to meet his, and the two weapons meet in mid air, my hand throbbing with the impact. The eyes of my enemy protrude a little, and a small cry rips from his mouth as the clang of the weapons meeting reverberates down his arm to his bleeding wound. He tries to work his shield between us but his right arm has lost its strength with his injury, and I just need to decide how best to kill him.

Our war axes are still entangled, the strength of my arm far more than his own, but he's not yet prepared to give up. His shield hangs limply between us as I swing my sword back towards him. It's not the most comfortable of moves as I'm too close to raising my arm as I normally would but with a little strain, I manoeuvre it so that with one slice I might just sever his head from his neck.

He tries to force the axes down, step away from me and make my movement ineffectual but he's too weak now, his breath coming in short rasps, and I wonder if he was already injured before I came upon him, perhaps down his back, or through the right side of his body. It seems to have been too easy a kill.

I hold my ground, and acceptance comes into the clouding eyes of the man. With a heave of effort, my sword comes full circle, meeting the resistance of the man's neck and I exert my strength to cleave it entirely through his exposed neck. Halfway through I realise I'm never going to complete the move, and the man is long dead anyway.

I let the body tumble to the ground, and using my boot as leverage, I force the sword out of the neck. Another kill, and I'm feeling strong and keen to kill everyone who's come against me.

The ditch that Constantin and Olaf hoped to use to their advantage is filling with the bodies of their warriors, and my men are stepping over the dead to face any who still live and still have the will to attack us.

Amazingly the retreat has not yet been called, and I wonder if Olaf and Constantin have fallen and none of their men have noticed.

And then another man stands before me. His sword raised menacingly with blood streaking its dulling surface, and his shield firmly in place. I imagine he's watched how I killed the other two men and had no intention of falling victim to any of my ploys.

He's a smaller man, compact and wiry and when he moves to step towards me, it's as though he moves with the stealth of a wolf. He's a warrior of much cunning, but I'm happy to find someone who might challenge my skills.

Never one to falter, I step closer to him, making him reconsider his move. No warrior likes it when you step in too close, and he must decide whether to take a step backwards or meet my challenge by trying to take advantage of my movements.

He chooses the latter, and I smirk at his manoeuvre. We are now so close we could be lovers. In such a confined space it's difficult to kill a man, and so I take a decision, and quickly lunge my head forward, snapping it down on the other man's exposed nose. He howls with anger, while blood bubbles from his nose. I wear my helm with a nose guard; he doesn't. Inadvertently he steps back, licking his lips as he does so, tasting his blood and swallowing it down so that it won't choke him.

I still hold my axe and my sword, he holds his sword and his shield, but he's already bleeding.

"My Lord Athelstan," he says through gritted teeth, and I note the roll of his words and know that English is not his first language. He must be one of Olaf's allies from across the sea in the rough and ready lands of the Irish.

"And you are?" I ask, acutely aware that around us other men dance and die while we make introductions.

"Cellach," he says quickly, and he need say no more. He is one of Constantin's sons. An excellent catch if I can kill him. His mother was a woman of the Irish dynasties, and that explains his strong accent that I don't think his father shares.

"I'm come to avenge the death of my nephew," he spits, and I laugh openly in his face, my battle rage roused for all that normally I'm a calm man.

"I didn't kill your nephew. His youth and his inexperience and his father killed him," I cry, knowing full well that Cellach will take offence, and hope to knock him a little off balance, make his anger fuel his moves, not his training.

His eyes flash with anger, and he tightens his stance, but the hoped for anger does not surface. Instead, he grins abruptly and lashes out with his sword, a movement so fast it surprises me, and for a moment I'm aware of it hovering dangerously close to my exposed body.

Quickly, I step backwards, moving out of the reach of his sword, hoping I won't trip over a body or a discarded sword.

Luckily nothing gets in my way, and I quickly reappraise my next movement. Cellach seems to be imbibed with the stone cold desire to kill me in revenge for the death of his nephew. Undoubtedly he'll not turn angry with any of my words, his resolve written across his bleeding face.

He's watching me with interest, having brought his shield back close to his body, holding it loosely; ready to strike at a moments notice.

My weapons are just as ready, held before my body. And I think it's just a matter of who strikes first.

"Anyway, surely it should be your brother who seeks his vengeance on me, and shouldn't it be against my brother? After all, it was he who killed the boy," I taunt, as though discussing my death is an everyday occurrence.

"You ordered the attack; you marched into our lands. If you'd not, the boy would still live," he leers at me, and I see that he'd made his mind up about who is to blame long ago.

"If your father had stayed true to his word, I'd not have needed to come and visit him within his lands."

A bark of laughter erupts from Cellach, and I smirk openly in his face.

"You're quibbling over nothings," he growls, raising his shield into a defensive position. "I'll take pride in your death, and then my brother will rest easy knowing that he's vanquished his son."

"As you will," I mutter back, and then I'm rushing towards him. I need to make the first move, or I think we might reach a stalemate, and then, he might be the better man.

A slash with my axe across his shield and it drops just enough that I'm able to see Cellach's neck clearly, but I'd already decided not to go for such an obvious move. His eyes are watching me impassively, although he's stepped back on his right foot to brace himself against my attack.

Lightning quick I pull my axe clear, and aim for his sword arm, just below the shoulder. He's expecting me to aim across his body from my left, and instead, I reverse the angle of my swing and slash at his right shoulder. My weapon grates across his protective coat of rings, loosening them, and his eyes open a little wider in shock.

Now he bleeds from two wounds, but I know I've barely touched him.

My axe, glistening once more with the enemy's blood, lashes out towards his neck, and he jumps back, out of my reach, and something like fear touches his face. Perhaps, after all, he's not the warrior he thinks he is.

Before he can reappraise the fight, I step close again, repeating my movement of moments ago, and then reversing the axe and aiming for his left shoulder. My abrupt change confuses him, and his shield is trying to cover his right shoulder, while I aim for his left.

Once more I move before his eyes can focus on me, a sharp slash with my sword to his exposed ankles, and he staggers a little under the onslaught. I imagine he's practised since he was a young boy with his sword and his shield, but not how to use both as shield and weapon both. A veteran of my grandfather's wars taught me all his most effective aggressive moves, and his defensive ones too, but clearly, I'm the aggressor here.

He's not given up yet. I'm watching his every move, and still, he wrong foots me by stepping towards my axe hand, and then changing direction, and aiming for the arm where my sword is pointing towards the ground. He tries to slash at my side, but my axe is suddenly there, once more playing the part of a shield, and the axe head, close to my shoulder, stops his sword. He holds it there, hoping to force my left hand against my body and then wrench his sword free. He still thinks that my left hand is the weaker of the two.

While he focuses all of his strength into pressing his sword against my axe, I lazily move my right arm, my sword not quite tight in my grasp, but enough that I'll be able to strike him with it if I can just force him back a step.

His breath is in my face, his crazed eyes boring into my own. The sounds of battle have faded to nothing, and yet, I know no fear.

With a roar of rage, I apply all my strength to my axe, first letting it fall a little, as though my arm is weakening and forcing him off balance. As soon as that's done, I step back, half a step, just enough room to swing my sword, and then it strikes the side of his head, his close fitting helmet almost of no help against such a near blow with a heavy object.

I see his eyes lose their focus as I feel the grate of bone on blade, and then he's gone, my sword digging into the side of his ear just above his neck, not severing his head, but playing havoc with the life blood that flows there. He's dead before he hits the ground, and a growl of real triumph erupts from my throat.

Breathing heavily, I look around me. The shield wall is gone, wasted away to nothing as men face each other, generally one on one, but occasionally two to one, or even three.

In my ear, I hear Guthrum's deep voice.

"A good death," he rumbles, and I meet his eyes grateful to know that throughout that brief interchange he was there, ready to intercede if necessary. I'd almost forgotten I was the king then, so intent on my altercation.

"My thanks, Guthrum," I breathe, trying to determine how the battle is proceeding.

"Your brother is fighting well," he says, pointing with his bloodied sword to a press of bodies on our side of the ditch. Edmund is there, I can tell by his clothing, but other than that, the men have all merged into a brown mass of living, thrashing beasts, the only identifiers their eyes and their voices.

"Good but there are still many of the enemy?" I query, hoping that he's a little more aware of what's happening around us.

"Yes, but you have rid us of Cellach, and over there, Edmund and Eadric face Gebeachan, king of the Isles, and the few of his men who remain. And over there," and he points towards the flank of the original shield wall, where Ælfstan had been commanding his troops, Olaf of Dublin is facing Ælfwine."

"And Constantin?" I ask, wondering if the old bugger has deigned to get off his horse and join the fighting.

"He still sits and watches," he says, indicating with his head where a solitary horseman can be seen on a far away rise in the land.

"He's unprotected?" I query, surprised by the apparent confidence or desperation.

"It appears so," he says, and I know what I want to do now.

"Then we must make our way towards him."

Guthrum nods his head in agreement,

"A bold plan, my Lord, and one I'll happily accomplish for you."

"No, but my thanks all the same. I wish to face him. Knock him off his horse and have him face me with his sword."

"As you will," he accedes without further argument. Now is not the time to argue about who should have the privilege of killing the lying Scots king.

But before I can take even one step, attempt to cross the ditch that has been my enemy's downfall, a wild-eyed man steps into my line of sight. He looks like the man I dispatched moments ago and my eyes betray me and glance to the dead body on the ground. It's not moved so this must be another of Constantin's by blows.

"Athelstan," he growls, his own eyes flickering over the corpse and showing remorse for the death.

"And you are?" I ask, feeling Guthrum tense at my back.

"Your worst nightmare," the man says, his own back suddenly protected by a small collection of bloodied warriors. Not one of them is devoid of another man's blood. This must be one of Constantin's better sons, Ildulb I imagine, the father of the boy Edmund killed no less. His rage emanates from every muscle.

He runs toward me, leaping over the ditch and landing, axe raised in front of me. Fumbling, I replace my sword and finally reach for my shield. If he's been watching me fight, I need to change my methods.

He smirks at my shield, throwing his own to the floor, and I wonder what sort of fool he is to defy me so openly. And then I know. He's a man who thinks enough to try and force me to a bad decision, just as I have sought to do with those I've already slain.

Calmly, I raise my shield before my body, my axe in my left hand, my back covered by Guthrum and my household warriors. This altercation could end this battle if I kill Ildulb. I can't imagine the old bastard Constantin fighting on if two of his sons are dead, and God alone knows how many of his grandsons.

Behind me, the cries of other men calling my name alert me to the fact that this might be more a spectator event than I'd have liked, but then, my men deserve to see me fight and win. That is after all why they're all here.

The ground is damp with blood and piss, but I step confidently into Ildulb, noting once more how much the Scots seem to hate this move. Surely someone has taught them the advantage of constricting the opposition's actions, forcing them to consider their every more? Not.

My axe streaks through the air, landing cleaning on Ildulb's head, the blunt force knocking him sideways a little. But his counter movement had already started, his sword sneaking its way past my shield, and grazing my chest. He pulls it back, as I do my axe, and then I strike again. The axe this time, aiming to draw blood not just stun. In mid-air, I twirl the weapon so that the sharpened edge is now aiming at the man's hand loosely holding his axe. He doesn't even attempt to defend himself, instead using my moment of temporary distraction to force his sword even closer to my chest, hoping to catch me with the sword's edge. He succeeds, a little, and I feel the impact as a brief quiver up my side.

Changing tactics, I drop my shield to the side of me knowing that it's hampering my attack. My small dagger in hand, I fend off his third attack with his sword with my dagger, ensuring the two hasps tangle, his sword the longer of the two and harder to extricate. As he tries to pull his sword back, I aim again with my axe, this time for his arm where it crosses his body.

The weapon bites deeply into the gloves he wears, but I can't tell if he bleeds or not. The leather is good, and it might just have stopped my weapon.

His sword, finally released, is shining through the air, aiming for my neck, and I step out of its reach. He's a strong man, and I imagine plenty capable of severing my neck if I give him the opportunity.

Behind him, his warriors are glaring menacingly at me, and I wonder when Guthrum will command the men who protect my back to attack. I'd like it to be sooner rather than later, while they're distracted by their Lord's fight to the death they'll make easy pickings.

He laughs derisively at my avoidance of his sword and readies himself to swing again, thinking that I'm scared of his sword without my shield in my hand. Perhaps, after all, he didn't watch me tackle his brother and the other men who now lie lifeless on the ground.

I decide I'd rather bring this to a rapid conclusion, and so once more, I step forward, my foot rising off the ground and tensing to strike his knee with as much force as I can muster. He grins again, perhaps thinking that I've tripped. I push my weight onto my back foot so that I can raise the other off the floor, but the blunt force hitting his knee cap knocks the grin from his face instantly. He staggers back, and then my axe is behind his other knee, my head level with his sword hanging lifelessly in his hand, and the sharpened edge of my axe digs deeply into his shins.

I step back quickly, I need to follow up this advantage, and I raise my sword to do some more serious damage, to slash at his arm that has snaked down his shin and will come away sticky with blood.

A howl of rage erupts from my mouth as another man rudely pushes his Lord aside, sending Ildulb tumbling to the ground, where he's quickly protectively surrounded by four men, and a man with his axe twirling in his hand as he taunts Guthrum with his presence.

The new warrior roars with rage, and I use my already in play sword move to attack the giant of a man in front of me. As I do so, warily watching his next move, Ildulb is being escorted from the battlefield, and annoyance floods my actions. No matter the size of the man, I don't want to waste my time on him. I want the son of Constantin, another one.

My axe flies through the air, first biting into the flesh on his left shoulder, and then on his right, and then slicing across his waist, and all before he's got his shield in place to protect himself. He eyes me with anger mixed with pain, and I spit in his face. Sod him and his interfering ways.

"You'll die for that," I shout, knowing that rage is making me irrational, but I've been denied an easy kill. A short, sharp tap on the man's nose with my dagger, forcing blood to well and my axe is buried deep within his chest. I yank it out harshly, watching the blood and bone that leaves his body dispassionately, and then I walk away in disgust. He's dead or will be soon. I hope it was worth his while to die at his Lord's expense.

I want to go after Ildulb, but the men who protected him have run from the battlefield, and more men are converging around me.

"We need to spread them out," I shout to Guthrum, only now noticing that Edmund has joined my attack as well.

With steps more akin to those in a dance, every warrior still standing chooses an opponent and taunts them into moving onto more open ground. With more space between them, it'll be harder for them to protect each other's backs and any reinforcements who race to help them will have to take valuable time to decide who they should protect.

I'm disgusted with Ildulb's withdrawal and want nothing more than to race after him and his cheating father, but know that the battle is, for the time being, here on the battlefield, not with the orchestrator of this fight.

A howl of battle lust leaves my throat, and I eye the men come to fight me with interest. Who will be my next victim?

Chapter 22 – 931 - King's Worthy – Edmund

The day has passed without any difficulties. Athelstan is happy with the success of his Witan and so too is Hywel of Dyfed. Idwal, Hywel's cousin, Morgan of Gwent, a more recent ally and of course Owain from Strathclyde are all in attendance and are being feted and feasted. With or without the tacit support of Constantin, Athelstan sits as king above all others.

I am sat beside Owain of Strathclyde at the feast, and at my side sits Ælfstan, one of my oldest friends and closest allies. Between us we keep the slightly nervous looking Owain amused and entertained. It's not that he's uncomfortable, or shifty with his looks, but there is something that makes me feel that all is not as Athelstan may have hoped.

I find it just as likely that Owain is here at Constantin's command, as he is at Athelstan's. I must remember to speak to him later before he does anything he might regret at a later date. And rumour had reached me, via one of Ælfstan's commended men, that Owain met with Morgan and Idwal before he arrived at king's Worthy. I wonder what they spoke about. There are plots a plenty stemming from the other subject kingdoms.

As always, our mother has decorated the palace spectacularly, and Hywel and Athelstan have already announced that they will be spending tomorrow morning examining some of Athelstan's newest relics and religious books. Both my brother and Hywel are avid collectors. I can appreciate the poignancy and legitimacy that the relics imbibe my brother with, but if I was in his place, which I hope not to be for many years, I don't think I'd enjoy spending quite as much time with the odd bone fragments he's amassed. Not that I say those words to him. It would be inappropriate if there were any rift between us.

The entertainers for the feast are noisily working their way into place before our feasting table. They will share epic tales from all of the kingdoms of our land, and then a skald from the Five Borough's will recount stories from the culture of the Viking raiders. I queried the wisdom of such a move with Athelstan, but he laughed my fears away.

"It's important to understand the motivation of men who've been enemies and who might be again," he offered by way of an explanation. I respected his argument but thought it a little ironic that he would equally share our heritage with men who might use it against our people in the future.

There are also other men and boys amongst the Witan who don't stem from our island. Athelstan has long been foster-father to Alain of Brittany and Louis of Frankia, our nephew, but he has also welcomed priests and poets from the continent. As I glance around the bustling hall, I can't help but be struck by how many different languages flow around the wooden walls. The voices of those speaking in the tongue of the Norse, or the ancient Britons or those from Frankia. Athelstan indeed presides over a multi-lingual and multi-national Witan.

Many of those, whom he's named as ealdormen, or his king's thegns, also speak with a slight tinge of accent, some heralding from the Five Borough's, the lands that the Vikings colonised. It's from there that the skald has made his way to Athelstan, filled will tales and stories and aware of Athelstan's close link with the king of Norway, he's come to seek my brother's pleasure.

Owain is watching everything through narrowed eyes, his shoulders set and his mouth stretched in a thin flat line. He's ill at ease and uncomfortable with everything he sees, although he tries to mask it.

"My Lord Owain, do you have many visits from over the sea?" I enquire, thinking he'll be pleased to speak of something, anything, other than the delicious food or the weather but instantly I know I've erred as he chokes a response.

"Not too many, Edmund," he stumbles, but I can't help thinking that he probably has a court filled with men from the Dublin Norse and the land of the Scots.

"We often have visitors from the Outer Isles," he offers as some consolation, as though he's realised he's being rude and abrupt and now gives more away by his surly answer than anything else.

"They travel by ship or over land?" I ask.

"By ship. They are men who live and die by their ships. A strange mix of the ancient races that inhabited the lands before the Norsemen came, and the Norsemen themselves. Much like our island," he offers, seemingly as an afterthought.

Instantly I wonder what he means by such a comment. Who does he think is the strange part in the mix of the heritage of the men in this hall? Ælfstan at my side cautions me with his eyes, and I realise that I shouldn't press the man further. After all, he's a king in his own right, unlike myself, and I shouldn't presume to have him answer my every question and whimsical query.

Still, I'll think about this some more. Owain may, after all, be a little more slippery than I expected. He may also be more his own man than I've given him credit for. Certainly, he thinks about the people of the island of Britain more than I ever have.

After the meeting at Eamont, Athelstan went to great lengths to discover all he could about the men who'd met with him. The relationship between Constantin and Owain has given him the greatest pause for thought, and he's spoken of it openly to his ealdormen and me. Eventually it became clear that Owain only held his place as king because Constantin had commanded it. Athelstan was surprised by the news. He'd not realised that he had a contender for his chosen role as Over-King of our island.

Since the discovery, he's taken extra effort to meet with Owain, have him a close ally. I think, if he could that he'd try to entice him away from Constantin. He'd like a partner in the northern lands as he doesn't have one. Ealdred of Bamburgh looks to the North, and Owain is allied very closely with Constantin, at least for now.

"Do you trade with them then?" I ask, turning the conversation back to Owain.

"Yes, for precious stones and furs. They like our furs. Apparently, the Outer Isles are not rich in trees and too small for forests, and they don't have bears and wolves as we do. And yet, their islands are cold for half of each year, and then for the other half, the sun rarely sets."

This is all news to me, and I find it fascinating.

"Then how do they sleep?"

"They sleep when they think it's night time, and wake when they believe that it's daytime. I would find it confusing," he offers, and I laugh along with him. I'd find it confusing as well.

"Does that mean that in the winter, it's always dark?"

"I assume it must do; I'd not considered that. No wonder they're a funny race," he jokes, and Ælfstan laughs along with him, while I try to think of some way of continuing the conversation. Only Owain seems more relaxed now, and his eyes sweep the room with interest.

"The king has many sisters," he says, a question for all that it sounds like a statement.

"He does, but three are now married, and a fourth lives in the lands of the Germans. One of our sisters is a widow, and another two have decided to retire to nunneries and devote their lives to God."

Owain glances at the table where the royal women sit with interest.

"Are any of them here today?" he asks, and I wonder what interest he has in the women, but as I still can't think of anything else to say to him, I point out my stepmother and my sisters and their children, if they have any. Owain is very intrigued by the youths who sit with my mother.

"They are your brothers?" he asks, and I nod.

"Two of them are, those two there, the other two boys are either our nephews or Athelstan's foster children."

"So he fosters but has no children to call his own."

"No, Athelstan decided not to marry. I think my father left him with enough sisters and brothers to contend with, without adding to his familial obligations."

"Your father married three times I hear," Owain smirks, "He was either an unwise man or one who liked women too well."

"I think the latter, but I could be wrong," I reply, not enjoying the turn of the conversation.

"Three different women," he muses, " he was happy to cause discontent in his own home if he had three different women to please at the same time."

I want to point out that my father did not marry all three women at the same time, but Ælfstan once more cautions me with his eyes. It's entirely possible that Owain is trying to upset me knowing only too well that my father's chequered history is a bone of contention within the kingdom. Luckily, the skald has taken his place in the centre of the hall, beside the roaring fire, and as I settle in to watch and listen, I notice that it's Owain who now looks unhappy. I wonder why as the words of the skald wash over me. I think he adds something new to his usual repertoire, but I could be wrong.

Brunanburh - Olaf of Dublin – 937

It didn't work, that's all I know. My great ploy to hack the English men to pieces using the ditch has faltered and now, back in the thick of the fighting, I am aware that one wrong move and I'll be dead, and this battle a shambles.

For now, I'm back with the dismembered shield wall, my men surrounding me, the cries of my allies reaching my ears although I'm unable to run to their aid. The English are everywhere.

And yet, a cold realisation settles over me. I can still turn the tide of this battle, single-handedly if need be. All I need to do is face the English king, for my man saw him enter the fray and now I'm searching for him, praying that I find him and that the honour of slaying the robbing bastard will fall to me.

I feel stronger than an ox, able to beat any who step before me. Even now as I consider where I will find Athelstan, my sword is raised, my shield as well, as I fight a stringy little man, with only half my attention.

Resolved, I slice him, cleanly through the stomach, watching with disinterest as I pull the sword through his body, leaving a bloody gaping hole through which I can see the red of his insides and the grey of his bowls. He howls in agony as I lower my sword with the weight of his body and let him slide to the ground. A kick to the face and his eyes shut down, his knees on the floor, his head won't be upright for much longer.

Athelstan, where will I find him?

A shout from one of my men and I follow his sword to where he points to a noble man, dressed in the finest battle gear I've yet seen and surrounded by men fighting as valiantly as he does, and as equally well dressed.

I've not met the English king before, but this looks as though it's him.

With determined strides, I slide past the sharp swords and hacking axes of any I meet on my journey to stand before him.

The men around him are shouting and jostling each other, making him aware of my presence. A brief grin lights his face, and I know then that this is Athelstan and my temper rises and then falls quickly. To kill this man, this great power of the English, I will need to recollect myself to the here and now and not think of my gains of tomorrow.

Done with dispatching the warrior he faced he looks me squarely in the face.

"And who might you be?" he spits into my face; the saliva mixing with the blood that already covers me.

"Olaf, my Lord Athelstan," I crow, "King of the Dublin Norse, and soon York as well."

He laughs at my words, and a cheer ripples through his men. He throws his head back, exposing his throat and I wonder at his laughter, but I'm too busy raising my sword and readying my stance to think more of it. If only I could take his head off now when he exposes his neck so enticingly. I hope a few sharp stabs of my sword will have him on his knees. For all his flushed face, and battle-bloodied weapons, he looks no more kingly than I when we're so close together. I'm his equal, and I'm about to prove that I'm his superior as well.

I swing my sword across my body, and he quickly covers his own with his shield. There's a crash of metal on wood but I'm already moving my arm back for another swing, and the impact barely registers.

But before I can complete the curve of my stroke, I feel a sword crash into my shield, and it knocks my stance, sending my sword-arm flying wild to the side. Annoyed I glare at Athelstan, noticing that his blue eyes are composed. Irritated, I raise my arm again, swinging with less force but more quickly.

His shield blocks my path, and then he's changed his weapon, holding an axe in his hand, which he uses to drive against my shield. His massive strokes dent my shield, and chunks of the wood fly free as the rivets holding the boss together crush the wood into my hand where I grip the handle. I grimace but remain holding on. Using his axe has brought him closer to me, and I know that I can use my sword or my helm to inflict some serious damage.

I lunge forward, trying to knock his head with my own, but he dances back, his axe still in my shield and a slight grin across his bearded cheeks.

I wonder what makes him still smile?

With a yank of my shield, I force his axe from my shield, and it's my turn to dance backwards, careful not to trip over any obstruction on the ground, my shield in front of me and free from the uncomfortable weight.

I weigh my sword in my hand. I want to give a wounding shot, perhaps down the side of his leg or his arms. Somewhere where it will hurt a lot and make him lash out in pain.

His thoughts mirror my own, and I see him attempting to switch his weapons again. Before he can complete the move, I knock my shield into his arm that reaches for his sword, and his axe falls from his hand and drops at my feet, the edge embedded in the muck of the field.

Frantically he searches for his sword on his back, but still, he smiles. I grin back at him, confused by his carefree manner. He does not seem to fear me at all.

As he fumbles, he steps into my shield, knocking it with his own and forcing me off balance and to my left. By the time I've righted myself, he holds his sword and is attacking me quickly, one, two, three crashes of his weapon on my shield.

Even above the noise of the battlefield, I can hear his ragged breathing. He's not such an accomplished warrior as his allies would have me believe. A few moments of close combat and he seems done.

Another crash on my shield, and it's my turn to count to five before I lower my shield and dance into the space between us, my sword slashing wildly from side to side, its sharp tip seeking the flesh of this warrior.

With a satisfied smirk, I feel the iron pierce the byrnie and then the skin of the man when I strike him down the right-hand side of his body, the part not covered by his shield. He exhales into my face, his spit once more merging with the blood and sweat and angrily, I turn my head to the side and wipe my eyes clear. At that moment, with my shield in my hand, and my shoulder up to my face, he knocks the shield, causing it to impact with my front teeth and I feel the scrape of my teeth shattering with the force of the metal rim of my shield.

Anger strengthens my arm, as I slam my shield into his and force it down and away from his body. He's weakened by the injury he has, and I can feel his strength waxing as I apply more and more pressure, until I have almost all of my weight pressed down on the shield.

A quick glance to ensure that no one is coming to his rescue, and I stab forward into his already bleeding wound. His face twists in pain, but he doesn't cry out. Instead, he takes the time to grab his sword and slash wildly at the side of my neck. As his guts spill over my hand, a momentary flash of heat runs up my arm, and I start to crow with delight. I've done it, I've attacked the bloody English king, and he kneels, even now, dying at my feet.

A sting of pain clouds my vision, and I feel rather than see, his sword slicing down the side of my face and across my neck. I jump back in shock, looking at the man who even now is forcing my sword deeper and deeper into his body, twisting it as it goes in, to hasten his death. I watch with horror as he opens his bloodied mouth, his teeth red rimmed.

"My name is Ælfwine," he garbles, and I lean forward to catch what he says.

"Ælfwine," he repeats, his voice wet and choking with blood, and then he laughs a gurgling breath.

"I'm not the bloody king, Olaf, and you'll never kill him."

His eyes close, and I look about in confusion. Not the king?

"Then who the fuck are you?" I shout, angry that I've wasted my time.

"The king's cousin, you arse," he laughs, his death almost upon him. "But thanks for the enjoyment of watching you not kill the king, you jumped up little turd." And with that, his eyes shut, and he slumps to the ground, and suddenly, five men are advancing towards me, menace in their eyes. Only, one of them looks just like Ælfwine.

"Who are you?" I shout, not wanting to make the same mistake again.

"Whoever you want me to be," he answers unhelpfully, his sword raised, his lips curling and his blue eyes clear with vengeance.

He rushes at me, the four other men behind him, and I snap my shield back to my body, my sword back to my side, not caring that blood and skin still dangle from it, or that my arm is tired and my back aching.

He crashes into me, deciding to use his weight, not his sword. His attack rebounds up and down my arms, and I feel a moment of genuine anger. Growling I reach for my axe and snake a quick strike at his shoulder where it's still virtually embedded in my shield. I catch his ear through his helmet, and he rages in anger, but quickly recovers himself, stabbing forward with his sword into my shield, uncaring of the blood pooling down his neck. I wish I knew if this was the king or just another cousin.

He steps backwards, and swings with his sword this time, raising his shield at the same time as he attempts to knock my face with the reinforced metal edges of his shield. If I duck my head away, I'll step more fully into his swinging blade so instead I stay still, allowing the sword to ineffectually hit me as opposed to the shield knocking me on the nose and momentarily blinding me as my eyes tear and blood spills fresh from my nose.

The man I face grunts in annoyance that I haven't fallen for his ploy. As he does, I hammer my sword into his shield, over and over again, not giving him time to react other than to hold his flimsy piece of wood out in front of him.

My arm quickly starts to quiver with the strain, but I'm not stopping until he falls to his knees under the blows of my frenzied attack.

Over and over again my sword crashes down, always from the right side and I hope that it's weakening my enemy, whoever he might be. I need to kill him, and then I need to find Athelstan and kill him too. And I need to do it before the enemy succeeds in forcing us to retreat. Already I know that some men have made a run for the ships. I'll ensure they're punished when I turn this battle aside. They should have more faith, even in the face of such overwhelming odds.

The man I fight is noticeably growing weaker, and with each stroke of my sword, I feel his shield drop a little lower, and a grin of joy fills my face. This old man is easy to kill.

I slow my sword strikes, and wipe the sweat from my eyes, ready to take the final blows, ready to watch the light of life fade from this warrior's face.

Only just when I think he should be weakened and unable to go on, he raises his shield abruptly, using it to knock my sword away, and it's I who struggle with the weight of my weapon. The pounding I've given his shield has left deep gouges in its surface, but not in him. He seems stronger if that's possible, and I'm weaker from my massive strokes with my sword.

He looks at me with a smirk,

"Still wondering who I am?" he says, stepping into my space, coming too close to me as my sword is resting its tip on the ground as I fight my exhaustion and try to find the will to resume my battle against him.

"No," I shout defiantly. "you're one of Alfred's or Edward's by blows, and I'll be pleased to kill you before I move on to your king."

His grin stays firmly in place as he exchanges his sword very casually for his war axe, which until now had been lost on the muddy ground.

"And I will have the joy of killing you, Olaf of the Norse, desperately trying to claw back land your father gave away to my king. I wish you luck with that."

And he's upon me, his axe against my shield and trying to work its way behind my shield so that he can severe my hand or my neck, or simply form a deep gauge down my right-hand side. The force of his attack is astonishing, and with every crash of his weapon, he laughs loud and long, a terrible cry that I'll not quickly banish from my memory if I should survive his attack.

His attack is as frenzied as my own; only he doesn't have anywhere else he'd rather be. He wants to kill me. I just want to kill him so that I can move on and find Athelstan. My frustration wars with my fear and suddenly I realise that I can cower behind my shield, or I can attack him and be on my way.

Growling with anger and rage, I thrust my shield aside, taking his axe, embedded deeply into the wood, with it, and he's standing without weapon or shield. I grin in delight at my ruse, and with a slow and steady step, I bring my sword around, and I ram it into his hard iron chest, forcing all my weight behind the move and hoping that it'll work.

His eyes never lose their joy in the battle, and he laughs the whole time I work my weapon deeper and deeper into his body, and then, as the man before him did, he grabs the sword and twists it first one way and then the next, hastening his inevitable death.

As blood pours from his mouth, staining his teeth with the bright fluid, he spits in my face.

"Go to hell you robbing bastard," and he falls at my feet, my sword embedded deep within his body and I know I'll not retrieve it now.

Without further thought I reach for his sword and pull it from his back, and pick my shield up, working his axe free.

Now I just need to find Athelstan. Wherever he's hiding.

Chapter 23 – 931 - King's Worthy – Owain of Strathclyde

A bead of sweat forms on my lip as I sit and listen to the great skald at work. He's a great man who can do things with words that conjure images within his rapt audience's mind, take them to long ago battles, and the times of our ancestors, and have us all believing we too are taking part in the story.

He is a wonder and a great man.

He is Constantin's pet and his being here makes me uneasy, squashed as I am between the king's brother and one of his newest ealdormen. The vigour of the two youths is sobering to my advancing years, and I feel as though they know every thought going through my mind and know what I'm thinking even before I do.

I fear they mean to trip me with their questions and I must consider every word I say while at the same time appearing as though my responses are flippant and casually given, as though they are the truth. My head is pounding, and fear makes me regret the multitude of good food and wine and mead that I've consumed.

And then to top it all the great skald himself approaches the king and begins to recite tales of the ancient Britons. He speaks of a long ago mythical king who will one day return and unite our lands and then, into the thick of it he launches into his poem, only a poem constructed on Constantin's orders. A poem I've heard before and wish I didn't know.

"The Awen foretells the hastening of

The multitude, possessed of wealth and peace;

And a bountiful sovereign, and eloquent princes.

And after tranquillity, commotion in every place,

Heroic men raising a tumult of fierce contention.

Swift the remorse of defending too long.

The contention of men even to Caer Weir,

the dispersion of the Allmyn.

They made great rejoicing after exhaustion,

And the reconciling of the Cymry and the men of Dublin,

The Gwyddyl of Iwerdon, Mona, and Prydyn,

Cornwall and Clydemen their compact with them.

The Brython will be outcasts, when they shall have done,

Far will be foretold the time they shall be.

Kings and nobles will subdue them.

The men of the North at the entry surrounding them,

In the midst of their front, they will descend."

I gasp with shock at the arrogant accounting, looking around frantically to see if the great English king is aware of the huge dishonour being shown to him here. He appears oblivious, thinking it no more than an extension of the tales of that same mythical king the skald first mentioned. He doesn't know that this is Constantin's attempt to undermine him, his call to arms for all of the people of this island who do not think of themselves as English.

I did not know the skald would be here. Constantin had sent instructions that I was to meet with the king's of the Welsh and inform them of the skald's actions, not to say that Constantin had anything to do with the poem, but to let them know that there was a subversive working to undermine the vision of Athelstan's united island. I was only to mention a few words, drop a few hints of the tales I'd heard, and see how they reacted. Nothing more. But Constantin, or his skald, or both, have placed me in an unenviable situation. I know this poem, I've learnt it almost word for word, and yes, I approve of it. But not here, not before the English king.

I've noticed that Idwal and Morgan are casting barely veiled looks of disbelief my way, amazed at the Skald's brazenness. I wonder if they think I should speak out, decry the man and what he's doing. But I can't. Constantin has played me for a fool, but I'll not undermine him and put an end to his schemes. After all, his schemes keep him away from my Court and allow me to rule as I wish. Athelstan is a blessing to me.

When the skald has finished the final five verses of his tale, he swiftly moves to another poem of our ancient kings, and I feel my frantically beating heart start to slow a little. At my side, Edmund has a fixed expression on his face, almost as though he's trying to look as though he listens to the words, even though he doesn't. Or, it could be that he's deciphered the meaning behind the words.

Ælfstan leans towards me; a bright drink infused smile upon his face,

"I've not heard that particular one before," he says, and at my other side, Edmund is nodding his head in agreement. I feel I should say something.

"I think it's an ancient version of the story. Perhaps that's why it sounds so strange to your ears."

Ælfstan considers my words with a drunken shrug of his shoulders and a downturned bottom lip.

"You might be right. These skalds seem to have an unlimited store of ancient stories. It's always good to hear something new though."

I laugh a little nervously and agree with the ealdorman. And then, and only then, do I risk a glance at Athelstan's face. He looks intrigued and not a little confused. At his side, Hywel is eagerly talking to him, no doubt of his much-mentioned travels, but Athelstan has his eyes firmly fixed on the skald.

I shudder with fear. This has been too bold a move on behalf of Constantin.

The eyes of Idwal and Morgan also bore into my own body, and I know I'll need to offer them some explanation. Only I don't know what to say. I'm not known for my ability to think quickly. I like to take my time to consider the options, knowing that when I've made a decision that will be the decision I stick with. This trying to decipher Constantin's moves when I don't know what they are is making my head pound in time with my heart.

I reach for my drink, noticing dispassionately that my hand is shaking a little. Cold fluid splashes equally into my mouth and down the front of my tunic, and I know that Edmund has seen my fear. His face has turned even more quizzical, and I desperately try to think of some way to have his attention diverted away from me.

I could do with some air, perhaps a visit to relieve myself, anything to get out of the suddenly too hot room and from under the gaze of everyone there.

Abruptly I stand and so too does Edmund, a frown of worry on his forehead.

"I need a little air, a little time to myself," I offer, and he smiles and waves his hand to show he's in agreement. My steps are as unsteady as my hand, but with the skald gone from his place in the middle of the hall, I walk as nonchalantly as I can outside, Edmund back in his seat and one of my servants at my side.

The outside air is cool and damp on my sweat stained face, and my servant looks at me in surprise when I make no move to visit the conveniences.

"I just feel a little ill," I say to the man, and he nods in understanding. He's my servant, a man I've known and trusted nearly all my life. Only, he does not know about the poem and the skald. Both of these developments have been kept from him, more to protect him than me for I would much prefer to have someone to share my worries with.

Inside the palace, the level of conversation picks up as they all take the time to move around and converse with others now that the more formal meal and entertainment are over. I'm pleased. It'll be far easier to make an early departure from the feast now and spend some time considering all that has passed here.

Only then Idwal approaches me, accompanied by Morgan and I realise that they've come to seek me out. Abruptly I tell my servant to return inside, that I'll be okay for a few moments while I converse with Morgan and Idwal.

They both mark the man's passing and then hedge me in, one in front and one behind. As always it's Idwal who does the speaking,

"Was that it?" he hisses, his words twisting as his anger seethes through his barely open mouth.

"Was what it?" I hiss back, trying to play the innocent even though I know it won't work.

"The Skald, did he happen to add the subversive poem you mentioned into his set pieces?"

"I don't know," I try again, desperate to avoid a confrontation.

"I think you do," Morgan says from behind, his voice a bored growl of annoyance.

"I've only heard rumours and snippets," I say, pleading in my voice.

"I don't believe you," Idwal says, his words getting angrier. "And neither does Morgan. So tell me, and Morgan, why you'd go to all the trouble of discussing your secret little poem and then have it presented before the bloody English king before we've taken the time to consider the wisdom of such an act."

I know it's useless to continue to argue, but I have little choice.

"Which poem do you mean? I thought I recognised them all."

"Don't be such an arse," Morgan barks in my ear, "Although if I must make it clearer to you, the one where the people's of our land are listed one by one and the downfall of the English king is discussed."

"I don't think I heard that one," I mutter, looking at the ground to ignore the fierce glow in Idwal's eyes.

"Fine," he responds, anger making his words spit from his mouth, "have it your way and deny all knowledge, but I suggest you tell Constantin that we're not happy at being played for fools."

And with that, they both turn away, their annoyance evident in their steps and straight backs.

Damn bloody Constantin. Why have me speak to them about it if he was just going to flaunt it in their faces? It makes no sense to me, and now I'm angry that I'm being used as a blunt tool in his power games and I'm helpless to act. Damn them all. I can't wait to get home and never visit with the English king again, and if possible, never see Constantin again either.

So resolved, I turn and make my way back inside. It's the turn of the man from the lands of the Norwegian king now, he's a poet in the true tradition of the Norsemen, and I know that when he speaks, I'll be able to relax and listen to his rich voice, even though I don't understand the words. He's visited my Court before, and I like him, for all that he's a funny rat of a man with no discernable Norse heritage in his bearing; his hair is dark black, his eyes a hooded grey and he has no muscles apart from those that work his jaw. I doubt he truly is a Norse man but no one else has ever commented, and I've long kept my thoughts to myself.

Today he has a new tale to tell, and for once, and despite my anger and upset with earlier events; I find myself drawn to the man's words, my head resting in my hands as I rest my elbows on the table. No one moves, few dare breathes, as he tells of men and women gone to start a new life in a new land far to the North of here. Again, I've heard tales and rumours of this 'iceland', but I wasn't entirely sure that the rumours were true. The way the poet speaks, the story he recounts makes me believe, finally, that men and women have merely taken all that they can carry in their ships and gone to start a new life in a new world.

I envy them their freedom.

Brunanburh – Constantin – 937

The shield wall is long gone, now it's one man against another. The voices of any commanders would be ignored no matter what they commanded, apart from 'retreat'. I think retreat might still be heeded. But only just.

This has become a bloody battle to the death; only I think the men aren't yet aware that we've lost.

I want to call the men to retreat, but I've lost sight of my sons, and I can't get a message to Olaf, who likewise is lost to my sight in the massive scrum of men before me. I can hear their harsh cries of anger and rage, I can listen to the scrape of weapons on metal and flesh, but they won't listen to an old man such as I above so much noise. We're being slaughtered like pigs and no one, other than myself, is even aware.

Owain of Strathclyde was right after all. Athelstan was not an enemy I needed.

And before him, Ealdred was right as well. He called on me on his death bed to ensure his son inherited and I failed to act to support his son and make myself a friend once more to the men and women of his land. His son rules now, with the aid of their leading men, but they wouldn't come at my summoning, just as I wouldn't come at his urging. I have only myself to blame for that.

I'm in two minds as to whether to retreat myself or stay, flee the battlefield while I still can and ensure my survival. But I can't turn my back on my sons, not while I hope they still live.

And neither can I bear to watch the massacre. I'm torn.

Messengers no longer come to tell me how the battle progresses, they are possibly all dead or too busy fighting for their lives against Athelstan's men, but I don't need their words anyway. I know this battle is lost. I should have fought harder to keep my distance from Olaf's fight. My plan to undermine the alliance with the Welsh has been advantageous. Not one of the Welsh king's is here with the English king, not a single one. Even Hywel, his long time ally decided against the move, and it's not just because they didn't want to fight Olaf. No, it's because they fear a backlash from their people should they realise how close their links with the English have become. The enemy who marched across their lands four hundred years ago and stole their wives, their farms and their prosperity, forcing them to the hilly lands of the far west, east and to the north. The people haven't forgotten that, no matter how much the kings might like to.

Every Welsh king has taken a huge step back. None have attended any of the English king's meetings for the last two years. I should have been happy with that success and continued to drive a wedge between the English king and his one-time allies. That would have been more than enough to ensure the freedom of my people and the independence of Bamburgh.

I only hope that I'll be able to rebuild the trust of my people after this debacle. I only hope that the losses I fear I've suffered today do not cripple me for the rest of my days.

Resolved I turn my back on the battle. I'll not be doing my people any more favours if I die here, no matter how hard it is for me to leave.

None of my warriors surrounds me, only boys and my youngest grandsons remain at my side, and I tell myself, it is also for them that I must turn my back and leave. They should not die here. They have many, many long years of their lives still to live.

I can see the men slowly starting to realise the futility of the fight. In dribs and drabs and then in more sustained numbers, they turn and run back towards their ships or their horses, and I don't blame them. I would have done the same had I been a member of the dismembered shield wall.

I hope they make it to their ships, or to their horses, but just as quickly as I note the men are running with their bloody weapons and shields, I also watch the English take barely a breath before they're racing after them. More of these men will die as they attempt to escape, and as much as it saddens me, I can't blame the English for this seemingly brutal attack. The men, after all, have decided to run for their lives. I wish them luck.

And then I see one of the Englishmen fix his gaze on my grandsons and me. The time for thought and inaction is over. Calling to the rag tag collection of ten boys and youths I direct them to race with all haste away from the place of slaughter. I only hope that we make   it.

Chapter 24 – August 932 – Kent - Hywel of Dyfed

I greet Athelstan warmly, as normal. I never tire of spending time with him and visiting his Court. I'd like it if he visited my own, but I know that would give the wrong impression.

I'm accompanied by my cousin Idwal and by Morgan and Gwiard. Between us, we represent every tribe from the Welsh lands. Athelstan has accomplished a real accord with us. We all smile and laugh and pay our tithes gladly. I'm amazed and awed both. I honestly did not think that an outsider could unite us, and yet, he has. Not since my grandfather's day have our people been so united in thoughts and deeds. And yet, I fear it'll not last. There are rumours and rumblings that not everyone is as happy as we king's think they are.

My sons and my men bring me details of the whispers they hear, and I too, put them to Athelstan, as I should as his subservient, but they worry me. The rumours speak of a united land of the Welsh, which we currently are, but also of an England in tatters, its rulers dead, and our people left to run free as they imagine they once did. I think the story nothing more than a tale to tell children before they sleep, but many are listening and planning. Our people have long thought that the English were the interlopers, that they stole our lands and pushed us to the inhospitable lands behind the border, where the hills are good for little but sheep and the farming land sparse and difficult to manage.

As I watch Athelstan and his brother, I think the English are capable of anything, but I have my reservations about this action. Once more I believe that it is a tale for children, not one for men.

For now, I push my fears aside. The king will not want to see my glum face or hear my concerns. We've come together to celebrate and feast for the summer has been good, the harvests huge and Constantin and Owain have been quiet on their borders. If this is what peace can be like, then I will gladly embrace Athelstan and offer him my thanks. I want my people to thrive, and my land to flourish and peace is needed for that. I want to be remembered with the same affection that my grandfather's name occasions. I want to be as great as him. I want my people to have law and order, and coin.

The coin is what currently drives me, and Athelstan has informed that I can make use of his moneyers and my precious metals to make coins for my people. This trip is to watch the work in progress, see how the gifted moneyers shape the coins that people use to live their lives. With a coinage system the people of Dyfed will rise in prosperity, be as powerful as the English, and I, well I will have my image struck on the coin, and then I'll be remembered for eternity.

The thought brings a smile to my face. Away from my lands and worries, this is a time to relax a little, enjoy being with other men as powerful as I and who, one day, will die and then I can have their land as well in the lands of the Ancient Britons.

The future is bright and full of possibilities. If these bloody rumours about the English would just vanish, my life would be much simpler, my future much easier to determine, but, as always, I trust in my God, and I know that as I do his work, he too does mine.

Brunanburh – Edmund of the English – 937

The shouts and screaming batter my head as I fight, almost without thought. I can taste our victory on my tongue, but it's not yet an absolute. Still, something could unhinge our greatest success.

I watched Athelstan fight the men he killed dispassionately, watching a great warrior at work, trying to determine his next move and marvelling at his prowess without fear or worry. Athelstan would never enter a battle he didn't know he could win.

Ildulb's hasty departure from the battle line has caused a genuine ripple of unease to run through the enemy. I know that Olaf still fights for I've just seen him take the lives of two of my cousins, but Ildulb, and also Constantin are conspicuous by their absence. We need to take further advantage of that before all the men still standing turn to flee and leave us with nothing but a mass of stinking bodies to bury, and the memories of how close we came to total victory.

Not that the English haven't suffered losses. As I said, my cousin's are dead, grandsons of the great Alfred, like myself, bled to death on this battlefield. Not that they weren't pleased to do so, for I know they were. They might have held only the slimmest chance of ever attaining the throne of the English, but they still protected it with their lives, proud of our shared heritage for all that they kept quiet lives on their estates.

Athelstan is fixated on Constantin, and so I walk passed him, my mind resolved to gain some vengeance for my dead cousins. Olaf of Dublin needs to feel the slice of English iron on his skin to know that his actions here are deeply, profoundly wrong.

Eadric stays close to me, but we've both sent Æthelwald on his way. He's fought well but he carries an injury, and with the battle so nearly won, he need not fight on to his death. I hope the healers will work on his deep cuts and gaping wound, and I hope I will celebrate this great victory with him when he's well.

The amount of men still fighting has dwindled far more quickly than I would have thought, but Olaf still battles on, no matter how hopeless it is, and with delight, I see him trying to make his way towards me, just as I am towards him.

I imagine he's looking for the king.

But, he's found me, and I will kill him for the work he's done here today. I'll be amused to see what happens to his precious Dublin when he's dead. I hope that Sihtric's son from his first marriage, my half-sister's stepson, is as bad a leader as his father before him.

Abruptly I stop before Olaf, and he does me the courtesy of looking surprised to see me, and as he grabs for his weapons, I'm pleased he sees me as a threat.

"Olaf," I begin, "were you looking for me?" It's a taunt, and a question all rolled into one.

Lazily he replies, his hands far tenser than his voice implies,

"No, but you'll suffice for the time being. The more of Alfred's blood stock I kill here, the greater the peace will be in my lands."

A burst of laughter jumps from my mouth at the cocky words of this upstart Viking. He doesn't have the blood of real kings in his veins. No, he's the descendant of a self-made Viking who stole his land and named himself king. There's no honour in such an act.

"I wish you luck with that," I say, deciding I'd rather fight than talk. I swing my sword forward into my waiting hand, and crouch a little, ready to attack or defend, depending on what he plans on doing first.

"I don't need your luck, I've already killed your cousins, and it'll be your brother after you."

Without pause for thought, I step into an attack position, my sword and shield ready. I don't want to listen to another word this man speaks. His breathing the same air as me offends me and I want him dead more than anyone in my entire life. Still, I hold my anger in check and use it to fuel my aching arms and tired legs. It's been a long day of battle, and it's far from over.

Surprised that I don't wish to dual with words, Olaf is not ready as I launch my first attack, my sword crashing into his shield, causing it to bounce a little shakily in his hand. When he speaks his voice sounds a little whistley, and I've already seen that his mouth is filled with blood and crushed teeth. I hope my cousin caused that injury.

Before he can have his sword back in place, I crash into it again, with my sword this time, gritting my teeth against the sharp pulses that race up my shield arm. I know I'll have hurt him more than me, but I can't deny that it does hurt. A lot.

Angry words erupt from Olaf in a stream so fast I can't make them all out, and I laugh openly in his face. Whether he's upset with himself or me, I don't much mind, but I need to make his anger count.

My entire body is being flooded with renewed vigour. I've gone from feeling invincible to shaky more times than I care to remember during this battle, but I know it happens to all warriors. The joy of the fight can be quickly replaced by fear for it. A true hero of the shield wall must learn to master those twin emotions, fight the fear and use the joy. It's a skill as important as how to use shield, sword and axe.

He steps out of the attack and then quickly lunges for me again, but I'm ready with my sword, and I hammer it onto his already beaten sword. He's made much use of his shield today, and I remember that fact. He's a man who must like to cower and wait for his opponent to be exhausted and then take advantage of his greater strength. I'll not be making that mistake.

I let him circle me then, let him think that he has some advantage to be played, but I'm watching his hands and his feet, waiting to see which tell tale sign will give his next move away first. And it's his feet. He stumbles on them a little, sorting out his balance before he dances forward two steps and attacks my right-hand side, trying to slide his sword between my shield and my body.

His eyes gleam with the ease of it all, and he doesn't notice that I'm exchanging my sword for my axe while he tries to worm his sword closer and closer to my protective coat.

Only then something in my movements gives away what I'm doing so that he can look surprised just before my axe slashes a wild strike at his exposed neck. He moves aside just a fraction, but it's enough to have my axe connect with his solid shoulder. My hand, with its firm grip on the axe, buckles at the unexpected resistance it encounters, and my fingers only just keep themselves wrapped around the wooden handle.

Olaf steps away from me, apparently not happy that he thought he was winning and his arrogance almost cost him his life.

Behind him, I can see his men torn between watching their Lord and their desire to leap over the ditch of dead and dying and flee to the safety of their ships. The river is a vibrant blue on the horizon, its surface sparkling with the allure of safety and home. As I take a long hard look at the retreating men, I recall myself to the here and now.

"Eadric, get the men running after those retreating. Don't let them reach their ships."

Eadric jumps to attention at my shouted words, and they have the desired effect on Olaf. His back to his ships, he doesn't know how many men are going. Is it a mass exodus or just a slow trickle? His head whips around of its own volition, and with his attention elsewhere I race toward him and knock him to the ground with my shield. His body was facing toward me, his head the other way and his balance was all wrong.

He squirms in the mud and muck of the battlefield, his one hand resting on the head of a dead man, his fingers sliding inside the open mouth and into the pools of crimson eyes. He visibly shudders at the horror of it and attempts to stand, only I'm above him, my axe at his neck, and there's nowhere for him to go. If he moves his head back to watch the lines of retreating men, ants across a sticky surface, he'll slice his own neck, and I'll not have to do anything other than claiming his death as my victory.

So focused on Olaf, I don't realise that my own men have run to do my bidding, chase the enemy and stop them from reaching their ships, and another man, an ally of Olaf's now has his own weapon levelled against my back.

"I suggest you move away from the king," a deep voice booms, and I turn carefully to meet the eyes of the stranger. I've seen him at Olaf's back all day. He must be one of his warriors.

As much as it angers me to do so, I act on his words. It's my own fault for sending Eadric away.

Warily, I take three steps away from Olaf and feel the blade of the knife come away from my back as I do so. The man I face watches me keenly. He is covered in blood from head to toe. His own or his foes I can't decide. He does not seem as robust as his voice implies, and I wonder if he's not run away in retreat because he's already dying from a wound, and that perhaps this is his final stand.

Olaf looks from me to the man, not exactly happy, but relieved.

The man steps forward and offers him his hand, and Olaf grasps it and stands.

"You need to follow the other men my Lord," the voice says urgently, his eyes on me while Olaf sweeps him from the sanctuary of his ships to the battlefield.

Few men remain from his side, but the English are still advancing.

"Are you not coming?" Olaf says to the man, his body language alluding to his acceptance that this battle is lost.

"No, not yet. I'll follow, my Lord."

And that's that. Before my eyes I watch Olaf grab his weapons and turn to break into a loping run that has him out of reach in mere moments. I could cry with anger and rage, but at least he's not heading towards Athelstan anymore.

The warrior is still watching me intently, as I look at him. His body sags a little as soon as Olaf is out of sight, and as he drops to his knees, I see the large slash of red across his belly. This injury could take days to kill him as it slowly drains his lifeblood.

Without further words, I step forward and raise my axe, cutting his through his neck with one mighty stroke. His eyes close at my action, but as he crumbles to the floor, I realise he intervened, not to save his king, but to hasten his own death.

And now I'm even more pissed off, and race off to find Eadric and the rest of my men. There's still a chance I can catch Olaf before he climbs onto his ship.

Chapter 25 – 933 – Edmund of the English

A stunned hush fills the king's hall. Edwin wobbles from side to side, so drunk that he can't even sit straight, let alone walk. I wonder what has upset him so much that he's turned away from the progress he was making in becoming a valued member of the king's close circle.

Athelstan sits regally on his throne on the raised dais; giving the appearance that Edwin has not perturbed him at all. Unlike the rest of us. The whispered conversations taking place are manifest and shocked.

The rumours had reached us, sure enough, of Edwin's attempts to both undermine Athelstan by calling on any of the kings of the other people on our shared island, but none had expected him to go so far, and so quickly. None had thought him capable of trying to murder his brother so that he could be king in his place, but that is what's happened. The proof is incontrovertible. The two men and the woman sent to watch and serve Edwin in equal measure have made their case before the king and with a heavy heart; he's decided what must be done now.

Still, Edwin's appearance before the king has dismayed many. It had been assumed that Edwin would slink away to his death without involving anyone else. He has other ideas.

He's so drunk that he can barely speak and still he tries to.

"My Lord Athelstan," he slurs, attempting to bend his knee and falling onto the wooden floorboards instead.

"My dear brother Edwin," Athelstan replies, his tone severe. He's not amused, and he won't be changed from his decision. It took him ten days, and the advice of every holy man he could summon for an opinion before he reached his decision. It's final now, and Edwin surely knows it, and yet is prepared to make even more of a spectacle of himself.

"I've come to make amends for my hasty words and actions," he continues, oblivious to the king's simmering anger. Perhaps someone should step forward and inform him that he has no hope of turning the king aside, but none are brave enough to stand between the king and his pathetic wreck of a half-brother. Not even I. And every time I try to, my mother's hand is on my arm, warning me and stopping me. I'm grateful she's here. I don't wish to do anything I'll regret at a later date.

"Your words will have no impact on my judgment, but you're welcome to utter them all the same. An apology would be a good start."

Edwin begins to chuckle, a long evil sound, all of his remorse gone in an instant.

"I'll not apologise for failing to do something that should have been done to you at birth," he snaps, all his drunken stupor fallen away in the face of his intense anger. "Father was too caught up in the idea of you being his first born son to think clearly. I'd not have made the same mistake and nor would my mother."

"Our father loved his children equally. He provided for all of us, and I have continued to do the same. He would not have welcomed us turning on each other."

"He was blinded by his feelings for you."

And now it's Athelstan's time to laugh mockingly, his angry face terrifying to behold. Athelstan does not let his emotions run away from him, but Edwin, as Edwin always has done, makes Athelstan reveal things he'd rather keep hidden.

"Our father had a strange way of showing his feelings towards me. Do you forget that he had me raised in the Mercian lands of our Aunt? Do you forget that he bequeathed the throne to your full brother and not me? Do you forget that it is I who he sent into battle to fight his wars against the Vikings? Do you forget how he cast aside my mother to make way for your own?"

I've never heard Athelstan speak in this way. Never has he criticised our father before, or shown his unhappiness at the way he was sent to war when all of us other children were pampered in the safety of the Wessex lands. I look at him with renewed interest. Even now my brother surprises me.

"And you think that was a punishment?" Edwin shouts, his anger as bright as Athelstan's. "You, he allowed to fight and train and live away from the confines of the Court. You, he gave as much freedom as he could to, and you, he spared from the politics of the Witan."

Athelstan shuts his open mouth at those words. It's obvious he's not considered it in such a way before.

"And I, brother king, I was to live my life in your shadow, always. You did not hear father praise you at each festival and gathering of the ealdormen; you did not hear how he relished your prowess with the sword, your understanding of politics. Oh no, you were too busy playing abandoned child in a more loving home than I ever knew. Just as your mother was replaced, so was mine."

I feel my mother stiffen beside me, and now it's my turn to hold her arm and stop her from any rash actions. Edwin has always been resentful, but with the herd of children my father sired, it's never surprised me. Athelstan and Edwin are more alike than either would like to admit.

"And through all that, everyone knew that you would be the king one day. You. You might have to share it with your brother, but Mercia would be yours. Only then my bloody brother died, and you got it all. And you didn't even once think of sharing it out a little, giving to me what our father denied me."

"You'd done nothing to prepare yourself for kingship. Nothing."

"Because bloody father wouldn't let me," Edwin screams, angry beyond coherency.

"Brother, if you think to make me have any sympathy for you, you are an even bigger idiot than I thought possible. You can't plot to kill me and expect me to forgive you. You have to die," Athelstan spits with rage.

"So I'm to be punished for our father's sins?"

"No, you're to be punished for attempting to attack your anointed king. That we're related makes no difference to me. And to the religious men of our land, it makes it far, far worse. I will let you choose the way you die if you prefer that."

Edwin suddenly slumps to the floor, as though he's dead already and Athelstan's face softens a little. He stands and walks towards Edwin as men all around reach for their weapons, far less trusting of Edwin than Athelstan. The king waves their weapons away. Even now, he's far more trusting than anyone else in this room.

He slumps to his knees before his brother, reaches his arms out to either side and embraces the lifeless body of Edwin, and now we can all see that Edwin is sobbing uncontrollably. His games might have passed the cold winters away from the Court, but he knows that he's acted against every rule of his family, against every rule of his king. He plotted to kill the king, and he must be punished.

Athelstan whispers something to him, an exchange too quiet for anyone else to hear, but I watch as Edwin's body regains its substance, appears to grow in stature. And then his eyes sweep the room, taking in all who watch him, and resting his gaze on me.

It's like looking into my own eyes. They're the same deep ocean blue, crowned by the same thick eyebrows with the same firm chin and long beard. His mouth is like my own, a pale pink with straight, white teeth underneath it. He must be thinking as I do. Our positions could so easily be reversed.

But then his eyes continue their sweep, resting instead on his sisters who still live in our household. Then he's on his feet, standing as a king should do, or as the case will be, standing as a would be king should, one who has only himself to blame for his execution at the hands of his brother.

I don't envy Athelstan or Edwin, and I never will.

Brunanburh – Edmund of the English – 937

The ground is awash with discarded weapons and bodies. None have stopped to pick up extra weapons, every man instead fleeing as quickly as they can across the blood-soaked grasses.

The ditch where they all stumbled does not bear close examination, and so I manoeuvre my way around it, mindful of any sharp objects, and then I'm one step closer to the retreating men.

And then I remember whom I am and what I'm supposed to be doing here and stop abruptly, Eadric almost slamming into my back.

He stops quickly and looks behind us as well.

"What are you doing?" he asks with exasperation, his dagger in one hand, and his axe in the other. Killing men by striking their backs can be done far more efficiently with a smaller weapon.

"I need to check that the king is protected."

Recalled to his duties as well, Eadric squints along with me into the distance, and then he points,

"Yes, look, his standard bearer is with him, and a few of the men. And look Edmund; none of the enemy is still standing. They're all dead or fled."

I see he's correct and happy that my brother won't be harmed in my absence I turn and begin to race after the retreating backs of the enemy.

My limbs are tired and my weapons heavy, and I can't help wishing that I'd thought to retrieve my horse to race after these men, but I'm too far gone in my running now. It's as far to go back to get my horse as it is to reach the river and the enticing ships.

Already I can see that one of the ships has made its way into the channel of the river while men row with all the energy they have left, and others try to raise the sail to take advantage of the stiffening breeze now that I'm close to the water.

"How many men in a ship?" I huff to Eadric, I know the answer but I want him to confirm it for me.

"Up to sixty," he says, and I look with narrowing eyes as another ship begins to force its way into the channel.

"So that could be a hundred men already who've escaped," I shout, trying to force myself to run faster and also offer some incentive to the other tired men from the English side who are mirroring my actions.

"Yes, a hundred or more, if they've had the balls to wait until each ship is full. Let's hope that instead, the men are jumping in any old ship they can find, and pushing themselves off even if there aren't enough men to power the ship."

I like Eadric's thinking, and it gives me an added impetus to reach the riverbank. I want to kill as many men as possible. I want the river to run with their blood. I want not a single soul to set foot in their homeland again.

We're racing through the campsite now that the enemy had lived within for the last three days. There are smouldering fires and discarded clothing and possessions everywhere. There are even a few women and children, huddled together and crying in fear. I ignore them and hope my men do as well. They are not our targets here.

And then, forcing my way over a falling tent, I happen upon a man with his back to the ships, blood dripping from a wound on his forehead, as he works his axe backwards and forwards in the soil beneath him. I think I know what he's doing and he's an idiot. Better to escape with your life than with your buried silver.

Eadric takes one huge swing of his axe and aims it at the man's already damaged head. His eyes glaze instantly, and he tumbles forward, his arms falling into the mud at his feet. I can only hope he died clutching the silver he thought so important.

We're still racing onwards, the distance I thought only small from our place of encampment, but it's much, much further to the river than that. I wonder why the men left their ships so far behind them. It would have made more tactical sense to keep the river at their back and then they could have escaped far more quickly. The arrogant bastards didn't think that the English would carry the day.

Slowing, because I can barely breathe as it is, I see a small collection of men down a small rise. Quirking my eyebrows at Eadric, he follows me as we walk to investigate what's happening. The men are shoving and fighting amongst themselves, unheeding of the menace at their back. Abruptly, one of the men turns and sees us, and then darts away from the others and begins to run towards the ships.

The man next to him looks up to see where his friend has gone and likewise runs off. We let him go. I imagine this is a group of men robbing their dead Lord before they try to make good their escape.

And I'm proved right when yet another blood stained man sees us and makes a run for it. Where he was standing, I can see the naked body of a man, and I can see three men arguing over arm rings, and jewel encrusted clothing.

I don't know who the man was, but he must have been out of his mind to come to a battle with all of his wealth so prominently displayed.

Without pausing for other men to make their getaway, I step forward and slice through the exposed neck of one of the men, while Eadric does the same to one of the men arguing about the armbands. Their words die on their lips as their blood begins to pour down their backs and then the remaining three men are running, and I let them have their way.

Bending down, I pull one of the dying men from the body and gaze down at it in interest.

"He looks like a Norseman," Eadric says matter-of-factly.

"A very wealthy and stupid Norseman," I counter and Eadric smirks.

"It must have been that bloody fool Ivarr from Denmark. Athelstan had heard rumours that he'd been banished by his father and was looking for more suitable employment."

"Well, he's bloody dead now and robbed of all his wealth as well. Come, I still have an urge to face Olaf again."

Eadric grins at my determination, and we continue to walk the path that the retreating host has taken.

Now we walk though, grown tired by our activities.

"How many men do you think you've killed?" I ask Eadric; curious to know what wild accounting he'll give.

"At least fifteen," he smiles with joy, and not a little self-importance.

"And you my Lord?"

"At least bloody thirty," I say laughing loudly, my relief that this battle is almost over and that we've won it makes me a little giddy.

"You're joking?" he says, his eyes losing their good humour and now I can't stop laughing.

"Of course I am, but it was good to see the disappointment on your face."

He smiles again now, and suddenly we're walking amongst another battle line. The shore has been reached, and it's almost a replay of the shield wall again. The English attack the Norse who're trying to retreat onto their ships, and they hack at any body part visible.

I look around for Olaf. I want to make sure he dies, but up and down the shoreline there are at least a hundred ships, and I can't see Olaf on any of them. Eagerly, Eadric and I walk up and down the line of ships, ignoring the fighting unless a Norseman walks into our ready weapons, as we search for the bigger prize. I know that Athelstan would like Olaf alive, or dead, but probably more dead than alive.

Some of the ships are being set on fire by our men, better to have them burn than escape, and still, I can't see Olaf, the smoke making it even harder to see.

Chapter 26 - 934 – Constantin – His Royal Palace

My palace is in chaos. Messenger after messenger rushes in, most contradicting each other so that none truly know what's happening.

The only certainty is that Athelstan is coming to my lands with a full ship and land army.

I don't know whether to be outraged or incredulous. Who does Athelstan think he is, to dare step even one foot inside my kingdom?

And under what pretext does he come? He says I've broken my word, my treaty with him, and worse than that, that I seek to undermine his supremacy using the words of a poet! I could laugh out loud if only it weren't true. But this, this response is preposterous, completely out of all proportion. All I did was flavour the game with a little spice, see what trouble could be caused.

My sons, my councillors and my successor all watch me intently, wondering what I'll do to counter this threat.

"You must raise the war band," Mael Coluim demands, his face flushed with his anger. He doesn't know that my protestations of innocence are perhaps too vehement.

"I have every intention of raising my war band," I growl, stressing the 'my'. Mael Coluim's not offered to raise his own, the pompous arse.

"And I'll raise my own as well," Ildulb announces, glaring at Mael Coluim. There's no love lost between my eldest son and my heir, and there never will be. They both hope the other will drop dead before them, but while Mael Coluim wishes for my death as well, my son actively labours to keep me alive. He doesn't want to lose his position of power within the royal court.

I nod in thanks and stand abruptly. It is warm in my hall, and I feel the need for some fresh air.

The men who support my kingship watch me with eyes that show fear, horror and anger. None of them, apart from Ildulb, know the truth about Athelstan's claims, although not one of them has advised me to hold myself true to the alliance. They've all been busily voicing their belief that I was right to keep myself at arm's length to the treaty forged at Eamont. That was until now. Now I know that their memories will be short and their comments vocal and widespread.

"Do we know where they are?" I ask. It's important to stop them as close to the border as possible. I have no ship army to call my own, but I can call upon some of the traders. I'm sure they'll happily watch for the ships of the English king even if they don't want to attack them, they'll at least inform me if the ships come too close to my land.

"Yes," Ildulb says, he's working hard to make some order out of the messages we're receiving. "He's heading towards Bamburgh, north of York at least."

I hold my anger in check. Ealdred is ill, close to death. He sent to inform me of his predicament; a son too young to sit on the throne and a wife too far gone with madness to offer her son the support he needs. He begged me to intervene for his son, send one of my sons to rule for him until he was of an age. I'd been putting off making the decision, but perhaps now it would be prudent to have my own eyes so much closer to Athelstan.

The most important thing is to keep him from my lands, and if that's not possible, then I must mount a defensive attack.

"Ildulb, please collect your war band and head towards the border between York and Bamburgh. Take messengers with you and fast horses so that you can keep us appraised of Athelstan's actions." Ildulb doesn't even falter in his current task as I speak. Instead, he hands the scraps of parchment to my next son, Aed and strides confidently from my hall. He is a man of action, never happier than when hunting, riding or fighting.

Mael Coluim watches me with narrowed eyes, and I meet his gaze evenly. He thinks that I can't send him out, as I would my sons, but he's not right. I can and I will.

"Mael, collect your war band and take them to the borderlands with Strathclyde. Meet with Owain if you can and ensure that Athelstan doesn't sneak into our lands that way." I use the word 'ours' on purpose, reminding him of his obligations and aspirations. He draws a breath as if he's going to speak, but then he thinks better of it and only bows to me and walks away, not quite with the sharp snap that Ildulb had, but I'm just pleased he's gone without too much of a fight. I regret the opportunity of amassing his warriors that I've given to him, but I need him to hold Athelstan off. And I'll just have to hope that's all he does.

The other men within my hall are nodding or shaking their head, depending on whether they agree with me or not. My other sons are talking amongst themselves, discussing tactics and trying to decide who should go where. No one addresses me directly. In this moment of crisis, they all know that it's vital only one man makes choices and decisions. There's to be no second-guessing, even Mael will know that. It's after Athelstan has gone home that I'll worry about Mael's actions with his warriors, not during Athelstan's attack.

"Aed, you must collect your warriors and head toward the coast. Gather as many ships as you can and load them with your men. If you see Athelstan's ship-army, engage them or watch them and inform me of where they are. Count them, see how well they're armed, and keep me informed of what you think they're going to do next." Aed, like his brother before, leaves my palace quickly, he has a job to do, and he'll do it well.

That leaves me with a decision to make about Owain's Bamburgh, but I think I need to think about it a little more. For now, the knowledge that Athelstan has gathered his men and is marching towards my border fills me with fear and anger in equal measure. Abruptly I stand and signal for my priest. I need to pray.

Brunanburh – Constantin – 937

Stunned by my defeat once more I stop my horse's rapid canter, and gently turn him around, to face back the way we've just fled. The enemy didn't have time to retrieve their horses, rushing to strike down the retreating warriors with only their weapons and their shields. My escape was easily achieved, for all that I feel as though it was I who died on that field of carnage.

Men will write of this day within our land, their grief will make words flow from their mouths, their pens will flow with blood, and it is my arrogance that brought my people to this. My sorrows may mean that the outcry is slightly tempered, but I think I want the anger of my people to hit with the force of a blunt sword, strike my head from my shoulders, my arms from my body, my hands from my arm. It should have happened here today. I should have fought beside my men, my sons, my grandsons. I should not be alive to flee the field of battle.

My sorrow and my soul lie behind me, discarded where my sons fell, my grandsons, and I must take a moment, or maybe five, to collect my thoughts, and say my goodbyes. I little doubt the English king will send the bodies of my dead home for burial. Instead, they will lie on the field of battle until picked up by the victors and tossed into an anonymous mass grave with their friends, their allies and their enemies alike.

I know for I have ordered the same on my victorious battlefields.

I wish I'd acted differently now but winning a battle does strange things to a man's usually even soul. It makes him behave as a vicious bastard, an unfeeling bastard. Victory makes a person invincible. Always invincible.

The sun is almost gone, the light bleached from the land, the carrion swirling around the battlefield, viewable even from this great distance.

My son lies there. Dead.

My grandsons lie there. Dead.

My friends, my allies, my enemies.

Battle is wearisome when you're the loser.

With no consolation, I turn my horse towards the lands of the borders. Those who live and those injured, but who hope to live, escort me but we are a band of weak old men and injured young fools. I offer a brief prayer that Athelstan will be content for now with his total victory. If his men followed me and tried to attack our small host, I would do nothing but offer up my throat for the killing stroke. I've little enough to live for now and would welcome the respite from my all-consuming grief.

A cry in front of me, and I turn my dull grief filled eyes to the young man who shouted. He is streaked with blood; his nose knocked out of position, his lip and chin covered in his dried blood. He looks like a messenger from Hell.

"My Lord," he cries again, and I focus on him, trying to summon enough enthusiasm to listen to his words.

"In front, look."

And so I do, and the sight that greets me is a balm for an old man's aching heart.

Ildulb.

He lives, and he has stopped to greet me.

Ildulb. One son has been rescued from death.

Chapter 27 – 934 – Caithness (far north of the land of the Scots) – Athelstan of the English

My men assure me that the haze I can see far out to sea are the Outer Isles. I squint into the setting sun, trying to see the green of an island but it's no good. I can't see any features.

Beneath me, my horse shifts under my weight, and I pat it reassuringly on the neck. We've come a long way, from the borderlands right up to the farthest reach of the lands of the Scots, but my horse hasn't enjoyed his ship journey, for all that we stayed within sight of land the beast had been restive until his hooves touched solid ground again.

My force is not quite as huge as I would have liked. Not all of my ealdormen wanted to journey across the border, and I understand their reluctance although I'm not best pleased by it. They'll have to work hard to regain my complete trust, and yet in the meantime, they still serve me well by protecting the royal court.

Edmund has accompanied me, and he has a restive animal to calm as well. What we all need is a good run out, and I would welcome the opportunity to explore Constantin's lands a little more. But until I'm sure of our reception I'm happy to wait a day or two longer. We will pitch our tents, ensure we have a defensible position and then I'll be glad to explore more. For now, I'm going to enjoy the knowledge that no other king of Wessex and Mercia has ever been this far north. None before have stepped foot on the northern most tip of the land of the Scots.

A gentle breeze blows my hair as I gaze into the distance of Constantin's land. During the journey, we've hugged the coast, just far enough away that we couldn't be attacked by any of the local population. But I've seen the stark coastline, the soaring mountains and the rushing rivers. Constantin, for all that I'm here to show him my strength, is king over an enormous and productive kingdom. Fish have swum close to the sides of our ships, almost leaping into our hands so keen are they to be caught. And we've seen other sea animals as well, their noses showing above the water line, or their slick bodies shimmering just under the surface.

I'm not jealous of Constantin's good fortune in being king over such a fertile land. I know my own is just as full of good farming land, and natural resources such as tin or stone or precious gems.

What it has shown me is that Constantin has played me for a total fool. His failure to meet the terms of our treaty, to forward the tithe to me as and when he should, has all been intentional. His land is rich, his people rich in resources. My anger at him has already peaked, and yet, if I could get my hands on him now, I'd still be furious enough to inflict personal injury. He needs to know that I'm not to be treated in such a way.

Edmund has brought with him one of the brother ealdormen, Ælfstan, and he sits upon his horse beside him, keen to see and absorb as much as he can. I'm not entirely convinced of his total loyalty to me, but now that he's seen the land, seen the roaming cattle and magnificent fields of trees and crops, I know that he must be pleased he came.

A commotion in front of me, and a man rushes toward me, only stopped when Edmund kicks his horse forward to prevent him getting any closer. He's not someone I recognise, but he knows who I am.

I watch Edmund speaking to the man, wondering what this could be about. We only made landfall half a day ago. Surely news of our arrival can't have reached Constantin already?

Edmund looks at me and then moves aside to let the man through. He carries words that I need to hear.

He walks towards me sedately, Edmund at his side, still mounted on his horse.

"My Lord," he says, sweeping to his knees before me. With a raised eyebrow at Edmund and a reassuring nod from him, I tell the man to stand.

"And you are?" I inquire, and the man looks nervously around before replying.

"My name is not as important as my message or who sent me," he finally says, and again Edmund nods at me. Clearly, the man hasn't told him his name either.

"And what is that message?" I ask, more than curious by this strange man.

"Constantin's son is coming, with a war band. They've been following you ever since you sailed past the border."

Now, this is something worth knowing.

"And when will the attack come, and which son is it?"

"Ildulb my Lord, and tomorrow, before first light I would imagine. And my Lord, the first light here is very, very early. I would keep a guard all night and be ready for anything."

"And who sent you?" I ask, and the man grins and bows once more.

"Someone who would be happy to see Constantin and his herd of bastard sons dead." And so, his message delivered, the man turns away, and I watch him with interest. What strange trick could this be or is it the truth and why would he tell me? The man was one of Constantin's people for all that he spoke my language well.

I ponder the implications as Edmund comes closer to me.

"A camp and a defensive formation?" he enquires lightly, and I nod in agreement. Whether the message is real or not, I can't ignore it.

"And send some scouts out as well, one to the south, east and west, and one back along the coasts in each direction."

Edmund kicks his horse, and it starts to canter towards where the main camp is being raised in a more defensible position. I didn't expect to not meet with Constantin on this journey, but I'd thought it would be closer to home. I'm curious as to what the morrow will bring.

Brunanburh – Athelstan – 937

My breath is harsh in my ears, my anger slowly dissipating.

I stand virtually alone on the battlefield. Everyone has fled.

In the distance, I can see fires starting amongst the line of ships that the enemy hoped to use to escape. I doubt many of them will make it home and I'm pleased with the overwhelming success of this battle.

While I still feel fuelled by the joy of battle, I walk amongst the bodies, looking for any I might know, and hoping I don't see them.

It's no joy to come across my cousins bodies, both dead from a variety of wounds. I signal to one of my few remaining men that these bodies should be gathered and returned to our campsite. They will need a burial fitting of their ancestry.

I walk further away from the ditch where so many met their deaths, and I look, as dispassionately as I can on the faces of those who've died here. Young, old, thin and fat, every size of man and boy has perished, but as yet, I feel no remorse, only joy in the victory.

I didn't ask for this battle; I didn't taunt my allies to bring about the great rift between us. In fact, my alliance of ten years ago was designed specifically to prevent a battle on this unprecedented scale from ever happening. I was wrong to think that a man's word had more force than his sword.

Chapter 28 – 934 September – Cirencester - Constantin of the Scots

I can barely meet Athelstan's eye, my anger and resentment are difficult to contain. I'm here, as he bloody commanded, but I'm about as happy as a man about to be executed.

A full week it's taken me to reach this place deep within the heartlands of the English, as far from the coast as it's possible to be, and as far from my kingdom as I've ever travelled. And with a heart full of anger and grief, it's been a long week. If the pomp of his palace is anything to go by, it will be a long two days here, and then a long journey home to a kingdom still reeling from his lightning quick attack and my resubmission to his overlordship.

My son Ildulb has accompanied me, and I wish he hadn't. The grief for his son, killed in battle against Athelstan at the top of our land, is a heavy burden he carries with him. He neither smiles, nor cries, but he's sullen and uncooperative. He has been for the whole two months since his young son met his untimely death on a battlefield against the English.

I should have refused him permission to attend when he asked, but I didn't have the heart. In my place as a father I've always felt out of my depths, as a grandfather, I was better. As a grieving grandfather and father to a grieving son, I know I'm next to useless. I'd give Ildulb anything he asked of me now. Anything.

I know that I can't pray his son back to life, but I'd happily exchange my own life for his son's. I've found it difficult to maintain my faith since the boy's death. My prayers seem to go unanswered, and I can find no inner peace. My God appears to be a man who expects too much from a mere man, even if he's a king.

Athelstan's palace is no bigger than my own, the wooden hall an adequate structure, well decorated and pleasing to the eye, surrounded by a large selection of sunken buildings and cattle barns. It's a strange cross between a farm and a royal palace. But it's not my home, and I could laugh at the small feminine touches his stepmother has littered the place with. I don't care for flowers or sweet smelling herbs, or Athelstan's extensive collection of holy relics. I only want to show my face before his people, have them know that their king has gained the upper hand over me, and be gone again. The smell of winter is in the air, and I don't want to be caught away from home should the snow come early.

And I don't want to be here at all.

The only possible piece of good news about this summons is that I've come alone. None of the other kings of the island is here, and for that I'm grateful.

I'd not be able to take the smug expression on Owain of Strathclyde's face. He warned me about Athelstan, and I ignored him. I thought my lands un-approachable; after all, what would an English king be doing in the lands of the far North? Athelstan seems to make decisions that I don't think him capable of, and even now, I know that he'll do it again in the future. No matter how many times I think I've understood his motivations and his desire, he'll show that I know him not at all.

"My Lord Constantin," Edmund says, stepping towards me in his beautiful clothing. Does he know he's the one man I hope never to see again? Ever. He looks older and cleaner than when I last saw him, devoid of his weapons of war I could almost forget who he was. Almost.

"Edmund," I reply as civilly as I can, my hand reaching for a sword that's not on my belt as I'm in the presence of the king and his family.

"You had a good journey?" he asks, making polite conversation even though I don't want to.

"Yes, your lands are fertile and well guarded, your roads straight and well maintained," I offer a little grumpily. I've seen as much of Athelstan and Edmund's lands now as he's seen of my own. The fact that I come as a subservient whereas he strode through my lands as though he owned them is not lost on me.

"We've spent much time and effort in reinforcing our borders, making our people feel safe with good law and order, and many coins in giving our people the ability to trade well and with men and women from far afield."

I don't comment that I've done the same. All my hard work seems to have fallen apart since Athelstan attacked my borders and messengers have chased me to Cirencester, telling me stories of problems that now infect my land. For much of it, I blame Mael Coluim and his ability to turn these problems to his advantage. I've even heard the words 'abdication' on the lips of some of his supporters. If they can't rely on Athelstan to kill me, then they're prepared to explore other ways for their man to gain power in our homeland.

My head is so filled with ideas and images, half formed thoughts and regrets that I don't know what to think of first.

"Athelstan is pleased that you've come," he offers, as though it was an invitation I could have chosen to ignore if I'd wanted to. Perhaps he's forgotten that Athelstan had one of the ealdormen escort me here, almost under armed guard. I can't say that I don't like Ælfstan, he's, after all, a robust and brave warrior, apparently high in his king's regard, but I'd rather have been allowed to give the impression that I'd come willingly.

"And I'm pleased to be here," I offer, hoping the young Prince will change the subject soon. At my side, Ildulb huffs in outrage, and I turn to caution him with my eyes, only in that instant Edmund has realised who stands beside me.

"Ildulb," he says, his voice suddenly thick with emotion, "I wish to express my sympathies for your loss."

And that is too much for my son to take. To hear those words from the man who's made his grief a reality. Without my leave or that of the English Prince, he's striding from the palace. I hope he won't go far, but there is the possibility that I might not see him again until I return to Scotland.

"My apologies my Lord," Edmund offers, his voice still thick, his grief evident on his face.

"War is a bloody business," I offer the only words I can force passed my throat that doesn't choke me with hypocrisy.

"Yes, it is," he replies, "let us hope that we never have to meet in battle and strife again."

I don't share his hope or even his desire for a future where I can't unleash my revenge on the English bastards. The day is coming when the Scots will lay waste their land and their hopes and fears. I can assure him of that. If I weren't acting as the submissive in a hostile land with a handful of warriors at my back, I'd take his head, here and now.

Brunanburh – Olaf of Dublin – 937

As my ship readies itself to take to the open sea, I look back in shock and dismay at the site of the bloodiest battle I've ever seen. The only one I've ever lost. That I'm escaping with my life is a miracle, and I realise how great that miracle is when I see the king's brother and his warrior searching the coastline for me. He truly intended to kill me.

I'm bloody and bruised and broken in places, and there is no joy in running from the battle like a scolded child.

All my hopes and dreams of the last ten years lie shattered and ruined.

I want my kingdom back. I want to unite Dublin and York once more, but this English king is too great a warrior. He has accomplished what I didn't think possible, and the fact that as many of his men as my men must have perished is no consolation.

He had only the support of his countrymen. I came at the head of an army of allies. I had king's sons and earls by the handful, and still, he beat us.

As soon as we hit the open sea, I slouch down into the swaying hull of the ship. I'm exhausted and worn out. Those men who power the ship are in no better condition, and yet, I owe them my life.

A horn of mead is offered to me by one of my men, and I don't want to take it. It should have been to toast our victory, but I'm thirsty and hungry and bone weary.

I grab the drink and gulp it without tasting it.

The drink hits my empty stomach forcing a belch straight out my mouth. Now I can taste my lost victory gone sour as well.

Aggrieved, I stand and throw the horn into the crashing waves around the ship. And as I stand I see the few straggling ships leaving the English shore, and I note the mighty blazes engulfing the ships that did not make it.

My anger burns fresh and bright. I'm beaten, for now. But I'll be back as soon as I can. I have land to claim, and an English King to thwart.

Chapter 29 – 936 – York - Hywel of the South Welsh

I ride into York with interest. It's the settlement that has caused so many problems over the last nine years, and I fear, still does. It seems no different to any number of places I've visited on my travels and within England. I wonder what the special lure of the place is because, at a moments glance, I can't see anything that would make me want this place so much that I'd kill for it.

The rumours coming from the Dublin Norse are that Olaf is close to becoming both king and overlord. He has men falling at his knees to pledge their allegiance to him, keen to be seen to be the ones that backed the ultimate winner in the contest of king's that been played out over the last five years.

I can't see that it'll be too many more years before Olaf turns his sights on York. He's made no secret of his plans to regain the land he feels Athelstan stole from him and it all makes me very uneasy. I joined this alliance for peace, and it's been in short supply in the last few years. And now that I've made my trip across the seas I'm not convinced that staying such a close ally of Athelstan serves my people well. And yet, neither do I want a war with the king of the English.

My decision to come here today is two fold, to sound him out on his plans for the future and to make him aware of the situation within Dublin and the one brewing in the lands of the Welsh kings. A day of reckoning is coming, and I need to know everything before I decide which side of the divide to stand on.

Athelstan is presiding over his Royal Court in the old palace that the Dublin king's used to use. It's a building in need of some repair work, but on a bright summer's day, it's a stunning building, huge and dominating. I wonder what it will be like inside.

My horses are lead away, and Athelstan comes outside to greet me. The day is still early. I've travelled all night to get here now, hopeful that Athelstan will speak with me before the business of the day is conducted.

He's aged since I last saw him, but he walks with the strength and vigour of a younger man, and I think that his hair turning to grey is ironic.

His eyes light up when he sees me, and a smile tugs his solemn face.

"Hywel," he says, "I wasn't expecting you to arrive until much later."

"Well my Lord Athelstan, the night was light, and I needed to speak with you, so here I am."

His face clouds at my serious tone but the smile remains firmly in place.

"Then come, we'll eat and talk in what privacy we can muster."

The few men who'd been following him stop a reasonable distance away and then start to file back indoors when he leads that way. My escorts stand around; unsure what to do next until one of Athelstan's men realise their predicament and come to their rescue. With an open face, he begins to talk to my second in command as they walk towards one of the animal barns.

The inside of the palace is much the same as the outside. A little tired in places, but full of warmth and people. A handful of men are eating around the open fire, and they watch Athelstan and me with tired and sleepy eyes. I think they've been on watch all night and are eating a meal before they get some sleep.

A servant watches Athelstan and picks up some signal that I don't see for we're barely seated before food and drink are being placed before us. I reach for my goblet greedily. I've ridden nearly all night, and I'm hungry and thirsty in equal measure.

Athelstan watches me eat and then asks what he must have been wondering ever since I arrived.

"What brings you here so early?"

"Rumours Athelstan, and worries and a desire to share the rumours with you that I know."

"About Olaf of Dublin," he asks, picking at a piece of bread and chewing slowly.

"Yes, and also about unease in the Welsh lands."

It is that news that surprises him.

"Again? I thought the problem dealt with."

"And I, but since Constantin's defeat last year there's been a resurgence in discontent. My men keep coming to me with stories, and half formed tales. I think there must be a skald working against us all."

Athelstan is intrigued by my words.

"A skald?"

I nod quickly, looking back at my food. The bread is good, the cheese even better, and my stomach is slowly settling.

"You think that someone has directed the skald?" he asks, and I'm relieved that the king still has his wits about him. This is my thought, and I think that Constantin is the one who's directed the skald. I wish I'd managed to find the man, but he seems to be staying far away from my lands for the time being. No doubt Idwal is protecting him just for the pure fun of it. He likes to cause trouble.

"You think Constantin has?" he finally realises, and I nod my head to show that I do. "The conniving bastard," he says, and I smirk at his obvious respect for the move. "Well, I never heard anything like this," he continues, "although it's an ingenious device to employ."

And there it is, the thing I like most about Athelstan. Even now, even here, when I've just told him of my fear he can still admire the man who's the cause of so much unease. He's not the sort of man who'll undermine another by trying to belittle his accomplishments. No, he's the opposite. He will laud them and admire them, even when they might be detrimental to him.

"And what would you like me to do about him?" he asks, going that next step that I'd hoped he would.

"He needs to be hunted and caught, and his words need to be defused." He nods in agreement once more.

"I could have one of my poets come up with a counter to his words. Do you think it was that poet who came to my Court a few years ago?" he suddenly asks, and I'm grinning with delight. Athelstan has put together all the pieces of the puzzle in a matter of moments. It's taken me at least a year for my worries to coalesce and take form and for me to decipher how it had all been brought about without my knowledge.

"That would be a good idea, but perhaps, one of my poets should also assist, ensure it sounds patriotic enough to the people of the Welsh lands, and not just the English."

He smiles at my words, "Of course you're correct. I should not have my poets laud me too greatly or speak of the English in too complimentary a tone as it will turn your people against me more. And, perhaps you would like some of my men to join your own in the hunt for the man?"

"Again I do, and my thanks for your offer, but they must be men who can blend in well in my lands."

"Yes, they must be men raised on the border and used to the ways of all our people. And you Hywel, what do you say to this attempt to infiltrate our alliance."

My face turns serious now. I knew he'd ask me for my opinion, and in all honesty, I'm not sure how to respond, even after the days of thought I've given the matter.

"My Lord Athelstan," he shudders at the use of his proper title, knowing that it means I've gone from his friend to his inferior in the blink of an eye.

"If the skald and the poem continue to work as well as they have been doing until now, and if Olaf of Dublin comes to claim York, and if Constantin of the Scots continues to work against you, then we will have problems, and I'll need to stand aloof from our alliance."

His face clouds at that, his mouth forming into an angry red line.

"But in all honesty, I find it difficult to imagine all those things happening, one after another, and falling into place so that you are left fighting for this great town." I indicate York by sweeping my hand behind me.

He stands abruptly then and paces back towards the doorway that's just opened and admitted my men.

He turns back before he leaves the palace,

"You have my greatest thanks and my greatest support for your words Hywel. I hope we remain as allies. But now, now I need to pray."

And with that he's gone out of the door, probably returning to his errand that I interrupted earlier. I can't say that I'm delighted with our conversation, but I know that he'll work hard to keep my kingdom as his ally. In this strange world of rumour and battle, where one scandal can lead to bloody battle, and bloody battle can lead to rumour, I'm not sure I could have achieved more than I have.

Brunanburh – Athelstan – 937

Exhausted, bloodied and broken, I watch with pride as my men continue to chase the enemy from our land. There are few enough of them left, and fewer yet will reach their ships.

The field is a sea of broken and bloodied bodies, horrifying in its contrasts of bright red, dead white and dying grey, but a necessary evil. As soon as the enemy is confirmed as gone, I will allow my priests to walk amongst the dead men and offer prayers for their souls.

Edmund is gone, chasing the enemy. My ealdormen are gone, chasing the enemy, but I remain looking at the triumph we've earned today. If I weren't so convinced that I laboured with God on my side, I'd be in peril for my soul. The destruction of so many men in one place has placed a heavy burden on me. When I return to my Court, I will arrange for grants of land to my favourite monasteries, and I'll amend my will. More men will be needed to pray for my soul when I'm gone, and I must ensure they have funds enough to do so continually. Without their intervention I may not make it into God's Heaven. Not now.

The day has become quiet and calm, the gentle breeze caressing my skin as the sunlight slowly begins to bleed from the sky. At my side, young Alfred is handing me a horn of mead and a lump of bread and cheese. I swallow hastily and eat as quickly as possible. I am starving and thirsty in equal measure. War mongering is a hungry profession.

In the distance I discern the noise of a troop of men advancing, and I look frantically around me, pulled abruptly from my reverie. My men are all dispersed either back to their tents to tend to their injuries, or gone to ensure no more of the enemy reach their ships. I stand alone ruminating on my victory, all apart from young Alfred leaving me to my thoughts.

For a long moment, fear stills my heart. I'd thought my enemy run away back towards their ships. Only then I discern the man at the front of the rapidly approaching force, and my body relaxes, all tension draining instantly away. I'll not have to fight for my survival again today, thank goodness. My arms ache, and my head is ringing with the cries of dying men.

Before me sits Hywel on a magnificent horse, deepest black with no hint of another colour, a smirk across his uncovered face, lined and illuminated by the sun as his gaze takes in the same scene I've been considering.

"I see I come too late, my Lord Athelstan," he calls jauntily as soon as he's within earshot.

"Yes you do, the enemy is vanquished. Hundreds, if not thousands lie dead before us. See."

I hide my surprise at seeing Hywel come to fight for me and point towards the field of death. I watch with some satisfaction as he gulps around the all too visible scene of my greatest success.

"Athelstan, this is a great victory for you, and now I'm even more aggrieved that I didn't arrive sooner," he says with all seriousness.

"Is that why you're here? To join the battle?" I ask with interest, but hopefully, not too keenly. It would be wonderful to know that he'd changed his mind about supporting me before the victory was won.

"Yes my Lord, of course," he quickly assures me, his voice still serious. "I realised the error of my judgment. Our island has grown quiet under your guardianship, and I shouldn't have turned ambivalent at the thought of proving my loyalty to you."

I'm too tired to mask my surprise at the words and Hywel starts to chuckle, his serious expression evaporating in the face of my obvious joy at his words.

"I mean no disrespect my Lord, but it's the first time I've ever truly seen you speechless."

"I won't deny that you've surprised me, in a good way. And you have my thanks for making the journey."

Hywel sobers at that, looking out at the field carpeted in bodies.

"You had an overwhelming victory?" he queries more statement than an actual question.

"It was a hard won victory. We must count the total number of dead and reckon up those we've lost on our side."

"I imagine that will take some time," Hywel mutters cynically, and I smile a small, sad smile that spreads across my face, turning it from winter's day to summer's at the thought of those I've lost on the battlefield. They all died for me, but they wanted to, and they had good deaths. All of them.

"It will, and there will, of course, be many graves to dig." The reminder of that unhappy task turns me even more sombre.

"My men are good at digging graves, and looting a little as they go, I can't deny that and so I won't. If you allow us, my Lord, we'll still set up camp and help with the cleanup operation."

"That would be most welcome. I imagine my men will not look with joy upon the task of preparing the dead for burial, not when they might fear who they'll discover next and whether they're kin or enemy."

Hywel bows low at the acceptance of his request.

"You have my thanks, my Lord."

"And you have mine. I've missed your company."

A commotion behind him and Hywel's impetuous grin is back on his face.

"I almost forgot," he says, his head turning to where a ragged man is being led forward between two of his men. He is a little beaten, although not too much, dried blood streaks his nose and his clothes are muddy from where he's been forced to march while Hywel and his men have ridden, but his eyes are clear and his face clean other than for the blood.

"I found something for you," he says, and I narrow my eyes and look at the man a little more carefully. I'm wondering if my guess as to who he is will prove to be correct.

"This, my Lord Athelstan is your little skald, the source of much of the discontent within the Welsh lands. And we were right; he's told me everything. His most famous poem was constructed on the orders of Constantin, a little something to worm its way into the minds of all those intelligent enough to interpret it."

I was right, and I'm overjoyed that Hywel has gone to all the trouble of finding the source of much of the discontent that has erupted from the Welsh lands, that, when combined with the honeyed words of Olaf of Dublin has forced all my allies to remain at home during this fight for York. I am equally relieved to know that my assumptions have proven to be correct, and ecstatic that Hywel has returned to me. Hopefully, the other men of the Welsh kingdoms will follow suit in the coming months.

Hywel reaches out then and grasps my arm firmly. I return the greeting wholeheartedly. After the day I've had, it feels good to have this further evidence of the righteousness of my kingship and overlordship.

"Come, my Lord, I'll get my men to set their camp and then we'll begin our grisly work."

I look bleakly out at the field of destruction and death; the blood churned bodies, the early evening sun dully shining on discarded swords and shields. Scraps of bright clothes catch my eye, the occasional glimpse of a pale upturned face, eyes now forever staring, and I notice for the first time the black crowd of birds who've come to the feast, their harsh ca-caring to each other belatedly penetrating my hearing.

"Tomorrow will be soon enough. There's no need to rush."

And with that, I resolutely turn my back on the battle site.

Brunanburh.

The name fills me with pride and disquiet in equal measure.

Brunanburh.

I know it will be remembered for a thousand years to come.

Historical Accuracy

First things first, no one actually knows where the battle of Brunanburh took place. No one. There are a number of different sites that have been suggested by historians from the one I've chosen, Bromborough in Cheshire and these are Brinsworth in South Yorkshire and Burnswark in Dumfries and Galloway. As one historian has commented, more discussion has taken place about where Brunanburh was than about its actual historical significance. In my role as writer of historical fiction, I chose the site that I thought offered the best opportunity to develop the storyline, and the one that intrigued me the most. After all, it does sort of make sense that any battle for York would have taken place close to York, but equally, why would the Dublin Norse have sailed all the way around the tip of Scotland to get to York from the East Coast?

Eamont itself is an accepted event in most histories of the time, and yet B Hudson, a fantastically engaging and easy to read academic historian, has cast doubt on it, saying there is no proof that Constantin ever made an alliance with Athelstan at Eamont. Again, Eamont sets the scene for Brunanburh and so I've kept it in.

An accounting of the Battle of Brunanburh survives as a poem in the Anglo Saxon Chronicle, a singular occurrence in a prose piece of writing, and this, I think, shows that it was deemed to be very important at the time. (A translation of the poem follows at the end). However other than the knowledge the battle lasted all day and that in the end Constantin and Olaf retreated, nothing further is known.

Where possible the events and the dates have been taken from known facts, more often than not the charter evidence for Athelstan, this is a record of who was signing charters and where they took place. Of course, the charters that have survived are small in number and have only survived because they benefited someone, somewhere, to keep a written record of the event being recorded. Our history is a series of chance finds and bias on the part of historians and Chroniclers. We're lucky we have as much as we have and can gain as much information from what we do have. And this is the work of a number of eminent historians working in the Anglo-Saxon field, Simon Keynes, Sarah Foot, David Dumville and many, many more.

The poem quoted as being invented by Constantin and the Skald did exist, and almost as much controversy surrounds it as the battle of Brunanburh itself. It has been variously used by many historians for different reasons. For the purpose of Brunanburh, I took the suggestion of Nick Higham that it was a poem devised in Wales from 930 onwards to show unhappiness with the links with the English. That Constantin had a hand to play in it, is my own invention, although, you just never know!

And yes, Athelstan's father, Edward, did marry three times and leave his son with a vast amount of sisters to marry. The truth about whether he had his half-brother, Edwin, executed, or whether he drowned at sea is open to interpretation. One historian has pointed out that being drowned at sea was an ancient Irish punishment for killing your brother (or plotting to).

The irony of Brunanburh is that it was the greatest battle to take place in the British Isles before the Battle of Hastings in 1066 and yet, before I researched the time period between Alfred and my Earls of Mercia series, I'd never heard of it and nor, more than likely have most of the people reading this. That can only be blamed on the rewriting of history that occurred after the arrival of William the Conqueror. I hope that this novel resurrects the battle for some of my readers and gives Athelstan his final wish!

229

Cast of Characters

The English

Athelstan – Initially King of Mercia and then King of the 'English' and 'Imperium' over Britain. Son of Edward the Elder and his first wife/mistress called Ecgwynn

Ecgwynn – Athelstan's only full sister – marries Sihtric of York but marriage does not last.

Ælfweard – Athelstan's half brother, ruled Wessex for only days until his death allowed Athelstan to become king of Wessex and Mercia (King of the 'English' at his coronation) (same father, with second wife)

Edwin – Athelstan's half brother and Ælfweard's full brother (same father, with second wife, Ælflaed who was the daughter of Ealdorman Æthelhelm)

Eadgifu – Athelstan's half sister and Ælfweard's and Edwin's full sister – marries Charles of the West Franks. Their son is Louis.

Eadhild – Athelstan's half sister who marries Hugh Count of the Franks

Edmund – his half-brother (same father different mother (Edward's third wife, Eadgifu)) and his designated heir

Eadred – Athelstan't half brother – full brother to Edmund

Eadgyth – Athelstan's half sister – full sister to Edmund and Eadred, daughter of Edward and Eadgifu

Eadgifu – third wife of Edward the Elder (Athelstan's father). Crowned Queen and still young enough to take charge of his Court. Edmund's mother. (daughter of Ealdorman Sigehelm)

Æthelflaed of Mercia – Athelstan's Aunt – sister to his father Edward, and daughter of Alfred of Wessex (already deceased)

Ælfwynn – Æthelflaed's daughter, Athelstan's cousin – 'disappears' before 925

Ealdorman Athelstan – at Brunanburh

Ealdorman Ælfstan – at Brunanburh (Ealdorman Athelstan's brother)

Eadric – Ealdorman Athelstan's brother

Ealdorman Osferth - at Brunanburh

Ealdorman Guthrum – at Brunanburh

Ælfwine – King Alfred's grandson/Athelstan's cousin

The Scots

Constantin – King of the Scots/or of Alba (no longer Pictland)
Ildulb – his oldest son
　　　his grandson
Aed – Constantin's son
Cellach – Constantin's son
Mael Coluim (Malcolm) – his designated successor
Strathcylde
Donald – previous king of Strathclyde (once allied with Constantin)
Owain – King of Strathclyde – subservient to Constantin
Jarl Sigurd – (made up character) his daughter marries one of Owain's sons
The Welsh
Hywel – known to prosperity as Hywel Dda – of Dyfed
Idwal
Owain
Owain, Rhodri and Edwin – Hywel's sons
Bamburgh
Ealdred – King of Bamburgh (dies 934)
Dublin Vikings and their allies
Ragnall – deceased before story commences – once allied with Constantin and Donald (the II) of Strathclyde
Sihtric – King of York – marries Athelstan's only natural sister before repudiating her. This is the claim that Athelstan uses to take control of York.
Olaf Gothfrithson – son of the Gothfrith who tries to claim York in 927 but is denied by Athelstan – leading to Treaty at Eamont between Constantin, Owain, Hywel and Ealdred.
Olaf, King of Limerick – captured by Olaf Gothfrithson in 937 – fights for him at Brunanburh
Ragnavaldrr – Olaf Gothfrithson's oldest son
Sigfrodr – Olaf Gothfrithson's older brother
Asl – Olaf Gothfrithson's brother
Guthrum – Olaf Gothfrithson's brother
Ivarr - son of King of Denmark, Gorm
Gebeachan – King of the Islands? (as named in sources of the period)

Note on names
It's been difficult to 'find' the correct names for everyone in this novel. Historians tend to use different spellings and translations in their work dependent on whether they opt for traditional or modern interpretations. That, coupled with the fact that the sources for the

period might be in English, Gallic, Irish or Welsh mean that its difficult to get an Anglicized version for every name. All mistakes are entirely my own.

Meet the author

M J Porter is an author of historical fiction novels set in later (and now earlier) Anglo-Saxon England. A keen history student, M J Porter has just completed an MA in History with an emphasis on primary source material and the way information is transmitted through time.

M J Porter also writes fantasy roughly based on Viking Age Iceland.

M J Porter can be found on twitter @coloursofunison, on Facebook, at www.mjporterauthor.co.uk, www.dragonofunison.co.uk and www.earlsofmercia.co.uk

Books by M J Porter (in series reading order)

Gods and Kings Series
Pagan Warrior
Pagan King
Warrior King

The Lady of Mercia's Daughter

Chronicles of the English
Brunanburh
Of Kings and Half-Kings
The Second English King

The Mercian Brexit
The First Queen of England

The Earls of Mercia
Ealdorman
Ealdormen
Swein: The Danish king (novella)
Northman Part 1
Northman Part 2
Wulfstan: An Anglo-Saxon Thegn (novella)
Cnut: The Conqueror (side story)
The King's Earl
The Earl of Mercia

The Dragon of Unison Series (fantasy)
Purple
Blue
Green
Red
Black
Silver
Orange (coming soon)

The Unknown Serial (young adult sci fi)
Part 1
Part 2

Stand alone short story (young adult supernatural)
Blue Sapphire

27146368R00131

Made in the USA
San Bernardino, CA
26 February 2019